Louisa Shelby's carefree life of elegant balls and beautiful frocks ended when her father died, leaving her penniless. With no hope of securing a proper marriage, the vivacious young miss accepts a position as a companion to an elderly viscountess. But temptation in a most unexpected guise awaits Louisa in the dowager's home ...

Once, Simon Wade was London's most eligible bachelor and most able seducer. But a tragic accident forced him into seclusion, away from prying eyes and questions. He thought he'd never again experience the tender touch of a beautiful woman. But while he yearns to hold the enchanting Louisa and taste the intoxicating nectar of her kiss, he will accept no woman's pity.

Louisa never desired a man the way she burns for Simon. And now her chance at happiness may rest in her ability to convince the stubborn viscount that her passion is real ... and her love is true.

UL 0 3 2007

Gayle Callen

THE VISCOUNT IN HER BEDROOM

An Avon Romantic Treasure

AVON BOOKS
An Imprint of HarperCollinsPublishers

This is a work of fiction. Names, characters, places, and incidents are products of the author's imagination or are used fictitiously and are not to be construed as real. Any resemblance to actual events, locales, organizations, or persons, living or dead, is entirely coincidental.

AVON BOOKS
An Imprint of HarperCollins*Publishers*
10 East 53rd Street
New York, New York 10022-5299

Copyright © 2007 by Gayle Kloecker Callen
ISBN: 978-0-06-078413-3
ISBN-10: 0-06-078413-X
www.avonromance.com

First Avon Books paperback printing: June 2007

Avon Trademark Reg. U.S. Pat. Off. and in Other Countries, Marca Registrada, Hecho en U.S.A.
HarperCollins® is a trademark of HarperCollins Publishers.

Printed in the U.S.A.

10 9 8 7 6 5 4 3 2 1

To my daughter, Michelle,
just beginning to go off on your own,
finding your way in the world.
Dare to dream big
and make those dreams come true.
You make me so proud!

Acknowledgments

I'd like to thank Dr. Sean Caples D.O. and Jean Caples, teachers of the blind and visually impaired, for their invaluable assistance on this book. I wanted Simon's injury and recovery to be realistic, and they answered all my questions patiently. Any errors are mine alone.

THE VISCOUNT
IN HER
BEDROOM

Prologue

London
September 1844

Simon, Lord Wade, was the most sought-after gentleman of Society, full of intelligent wit and sincere charm. Though young and handsome, he never neglected to converse with hard-of-hearing dowagers or dance with the plainest wallflower. Men found him such an easy companion, ready with a lightly humorous story or an opinion on a tricky investment, that they couldn't even regret his success with the fairer sex. Simon, grateful to be so blessed, thought his life could only get better.

Until he was thrown from his startled horse while riding through Hyde Park.

When he awoke, safe in his own bed except for a badly sprained ankle, he thought everything would be fine. Then he began to suffer horrific headaches, but the doctor assured him that this was normal with the several blows he'd taken.

Not only had his head hit a rock, the horse's hoofs had clipped him on the other side, leaving welts and bruises. His younger brother Leo joked that it might be a while before he would be presentable to the public.

But the headaches grew worse, and Simon's sight deteriorated. The doctor's reassurances became vague. Simon's family insisted that his sight would be restored when the trauma to his head healed.

But they were wrong. His sight faded until all he could see was gray darkness. Sometimes in very bright light, he could make out vague shapes. The only good thing was that the headaches had gone when his vision had.

As he lay in bed day after day, unable to walk on his ankle, he almost wished to see only true blackness, instead of this unending dark gray that gave him false hope, made him think his world might someday brighten again. But it wasn't going to, and he finally had to accept it.

The carefree life he had known was over. As the months passed, he put away the recriminations, the useless self-pity. In the beginning he needed a cane as his ankle improved, and he discovered that it helped to walk with it even when he no longer limped. He could feel furniture in front of him before he ran into it. Whenever Leo escorted him, Leo tended to forget to keep him safe.

Simon still had his work overseeing his many estates. He could be useful. His secretary and valet proved invaluable in his return to a somewhat normal schedule.

On the other hand, his ability to socialize was permanently damaged. He couldn't attend dinner parties—who would he let watch him eat? And dancing, something he had always enjoyed, was out of the question. He was no longer the recipient of dozens of invitations every day, though his true friends continued to encourage him without the pity so many of his dwindling acquaintances implied.

Simon retreated from London, where the busy city life reminded him too much of what he would never have again. He didn't want to go as far as the family seat of his viscountcy in Derbyshire, so he went to his grandmother's home in Middlesex, ten miles outside London. His whole family— grandmother, mother, brother Leo, and sister Georgiana—was with him for a while as he adjusted, but he sensed a distance from his mother that he'd never felt before. Simon was trying to be his usual, pleasant self, but she didn't respond as she used to, as if laughing at a blind man's jokes was too cruel. It made everyone feel awkward, but he resigned himself to it.

When his mother decided to go back to living her own life, Simon was relieved. He sensed her detachment, as if he was no longer of any use to her now that he didn't attend social events. Leo came and went, not bothering to hide his discomfort with Simon's condition, and Simon appreciated the honesty. Their sister, Georgiana, recovering from a disastrous first Season, was Simon's devoted companion. She became his eyes when he dealt with tenants and businessmen, and the two made a good team. Though his mother had discouraged him from working, Simon was not about to languish on a chaise lounge in despair. He would live his life to the best of his abilities.

His very quiet life.

Chapter 1

London
1845

The summons from the Dowager Viscountess Wade took Miss Louisa Shelby by surprise. She sat alone in the drawing room of Banstead House, her sister's home, and perused the letter a second time. She had met the grand lady on several occasions, but after Louisa's family had lost their fortune, their paths no longer crossed. Then six months ago, Louisa's sister, Victoria, had married Viscount Thurlow, effectively restoring their family in the eyes of Society.

But Louisa didn't feel restored. She felt restless, even ... bored by the parties and the life she'd once so loved.

"Louisa?"

Louisa looked up to see her sister Meriel, in London for her first visit since her marriage last autumn to Richard O'Neill. Louisa rose to her feet and hugged her sister, who stepped away, laughing.

"I've been here for several days," Meriel chided playfully. "You've hugged me at least once a day."

"I've just missed my sisters." Louisa sat down on the sofa and patted the cushion beside her.

Meriel joined her. "If I remember correctly, you always had more than enough friends to keep you occupied whenever I was studying or Victoria was immersed in her music. Surely that letter you're holding contains another invitation."

Louisa could have hidden her dismay, but this was Meriel, who would pry until her curiosity was satisfied.

"Lou? What is it?" Meriel frowned and put her hand on Louisa's arm.

Victoria suddenly sailed into the room, full of smiles and happiness. She was about to embark on her long-delayed honeymoon to the Continent.

Before Victoria could even open her mouth, Meriel held up a hand. "Shh, Vic, I was just persuading Lou to talk."

Louisa laughed as Victoria sat down on the other side of her. "Ladies, there are other seats in the room."

"But none right beside you," Meriel said firmly. "Lou just received a letter, and she doesn't look happy."

"Who is it from?" Victoria asked, her face full of concern.

Louisa regretted her transparent emotions.

She wanted them both to enjoy their happiness, not worry about her. "Lady Wade—the dowager viscountess—has offered me the position of her companion. It seems that she is good friends with Lady Ralston, my previous employer, who apparently gave me high praise."

"Surely that's not surprising," Meriel said.

"You are so good with people," Victoria added.

Louisa smiled distractedly. "But I left Lady Ralston so abruptly."

Victoria took her hand. "Surely she understood that once I married, you had a secure home and no longer needed employment."

"You know that wasn't why I left, or I'd have been here much sooner."

Meriel frowned. "Then tell us why, Lou. You actually sound like you're considering becoming a companion again when you don't need to. Enough with the secrets."

"I didn't mean to keep secret the reason I left Lady Ralston. It was just too … painful to discuss."

They sat on either side of her, holding her hands to give her support. They'd both gone through so much themselves these last months, from meeting their future husbands to finding love. Louisa hadn't wanted to burden them. But confiding in her sisters had always soothed her soul.

Meriel suddenly stood up. "There's only one place we can discuss secrets. Willow Pond."

Louisa chuckled and made a show of reluctance as they pulled her to her feet. "Have you forgotten that our cousin owns our old town house now? And he doesn't like us dropping by."

"He won't even know we're there," Victoria said, marching toward the door. "I know where the old gate is in the garden wall. David very sweetly had the lock repaired so that I could visit the pond when I needed to think."

"You mean he had the lock removed," Louisa said dryly. "I can't believe your husband condones trespassing." But she didn't continue to protest. She was reminded too dearly of her childhood, when she and her sisters used to retreat to Willow Pond whenever their parents argued.

Louisa followed her sisters out into the elaborate garden of Banstead House. In the silence, their footsteps crunched on the gravel path. No one spoke, as if they fancied themselves invisible. And then the spell was broken by a clatter of carriage wheels out on the street.

The gate, partially hidden by a fall of ivy, opened soundlessly, and Victoria gave a triumphant grin over her shoulder. When the three of them stood side by side on their cousin's property, their smiles faded and they watched the house carefully for signs of movement. Every window remained undisturbed, so they snuck down a path into the remotest corner of the garden, where the wall formed a corner and shrubbery hid them. Over it all was an ancient drooping willow tree, beneath whose draping branches they passed. Their bench was still there, standing guard over the pond, which was covered in a layer of stagnant green growth.

Meriel used the edge of her cloak to wipe the dirt from the bench, and they all sat down, shoulder to shoulder.

Meriel looked at Louisa. "Do you feel safe enough now to tell us what really happened when you were Lady Ralston's companion?"

Louisa nodded, but her hesitation must have been evident, because both her sisters took her hands in theirs and offered encouragement with their worried expressions.

"I liked working for her," Louisa began hesitantly. "It felt good to be needed, since she was confined to her sickbed and neglected by her family. I wrote letters for her, read to her, even sang when she simply wanted something soothing to drift off to."

"You once said she just needed you to listen to her talk," Victoria said, smiling.

"Yes, that's true, but helping her gave me true joy. And then I assisted her granddaughter, who was frightened of her upcoming Season. I never truly realized that some girls don't know how to behave amongst Society, and are afraid to talk to people."

"Now, Lou," Victoria began.

"I know what you're going to say," Louisa interrupted, "that I only had to look to you to see those traits. But I saw you as a woman who loved her music more than anything else, not someone ill at ease among people."

"Then I hid it well," Victoria said dryly.

"Or maybe back then I only understood myself, and couldn't see anyone else's fears."

"Why are you talking like this?" Meriel demanded. "You are the most sympathetic, compassionate woman I know."

In the dark of Louisa's mind, she saw an image of her father, who'd always confided in her, had trusted her sympathy. And she hadn't seen the truth until it was too late.

Louisa sighed and pushed the terrible memories away. "But not compassionate enough to remain with Lady Ralston. You see, I did not know how to deal with the men of her family."

"You, not deal with men?" Meriel said, clearly baffled. "But men liked you above all of us. You can ride with the best of them, and if Father would have given his permission, you'd probably have had your own pack of hounds for the hunt."

Louisa gave a bitter smile. "But that was when I was respectable. I had heard whispered rumors that certain men behave differently with female servants than they do with ladies. I honestly never gave it a thought. I was so foolish."

Victoria was holding her hand so tightly it was almost painful.

From the other side, Meriel spoke in a low, tight voice. "Did a man ... hurt you?"

She shook her head quickly. "Only my feelings. I resigned my position before things could become worse. Lady Ralston's grandsons and nephews regularly approached with lascivious invitations, as if I would be glad to accept whatever they offered me. I learned to pretend shyness to keep away from them, and I even learned to disguise my features."

"I had to do that," Meriel said grimly. "After my first employer's wife became too jealous—for no reason, I might add! Before we married, I even thought my husband was a predatory man. Because of Father, I had begun to believe that all men lied to women, but it's not true."

Louisa thought of the last time she'd seen her father, when she'd sat alone with him in his study one dark evening. He hadn't wanted to talk, as he usually did. He'd only seemed distant and sad. And then the next night he'd killed himself, leaving his daughters and wife penniless. Victoria had been shocked and confused, Meriel angry and bitter, but Louisa had felt ... sorry for Father. She still bore a terrible guilt that she should have seen his despair.

But even that tragedy did not make her feel badly toward men. It took learning the vulnerability of being a companion to do that.

"I still couldn't trust Richard," Meriel said with a sigh. "I was careful from then on, just like you, Lou."

"I guess I wasn't careful enough," Louisa continued. "They had a house party one weekend, and the men kept trying to corner me alone. Never before had I felt so lost—even the women looked on me with disapproval, as if the men's behavior was my fault. I was hurt and humiliated, and I finally had to leave Lady Ralston's employ." She blinked back tears. "I feel like I abandoned her."

Victoria put her arm around Louisa's shoulders and hugged her. "Don't feel that way. You had to protect yourself. And now you're staying here with me, where you can meet nice men and have a good life."

"Victoria, don't take this the wrong way, but I thought I'd be happy here." Her voice trailed off in a whisper.

"You're not?"

At Victoria's crushed expression, Louisa felt like the worst sister in the world. "Of course I'm happy!"

"But you're not, not really," Meriel said thoughtfully. "I had thought I noticed something when I arrived, but I couldn't quite understand what I was feeling."

"These strange feelings have nothing to do with you, Vic," Louisa said, her voice earnest. "It's me. I thought being back in London, with all my old friends, would solve my problems. But things didn't go back to the way they used to be. When we became poor, the women I thought of as my friends deserted me."

"We all experienced that," Meriel said, her face grim.

"But I've introduced you to new people," Victoria said.

"Yes, and they've been wonderful. But I've been so … restless and distracted."

"And we've been too busy with our own lives to notice your distress," Meriel said.

"No, oh please don't think that. I've been so happy for you both. It has been a relief for me to meet the two good men you married, to know that there really are heroes in the world."

"Surely the men you've met since you've been back in London have been kind," Victoria ventured hesitantly.

"Of course. And because of your husband generously insisting that I accept a dowry from him, I've even had two marriage proposals."

Her sisters gasped but held their silence.

"But I couldn't seriously consider them. I didn't love them, and I knew it was only the money they were after."

"Why didn't you tell us?" Victoria asked softly.

"Because I'm embarrassed!" she said, getting to her feet and beginning to pace. The cold stone bench had made her body as numb her heart had been feeling. "They wanted me for the dowry money, but I was once just like them. I thought money was important to my happiness, too. And then when Papa died—"

"Killed himself," Meriel said sadly. "We can't let ourselves forget what he—"

"Do you think we can forget?" Louisa cried in a soft voice, whirling to face them. They stared at her in shock, but she could no longer hide from them. "His death changed everything about each of us, and I didn't like what was revealed about me. I had thought Society was all that mattered. I loved having women friends and male admirers, and the dinners and balls that went along with all of it. When the money and the friends went away, I realized how shallow it all was, that I only truly had my family."

When Victoria tried to hide the fact that she was wiping away tears, Louisa groaned. She didn't dare tell her sister that she'd even felt in the way of her new marriage.

"Now you see why I didn't talk to you both about this. I don't know what's wrong with me, and I didn't want to hurt you. I only know that when I was helping Lady Ralston and her granddaughter, I found the first true peace I'd ever known. I had a purpose, and I don't have one here. I sometimes feel so old, so useless."

They enfolded her in hugs, and she welcomed their comfort.

"Trust me," Victoria whispered in her ear. "You'll meet a good man and everything will make sense again. You'll find a wonderful purpose—love and starting your own family."

"But maybe I won't," Louisa said, drawing

away from them. "Or maybe that's not all I want. I just need ... *something*, and I came close to finding it at Lady Ralston's."

"So you think becoming a companion again will help you find the peace you're missing," Victoria began slowly.

Louisa shrugged. "Maybe. I just know I have to do something, or remain miserable."

"You do know the tragedy that befell Lady Wade's grandson, my husband's dear friend Simon?"

Louisa gasped, even as his handsome face appeared in her mind. "I have been wallowing in self-pity so much that I'd forgotten. I'm going on about my own insignificant problems, when that poor man lost his sight. When I try to imagine myself in his position, how much everything would change, how people must treat him ... I am overcome with sadness and horror."

"Do you know what they call him?" Meriel asked, shaking her head. "The Blind Baron."

"How cruel!" Louisa murmured, her thoughts beginning to coalesce. Yet she suddenly frowned at her sister. "Baron?"

"It's his lesser title. And your problems are not insignificant!" Meriel added indignantly. "But you need to make an objective decision. Lord Wade is living with his grandmother, your prospective employer."

"He is such a kind man," Louisa said thoughtfully. "And he used to be so lively in Society."

"I used to think him a lot like you," Victoria said. "He knew everyone, and had friends everywhere."

Louisa frowned.

"David and I visited him before he left London, and he was trying to act like he could go on just fine."

"Was he really?" Louisa asked, shocked and impressed. "That is true courage: Even the disfigurement alone—"

"He's not disfigured in any way, unless you count a scar on one temple. His bruises have surely faded. He is as handsome as ever. But he wouldn't accept our invitations. I think he didn't want to be pitied."

"That is understandable. He must be led about like a child. Even something as simple as eating— do you think he has to be fed by someone else?"

Both Victoria and Meriel looked stricken and sad.

"He must be terribly depressed," Louisa said. She remembered his easy grin, the way he made every woman feel at ease and charmed. He had a shock of blond hair that occasionally fell over his forehead, and the deepest dimples when he smiled. She couldn't imagine his laughing green eyes vacant.

"He doesn't act depressed at all," Victoria said. "Resigned yes, but still struggling to be cheerful. I think he's very brave."

Louisa couldn't help her curiosity. How had

such a joyful man changed? Their home must be full of sadness after such a tragedy. Was that why his grandmother needed a companion, someone to lift her spirits?

And what about Lord Wade himself? Louisa remembered the way he'd helped Victoria fit into her husband's world. Victoria had hosted a reception to discuss the arts, and Lord Wade had made it a success by bringing all his eligible friends. He was a man who enjoyed helping people. Who was helping him?

Meriel rolled her eyes. "So do you need help packing your bags?"

Louisa slowly began to smile.

Chapter 2

Enfield Manor was a pretty little mansion in the country just north of London. Louisa waited in the entrance hall, her reticule in her hand, and felt more nervous than she'd thought she would. She didn't know what she'd expected—black crepe hung from the door as if someone had died? But the butler greeted her with civility, and the occasional servant who wandered by had nodded pleasantly.

But still her unease remained. She reminded herself that she wasn't desperate for the salary. If this didn't work out, she had a home to return to, even if it was her sister's.

But she didn't want this employment to fail as her last had. Her memories were overshadowed with the guilt of having abandoned an elderly, bedridden lady. Through correspondence with the granddaughter, Louisa knew that someone kind had taken her place as a companion, and she consoled herself with that.

But she realized that she was becoming far too

familiar with guilt. What had happened to her excitement about being useful, about seeing Lord Wade again?

She straightened her shoulders and waited for the housekeeper. She fully expected to be shown to her room and introduced to her employer at another time. Then a smiling older woman dressed in black with a white lace cap perched on her head entered the hall.

"Miss Shelby?" the woman said. When Louisa nodded, she continued, "I am Mrs. Calbert, the housekeeper. Welcome to Enfield Manor. I know you must be tired—"

"It wasn't a very long journey by train," Louisa said, smiling.

"Goodness, of course. I haven't managed to ride one yet. They seem so loud. Do you need to rest, or would you like to meet the family? They are gathered in the drawing room for the afternoon."

The family? Louisa opened her mouth, unsure how to reply. Was Lord Wade there? And she had just come in from the rain; the cloak over her arm still dripped, and her shoes—

"You look fine," Mrs. Calbert said, as if reading her mind. "I'll take your cloak and bonnet and show you in."

Louisa found herself swept up in the older woman's orderly speed. She trailed her through the hall, and then down a long corridor lined with Greek statues that stood on guard.

When they reached the threshold of an open doorway, Mrs. Calbert curtsied and said, "Miss Louisa Shelby."

She stepped back to allow Louisa to proceed her into a drawing room decorated in the warm colors of green and cream. Tall windows with sheer curtains before them let in the last gray light of the misty afternoon. But except for a few pieces of furniture and the paintings on the wall, the room was strangely bare of the decorative items a woman usually collected. No carpets covered the marble floor where the sofa and chairs were grouped.

Two ladies rose as she entered, both of them lowering their embroidery hoops to stare at her frankly.

To her disappointment, Lord Wade was not in attendance.

Louisa did not usually mind being stared at. Although she was not vain about her appearance, she knew that her features were never found wanting. But for some reason, she felt nervous about their stares, as if she had to pass a test—a test she wanted to pass, she realized with determination.

The dowager viscountess was a small, trim woman whose white hair was pulled back simply from her face. She had risen easily, belying her age. Her skin was lined with her years, but she smiled at Louisa in so friendly a way that Louisa could only smile back as she curtsied.

"I am Lady Wade, Miss Shelby. This is my granddaughter, Miss Georgiana Wade."

Louisa and Miss Wade curtsied to one another. The girl was plump and attractive, but without great beauty. Her gown was an ... unusual shade of purple. It clashed with her skin, and made her figure less appealing than it could be. Her hair color was somewhere between blond and brown, and her eyes were the same green as her brother's. As Miss Wade began to smile, the family dimples winked in her cheeks. She seemed like a good-natured young lady who would not abandon her grandmother to loneliness. So why would Lady Wade need a companion? Unless the granddaughter was only visiting briefly.

"It is so good of you to accept my offer of employment, Miss Shelby," Lady Wade said.

"It was kind of you to ask me, my lady."

"You received Lady Ralston's highest recommendation."

Louisa dipped her head. "That is generous of her," she said softly. "Is she still as I left her last year?"

"She is still confined to her bed, poor dear. But her letters, though dictated to her companion now, are as lively as ever."

"And her granddaughter is well?"

"Happily married, and it's thanks to you, from what I understand." Lady Wade glanced at her own granddaughter.

Miss Wade inhaled deeply, her expression full of forbearance, but said nothing.

"Miss Ralston attracted her husband through her own good nature," Louisa said smoothly. "I but coaxed her into showing the world. She was needlessly worried about her first Season."

She thought she heard Miss Wade mumble, "Needlessly?"

Lady Wade heaved a sigh and smiled at Louisa once again. "Do sit down, Miss Shelby. I've rung for refreshments, and while we wait you can tell us about yourself. You have sisters, if I remember correctly."

"I do, my lady. My eldest sister Victoria is newly the Viscountess Thurlow, and my youngest sister Meriel is now Mrs. Richard O'Neill."

"Ah yes, Mr. O'Neill is the young duke of Thanet's uncle and guardian. I understand he saved the little boy's life."

"He did, my lady, although he will hear no praise for his actions."

"You'll have to tell me the story someday. Your parents are well?"

This was the part Louisa hated—lying to people. But she and her sisters had sworn an oath to their hysterical mother to tell no one that their father had died by his own hand. Mama had wanted him buried in the church graveyard, his memory unsullied. "My mother is well, my lady, but my father passed on two years ago."

"I am sorry. I have lived long enough to accept that death will take us all one day."

"You are not old, Grandmama," Miss Wade spoke aloud for the first time. "Death doesn't even know where you live yet."

Lady Wade laughed. "Ah, Georgie my child, you amuse me."

Louisa smiled at Miss Wade, who blushed now as if she regretted her words. She bent her head over her embroidery again.

"And what are your accomplishments, Miss Shelby?" Lady Wade asked. "I'm always impressed by the talent of young ladies today."

"I, too, enjoy embroidery, my lady. I love to read and paint, and I'm told my speaking voice is pleasant, so whenever you'd like me to read to you . . ."

"Of course, of course. Do you play the piano and sing?"

Before Louisa could answer, Miss Wade gave a little gasp, then put her finger in her mouth as if she'd stabbed it with her needle. She glanced with a frown at her grandmother. Lady Wade continued to smile pleasantly, ignoring her granddaughter.

Louisa just blinked and smiled. "Ah, yes, I do sing and play, although my sister, Victoria, is the true musical talent in our family."

"Grandmama," Miss Wade said tightly, "did you forget that our piano is broken?"

"I had it repaired."

Miss Wade bit her lip and didn't reply. Louisa tried not to stare between the two of them with all the curiosity she felt. They didn't seem upset with each other, but the tension was palpable. Perhaps Miss Wade had not wanted her grandmother to hire a companion? Yet her smile had been so welcoming.

"My penmanship is perfectly legible," Louisa continued, "so I am able to write letters for you. And I enjoy traveling, and would accompany you anywhere—"

"Oh, I won't be traveling any time soon," Lady Wade said with a wave of her hand, "except through the surrounding countryside, of course. I have many friends I regularly visit."

Louisa frowned even as Miss Wade rolled her eyes. It sounded less and less as if Lady Wade was a lonely woman in need of companionship. Or perhaps she was realizing a frailty that she still couldn't admit to herself—or her family. Growing old must be difficult when one is strong.

"What will my duties be, my lady?" Louisa asked.

"Nothing very strenuous," said Lady Wade. "I will require your companionship for several hours in the morning and the afternoon, but you will always have time for yourself each day. Right now you can learn my schedule at a slow pace, since once my grandchildren leave, I'll surely occupy more of your time."

"I don't need to leave you, Grandmama," Miss Wade insisted.

"Someday you'll have a home of your own, my dear."

To Louisa's surprise, Miss Wade's hopeful expression soon faded.

A bewigged and liveried footman knocked and entered the room. "Lord Wade," he announced solemnly.

Louisa felt a rush of nervousness and curiosity as she rose to her feet with the other ladies. She had not seen Lord Wade since before his accident, and she wondered how much he had changed. She was prepared for a man in a state of disarray, sad, even lost.

She heard his voice, deep and amused, before she saw him.

"Bernard, I keep telling you that you don't have to introduce me to my own grandmother. She knows who I am."

Miss Wade giggled, Lady Wade smiled fondly, and Lord Wade entered the room, his hand on the shoulder of a plainly dressed man. He certainly didn't *sound* sad and lost, Louisa thought with relief.

Then she swallowed heavily, as the sight of him swamped her with memories and sensations from another time. She had always thought him a handsome man; whenever he had walked into a room, her gaze had been drawn to him. But unlike other handsome men, Lord Wade had always seemed like so much more. His humor and charm had been there on his open face, and she was gratified to see them still there.

And confused, too, because her reaction to him was still so very physical. She experienced a breathlessness that made her want to inhale too deeply, and suddenly the room seemed far too warm.

He wasn't limping, so the cane he carried must be an aid for his blindness. He was still so tall, so very fine of figure, wide through the shoulders where a man should be. He was elegantly dressed, but she should not be surprised at that, when he certainly had the services of a good valet. He seemed in robust health, instead of a man who must have lain abed a long while recovering. His wavy blond hair, cut shorter than the last time she'd seen him, shone in the light that filtered through the delicate curtains. He had a long, straight nose, and cheekbones that were rugged above the deep dimples in his cheeks.

But his eyes—his beautiful, green eyes, as colorful as the depths of a forest, were blank, vacant.

"Good afternoon, Simon," Lady Wade said.

When his grandmother greeted him, he looked straight at her, as if he could see.

Of course he would turn his head, Louisa told herself. He could hear where his grandmother was. Or perhaps that was even her favorite chair.

"Grandmama, it's always good to see you," he said, as his servant guided him nearer.

He had made a joke of his condition, Louisa thought with relief. He had always been a man who could enliven a situation with humor. She was glad that that had not changed.

Lady Wade swatted his arm playfully. "If you could but see the wrinkles on my face, dear Simon."

"Come give me a kiss," he said. "I'm sure I won't notice a thing."

When the servant halted, Lord Wade bent his head so that his tiny grandmother could kiss his cheek.

"And is Georgie here, too?" he asked, turning his head as if he scanned the room looking for her.

It felt strange for his eyes to pass right over Louisa as if she weren't there. And to him, she wasn't. Oh dear, shouldn't she be introduced? The servant's eyes widened upon her, but he only turned his head away. It wasn't his place. He waited in silence, his master's hand still on his shoulder.

"Of course I'm here," Georgie said. "When you don't need me in the afternoons, I'm always doing needlework with Grandmama."

Lady Wade gave a delicate snort. "Georgie my child, you need to be out and about, visiting friends and meeting new people. That's why I've hired Miss Shelby."

Louisa opened her mouth to say hello, but Lord Wade spoke before she could.

"You've hired a secretary?"

"No, a companion. I am getting on in years, you know."

He shook his head in bemusement. "That is the most foolish thing you've ever said. Your social calendar staggers me. You are the least lonely person I know. So what is your real motive?"

Louisa looked between them with interest.

Miss Wade darted her an embarrassed look, then said, "Grandmama, perhaps you could discuss this at another time."

"Of course, of course," Lady Wade said. She smiled confidently at Louisa. "Simon, allow me to introduce Miss Louisa Shelby."

Louisa saw his every muscle stiffen. She did not want to be the cause of his dismay.

"You met her before in London, did you not?" his grandmother continued.

But Louisa's attention was centered on Lord Wade, and she saw just a moment of embarrassed anger before his expression changed into the mask of pleasantry one would grant a stranger in a crowded ballroom. Did he wear that mask all the time, even around his family?

"Ah, I thought I smelled a different perfume," Lord Wade said smoothly. "Yes, I remember you, Miss Shelby."

He sounded as if they'd only met in passing, instead of sharing a conversation or two. She was surprised to feel hurt. She curtsied, then winced. He couldn't see it. "Good afternoon, Lord Wade."

He cocked his head toward Miss Wade. "Georgie, did she pass the curtsy test?"

Miss Wade covered her mouth to stifle her laughter. "Yes, Simon."

Louisa looked between them in confusion and saw Lady Wade's frown.

"The curtsy test, my lord?" Louisa asked.

"I'm always curious to see who curtsies to a blind man. So unnecessary."

She flushed, though she knew he was trying to be amusing. "Good manners are never unnecessary. They keep us civilized."

Oh heavens, had she just hinted that he wasn't? Miss Wade gaped at her, Lady Wade grinned, but Lord Wade only continued to focus his attention on her, wearing a half smile, as if she had not offended him. His regard was a different feeling than being stared at. This was an awareness that went deeper, as if he were ... focusing on her with his other senses. It felt far too intimate, a reminder of a time when the two of them had been different people.

"Good response, Miss Shelby," he said. "I like a woman who's not afraid of me."

And were so many? How distressing, especially for a man who had always been at the center of feminine attention and admiration.

"And is there a reason a woman should be afraid?" she asked.

"A certain amount of people seem to believe blindness can be contagious." Again, he tilted his head toward Miss Wade and laughed, as if she understood the irony.

But Miss Wade couldn't respond because she was blinking back tears.

"Simon!" his grandmother said sternly. "Save such foolishness for the men, who might understand your sense of humor. Sit down and have tea with us."

A maid had just entered, pushing a cart laden with a teapot and cups, and an array of biscuits. Louisa forced herself not to look at the viscount. She didn't think it proper that she be there while he did something so personal as try to eat.

"I am not hungry, Grandmama," Lord Wade said.

Lady Wade frowned, but said nothing.

"Manvil," he added, "guide me to a chair, and I'll release you to rest for a while."

The only other nearby chair was next to Louisa. The servant expressionlessly guided his master there.

"It is just behind you, my lord," he said quietly.

Lord Wade took a small step backward, and Louisa saw out of the corner of her eye the moment when his lower legs brushed the seat. Then he sat down smoothly.

Simon Wade controlled his resentment and frustration with a mastery that had been hard earned. How dare his grandmother hide the presence of a stranger from him? Even after all this time, he still felt shocked and strangely exposed whenever he discovered someone in his presence that he hadn't known about. As if he were an actor in a play he was unaware of.

He told himself he was being ridiculous; he had not embarrassed himself this time. Only a few sentences had escaped his mouth while he was ignorant of her. And if his grandmother had a secret motive in hiring Miss Shelby, the woman might as well know it. And why hadn't he trusted his own poor excuse for sight? Sometimes he could see vague shapes, and from where he'd entered the room, Miss Shelby would have been lit from behind by daylight. He'd probably seen a gray blob and thought it was furniture.

He could hear the clink of the china, smell the cinnamon in the biscuits. His grandmother was pouring tea and handing out plates. Georgie always refused to serve, since she inevitably spilled something.

He only hoped his stomach wouldn't rumble with hunger. He was not eating in front of them, especially not in front of a stranger, not until he knew he wouldn't make a fool of himself.

Miss Shelby wasn't exactly a stranger. He'd conversed with her at David Thurlow's home, and before that, seen her from across the room at several parties, although they hadn't been introduced then. But how could any man not notice her? She had flaming red hair, the color unfashionable yet wildly alluring. She'd worn it up in exotic twists and curls pinned to the back of her head, and he wondered if she still wore it so. Surely every man had fantasized about letting it down. And then there were her eyes, as blue as the lake he still rowed across, fringed in brown lashes.

For a moment, he wondered how long he would remember what people looked like. Would it all fade away some day?

He shook his head to clear it of such maudlin thoughts. He was trying to learn to take each day one at a time, to not dwell on things he couldn't change.

So he would think about Miss Shelby. Besides eating several family meals together, he had spent several hours playing croquet with her and her sisters at Banstead House, after her sister Victoria's marriage to his friend. He'd been impressed that a woman with stylishness and beauty had had such a ready opinion that she expressed with easy humor. She had talked of everything from railroad investments to fashionable bonnets with an interest that had been contagious.

He remembered her healthy laugh, no missishness for her. And while she'd bent over to play croquet, he'd found himself studying her as if they'd never met before. She had a compact figure on her small frame, but her breasts had pleasantly bounced when she laughed. And the smell of her perfume, roses and something else, even now teased him with its subtlety. He'd been resigned to his celibate life, but this wasn't helping.

Why had his grandmother hired her? Didn't she know about the subtle rumors that had swirled around Louisa Shelby?

As the ladies discussed the delicious flavor of the biscuits, he tried to remember everything he'd heard. More than one man had claimed her fast, though his brother Leo had been first with the gossip, as usual. She had the artistry of a born flirt, and allowed several men to call on her regularly. Someone had even kissed her, and it was said that it was only a matter of time before she became even bolder. Every man was hoping to be the one she chose for that experiment.

Ah, but it was only the men who talked of her, not the women. That's why Grandmama wouldn't have heard the rumors.

When he heard Georgie laugh at something Miss Shelby said, his concern deepened. Should his sister associate with her too much, it would not reflect well on Georgie. And Georgie was no beauty, to easily overcome such rumors. It could damage her chance at a good marriage.

If Georgie hadn't damaged it all on her own during her first Season.

He suddenly realized that his grandmother was calling his name. He'd been sitting there ruminating like a fool, and they'd just talked around him as if they were used to his silences.

"Forgive me, Grandmama," he said. "My head is full of business today."

"If you weren't going to entertain us," she said pleasantly, "and you don't want to eat, why did you come?"

"I was working far too hard today and needed a distraction. And Miss Shelby is certainly that."

"I'm not sure that's a compliment," Miss Shelby said dryly.

"Oh, it's a compliment." He had always liked the sound of her voice. He could hear her intelligence, her sense of humor. There was even the faintest huskiness that resonated inside him far too pleasurably.

But he couldn't dwell on that. He tried to remember the social niceties, which had become infrequent when one didn't encourage company. "And how is your family, Miss Shelby, and of course my friend David?"

"Lord Thurlow is well, my lord. My sister Victoria tells me it's a shame you do not accept their invitations."

He worked hard not to stiffen with uneasiness. "Then perhaps I should invite them to visit me here."

"Ah, but they've already left on their honeymoon."

He felt a twinge of self-pity that he quickly squashed. Of course the world went on without him. David and Victoria had struggled hard to find love; he was glad they were enjoying each other.

"So she got him away from his railway," Simon

said, shaking his head with amusement. "He must really love her."

Lady Wade said, "Simon, did you hear that Miss Shelby's other sister is also married now, to the duke of Thanet's uncle?"

He tilted his head toward Miss Shelby. "So you're the last unmarried Shelby sister. Is that difficult?"

He heard Georgie gasp, and he sent an annoyed look her way.

"Miss Shelby," he said, "I merely meant that I know how close you are to your sisters, and with both of them newly married, you must not be able to see them often. Is that why you accepted my grandmother's offer?"

There was an awkward silence that he kept expecting his grandmother to interrupt. But whatever she saw on Miss Shelby's face seemed to stop her.

"You are very perceptive, my lord," Miss Shelby said softly.

She didn't sound angry with him. "I'm only blind, not stupid."

"Simon!" Georgie said reprovingly.

"No, it's all right," Miss Shelby said. "Lord Wade is correct. My sisters have busy lives, and my old friends decided that my reduced financial circumstances last year made me unappealing."

Now she sounded embarrassed. Maybe she hadn't meant to reveal so much. It made him uncomfortable to be a part of such feelings. He'd forgotten that in pushing people away, he'd removed himself from emotions.

"Oh, Miss Shelby," Georgie said softly.

Their grandmother snorted. "Stupid girls."

Simon could only wonder if her lack of a dowry made all the men go away, too. But knowing David Thurlow's generosity, surely Miss Shelby had a dowry now. Then why wasn't she actively searching for a husband? Or had her dubious reputation become too well known?

"So when I received Lady Wade's kind offer," Miss Shelby continued, "it seemed the perfect opportunity to be of help to someone."

He concealed his frown, and had a startling moment of clarity where he realized that he was growing used to hiding what he felt. From his own family. "Grandmama, what do you have planned for Miss Shelby?"

"I have nothing *planned*," his grandmother said too brightly. "With Georgie soon to be busy with her next Season—"

He heard Georgie sigh.

"—and you distracted with your work, Simon," Lady Wade continued, "I need someone to keep me company. I am getting on in years, you know."

The two young ladies protested her statement in unison, but Simon wasn't fooled by the distraction. His grandmother was up to something.

"Georgie my child," said Grandmama, "I imagine Miss Shelby would like to rest before dinner. Why don't you show her to the blue guest room?"

Ah, now the old girl was trying to sidestep his questions by temporarily removing the problem. As if he was going to forget.

He heard Miss Shelby rise to her feet, and as she walked past him, he felt the brush of her skirts along his lower legs, inhaled the sweet scent that trailed behind her. These days, that was all it took to arouse him.

"Excuse me, my lord," she murmured.

"There's nothing to excuse." He waited until their voices trailed away, and he had mastered his distracted thoughts of Miss Shelby. "Are we alone, Grandmama?"

"You need not have that edge in your voice for me," Lady Wade said. "And yes we're alone, except for your valet."

"Well, I had to be certain." He cocked his head. "Manvil, please wait outside the door for me and close it behind you."

He heard the click of the door latch, but before he could speak, his grandmother did.

"Simon, forgive me for not introducing Miss Shelby earlier," she said in soft voice. "I admit that I just ... forgot I needed to."

He heard her sorrow, something she didn't normally reveal. Of all of his family, she'd been the one who'd most mastered the ability to act perfectly normal, as if he weren't blind. How could he remain angry with her? She was letting him

stay in her home, when his own mother hadn't
been able to get away from him fast enough.

"You're forgiven," he said gruffly. "But I still
don't understand why you hired a companion,
and Miss Shelby in particular."

"Lady Ralston recommended her to me as a
very compassionate girl. I need someone who
understands that although I may be aging, sometimes I don't want to be reminded of it."

He held his tongue, though he still wasn't satisfied with her answer. It was only what she wanted
him to hear. And there had to be another reason
why she had chosen Miss Shelby—and why Miss
Shelby had accepted.

Chapter 3

❧

Miss Wade escorted Louisa up to the second floor and down another long corridor, this one lined with doors interspersed with tall paintings. This last doorway led to a lovely corner bedroom, decorated in blue. Besides the large four-poster bed and all the basic furniture, she even had her own writing desk, which she well appreciated. Tall windows looked out over an immense park.

Miss Wade smiled at her and crossed the room. "One of these is actually a door to the balcony." She brushed aside the edge of the curtain to show the door handle. "It runs along the rear of the manor, so it is not exactly your own private balcony."

Louisa laughed. "I wouldn't need that much privacy, Miss Wade, not for the outdoors."

"There's a bathing chamber through the other door, with hot and cold water."

"I'll feel like a princess," she said. Even Banstead House did not have such luxury. "But I promise I'll remember my place."

Though Louisa was only teasing, Miss Wade's expression turned serious.

"Miss Shelby, I know that a lady's companion is not always treated respectfully, but you can trust my grandmother to treat you as the gentlewoman you are."

"I never doubted that," Louisa said.

"My grandmother is ... very different from what most people expect in someone her age. Her mind is still lively, and she has seldom been ill, so she enjoys paying her calls as much as ever. What has worried her the most is my brother. Simon, I mean," she added.

"You have another brother?"

"Leo, who is between Simon and me in age."

The name sounded familiar, but then she'd met so many men in the last several years.

"Leo has spent his life teasing me, and Simon has always been my protector." Miss Wade lowered her voice. "It's my turn now."

Louisa frowned. "To be Lord Wade's protector?"

Miss Wade sighed. "That's the wrong word, of course. I'm more of an ... assistant than a protector."

"I'm sure everyone wants to help him since his accident. His servant must be very dedicated. His valet, I assume?"

"Yes, Manvil helps Simon with everything he needs to do."

"If it is not too forward of me, how do you act as your brother's assistant?"

"I help Simon with his work. He has his secretary and steward, of course, to help him with all the duties of a man of property."

Louise felt foolish. Of course a blind man could still oversee all his estates and investments, as long as he had his employees to read the paperwork to him.

"I function as . . ." Miss Wade blushed. "Well, as his eyes. I sit in on meetings, and tell him later my impressions of what things looked like."

"You mean the expressions on people's faces."

She nodded vigorously. "Yes! You understand. And he manages so many properties, now that he's inherited the viscountcy, so there is much to do."

"And you attend all the meetings?"

She gave a cheerful nod.

"Then how do you have time for your own interests?" Louisa knew she was overstepping her bounds, but the girl's frank attitude encouraged it.

Miss Wade's smile grew sad. "I don't have all that much to do."

She looked away, and her shrug told Louisa that the girl was troubled about something.

"Except amuse Grandmama," Miss Wade added. "And now she'll also have you!"

Miss Wade seemed so happy to spend her hours at her brother's side. Louisa well understood the need for a purpose, but sacrificing one's own life and happiness seemed the wrong way to go about it. Of course, Miss Wade seemed happy with her new position, which meant that her own daily pursuits used to make her *un*happy. What young girl did not look forward to the excitement of the Season? Obviously Miss Wade's first one was uninspiring. Perhaps Louisa could discover what went wrong, and help her blossom this year. She'd so much enjoyed helping Lady Ralston's granddaughter. It was as if fate was leading Louisa to another troubled girl.

Meanwhile, Miss Wade was peeking into the bathing chamber to point out the tub and all the amenities.

"Perhaps you wouldn't mind showing me about the house?" Louisa asked. "I would hate to get lost on my way to dinner."

Miss Wade laughed. "Enfield Manor is not that large. But are you certain you wouldn't rather rest?"

"I'm too excited to rest."

"Of course you are. Coming to a new place and all. And not really knowing what will be required of you. We'll walk together and I'll tell you about my grandmother's schedule."

They walked through the house, and Louisa politely praised the conservatory, the library, and the ballroom, but she was really most interested in Lady Wade's day. The older woman spent her mornings writing letters and occasionally visiting several dear friends. In the afternoons, when she wasn't doing needlework or gardening with Miss Wade, she paid even more visits. After dinner, there was the occasional musicale or dance, but in the country, there was more time for simple evenings at home.

"And of course," Miss Wade said, as they walked through the dining room with its large table seating at least twenty, "one of Grandmama's favorite pastimes is listening to Simon sing." She suddenly broke off, and her face clouded with sadness. "But he doesn't sing anymore."

"And not because of the broken piano," Louisa said softly, not in the least surprised.

Miss Wade shook her head. "He says he can't read the music, so there's no point."

"But surely he knows many songs by heart."

"That's what I told him, but he refuses." She looked around and lowered her voice, even though the room was empty. "I think he doesn't like to be stared at." Suddenly she blushed and looked away. "Listen to me, going on like this."

"I don't mind," Louisa said. "If I'm to live here, I need to know what to expect."

A maid entered through a door, carrying a covered tray. They followed her into the corridor. Several doors down, she knocked and was bid to enter by the voice of Lord Wade.

Miss Wade took Louisa's arm and escorted her away.

Louisa glanced over her shoulder, feeling reluctant to leave when she could learn something about the man who so fascinated her. "Isn't Lord Wade to join us for dinner?"

"He doesn't eat in front of people," Miss Wade said with resignation. "Not even us."

As they entered the great hall, Louisa thought of the viscount eating every meal alone, with nothing to distract him from how much his life had changed. He should accept the company and conversation of his family—but that was easy for her to think.

The beamed ceiling of the great hall rose two full floors above them, and the high walls were decorated in shields and swords. Little groupings of furniture were scattered about, on noticeably bare floors. Less for Lord Wade to trip on.

Louisa felt very small in that massive room, but determined to create a place for herself in such an unusual household.

After a pleasant dinner with the Wade ladies, Louisa followed them to the drawing room. As an hour passed, and embroidery began to bore her, she admitted to herself that she was waiting to see if Lord Wade joined them. She cursed herself for selfishness, but she missed talking to men. Oh, she'd conversed with her brothers by marriage, but that was not the same thing. Men thought differently; they always said what they were thinking. It was refreshing.

It was not too shallow to like a man's attention— was it?

When the ladies rose to retire, Louisa said, "Lady Wade, would you mind if I borrowed a book from your library?"

"Of course not, Miss Shelby," Lady Wade said. "Would you like Georgie to show you the way?"

"It's just down the hall, isn't? Miss Wade gave me a fine tour this afternoon."

Miss Wade blushed.

"If you need company," Lady Wade began.

"Oh, no, please don't trouble anyone on my account. I could be browsing a long time. Have a good night, and I'll see you in the morning."

They parted in the corridor, and Louisa found the library easily enough. Oil lamps glowed softly on the desk and several tables. Books lined the walls, floor to ceiling, and she sighed with delight. She had never been a truly dedicated student, but she loved to read novels.

At the far end of the room, the double doors to the conservatory were thrown wide. Without the sun shining through the glass ceiling, it looked dark and full of shadows. But the odors of earth and vegetation after a cold winter drew her. She picked up a candleholder, lit the candle at a lamp, and walked into the conservatory. The paths were brick, the shrubbery so dark a green that they appeared black, even by candlelight. Fading into the blackness overhead, palm trees towered toward the glass ceiling. She was staring up at the stars, when she suddenly tripped over something in the path and went sprawling face first into a group of plants. Her candle went out even as she heard a man's startled exclamation as he fell onto the ground, their legs entangled.

"By God, are you all right?" he demanded.

Lord Wade. And she'd tripped over him as if he were a random piece of furniture.

"I am so sorry," she said breathlessly, trying to find a way to separate without touching him further. Touching him made her think forbidden thoughts about what he looked like under his clothing, something that had always been an embarrassing preoccupation of hers where he was concerned.

"Ah, Miss Shelby," he murmured.

She must have knocked him from the bench he'd been sitting on. When she turned onto her side, her face raked by fern leaves, she realized that her thigh slid up his as she moved. Her skirts were coming up as she struggled, and that only made her more and more frantic. Her heart was beating far too fast, her face was flushed with heat—but all she could think about was the hardness of his leg entwined with hers. No other man had ever been able to fluster her like he could.

"Stay still," he said, "and let me extricate myself. I'm not the one with my face in a shrub."

"How did you know?" she demanded, trying to push back her hair which had become caught on twigs. "It's so dark with the candle out."

"I know what's next to the bench I always sit on."

"Oh. Oh!" She gasped. "I didn't mean—about the candle—" Oh heavens, she was the biggest fool.

He drew his legs away. She thought he might have tried to save her from embarrassment by pulling down her skirts as he retreated. She should be upset—but she wasn't. She wished she had a fan to wave in front of her face.

"Think nothing of it," he said. "I tell people it's good to see them all the time. And that embarrasses them."

"Your grandmother finds it amusing."

"She's encouraging."

Louisa was finally sitting upright, her hands in the dirt behind her. Lord Wade rose to his feet above her, and by the faint light from the library, she could see him looking down at her.

Looking at where he knew she was. He wasn't really looking—thank goodness, because her knees were still showing. She tugged on her skirts.

"Does anything hurt?" he asked.

"No."

"Can you see?"

"A little. There's light from the library."

"Then give me your hand."

He reached down to her, and she reluctantly put her hand in his. He gripped it firmly and hauled her to her feet, then held her a moment too long. His hand was warm and large, and there were calluses across his palm, as if he physically worked for a living. That discrepancy in him had always intrigued her.

He let her go. "Are you all right?"

She nodded, then remembered to speak. "I'm fine. Did I injure you?"

"No, I'm quite healthy. The cane usually reduces the chance that I'll run into something. And of course Manvil protects me from that as well. But when I was first blinded, he occasionally forgot to mention the corner of a wall or a flight of stairs. The cane has saved me from a bump a time or two."

How helpless he must have felt, and yet he could joke about it. Her admiration for him only continued to grow. "You must have been quite bruised at first."

"Nothing compared to my head. A rock hit me on one side, and a horse kicked me on the other."

"Oh. How dreadful," she said softly.

A silence began and stretched out. Propriety told her she should leave him, but Fate seemed to be having its way with her tonight, or why else would she have stumbled over Lord Wade? She was determined to make the most of it.

"I hope I did not interrupt you, my lord."

"Only my thinking. Manvil will be back eventually to collect me."

"Would you mind if I sat with you until then?" There were so many things she wanted to ask him.

The silence thickened, and there was a new tension from him, although she didn't know why.

"Do you think I need to be watched over like an invalid?" he asked softly, a dangerous rumble in his voice.

"Gracious, no, my lord!" Suddenly he didn't seem like the jovial man he'd always presented to the world. Of course his experiences had changed him, and she wondered if he hid it from his family.

He reached toward her, and when his hand touched her upper arm, he gripped it, then caught the other one. She gasped, but didn't call out, didn't struggle, even tried to tell herself that she was offended, though she was more curious than anything else.

"I may be blind, but I'm still a man, and you've put yourself in a precarious situation by being alone with me. What about your reputation?"

Her mouth opened, but she could think of nothing to say. She was alone in the dark with a handsome man. His lips were closer to hers than any man's had ever been, and the warmth of his breath bathed her. She could feel each of his fingers imprinted on her flesh, but it wasn't painful. Her skirts swirled about his legs. It was suddenly easy to forget that he was blind.

"I—I only had questions about your family, about living here." She sounded breathless, but oh, it was not from fright. "But if you'd prefer that I ask tomorrow, when Manvil is around to protect you—"

He pulled her a little closer, and her hips brushed his. She felt a jolt of awareness that went beyond curiosity to something dangerous.

"To protect me?" he said huskily.

"I didn't come looking for you, my lord. If you fear that I mean to ... cause a scene, or allow myself to be compromised, I will leave this instant."

His hold loosened, and he sighed. "Forgive me, Miss Shelby. Something came over me when I thought you implied I needed a nanny." He set her away from him, then ran his hand through his hair. "So you think I might need a chaperone when I'm with you?"

She was beginning to see the pain he kept hidden. More and more she was convinced that he was a good actor. She kept her voice playfully serious. "It's the only way to protect yourself from me."

"And you're so very dangerous." He sighed again.

Louisa watched as he reached behind him to make sure of the location of the bench. After he sat, she purposefully sat beside him. He gave a start, but said nothing. It was a very small bench, and their arms brushed.

"I can't stop you from asking your questions," he said, stretching out his legs and crossing them at the ankles.

Which is how he must have been sitting when she'd tripped over him. If only she could be so relaxed—or pretend to be so. She wasn't sure which he was. Everything inside her quivered with intensity at his nearness. What was wrong with her? She'd been around many men—but only he had ever made her feel so attracted to him that all she could remember was the front of their bodies touching, however lightly.

He seemed different, here in the dark, alone with her. With his grandmother, he'd been the same man she remembered, cheerful, easy to talk to. Was it all an act for the benefit of his family?

She had to remember that he was not her purpose here. It was his sister who could benefit the most from her assistance. Or maybe the only sibling who would accept it.

"Wool gathering?" he asked.

She gave a start. "Forgive me, my lord. It's hard to know what I might be permitted to ask."

"I can only say no."

"Of course." She found herself longing to know how he was recovering, but that would be too personal a question to ask. Tonight it must be all about Miss Wade. She took a deep breath. "I sense a tension about your sister's first Season, and I don't want to cause her any distress by my ignorance. She's an intelligent, attractive girl. It did not go well?"

He didn't say anything at first, then gave a sigh and tipped his head back, as if he were looking at the stars. "She reluctantly came out last Season—and promptly fell on her face in front of Queen Victoria."

Louisa winced. "Oh, the poor girl."

"It got worse from there. At a ball, she tripped a duke's son when they danced. At a dinner party, she accidentally spilled her drink on the most sparkling debutante of the Season, leading to a rumor that she did it deliberately out of jealousy."

"Who would believe such a thing?"

Simon listened to the sympathy and compassion in Miss Shelby's voice. Though she had proved herself not so smart where men were concerned, it was obvious that she was a caring woman.

A woman who should have had her own household by now.

He hated how distrustful he'd become, how he now questioned the motives of everyone around him—everyone but family, whose motivations he understood. His family wanted to help him, and he was becoming tired of being their personal charity.

Now he had Louisa Shelby all concerned too. He didn't have to see her; the pity was there in her voice. That's what he inspired in the opposite sex now.

After several minutes, he realized she was waiting for him to say more about Georgie. But what was there to say? He was hardly going to tell her that he thought his mother was to blame for Georgie's lack of self-confidence. That would be just another reason to pity the whole family.

"So will she go to London this Season?" Louisa asked.

"I don't know."

And now he sounded surly, so unusual for him. Well, for the old Simon. The new Simon was sitting beside a beautiful woman he couldn't see, feeling sorry for himself. Miss Shelby reminded him too much of his old life. A year ago, in a situation like this, he would have been enjoying her company, making her laugh.

Now he was forced to wait for Manvil, when all he wanted to do was leave, to escape the tempting scent of her, the soft sound of her voice. He found himself wondering how often she'd "accidentally" been alone with men.

Her breath was sweet as perfume, and he could feel it on his skin. She was looking right at him.

"Why are you watching me?" he asked, hearing how husky his voice sounded.

She spoke steadily. "Because we're having a conversation. I don't usually look away from someone when I do that. And if you don't mind my curiosity, how can you tell?"

"I can feel your breath."

And then he didn't. "You can stop holding it," he said dryly.

She gave a soft laugh, and for a moment he was back in time, alone with a woman, his confidence as it used to be.

But he wasn't a part of that world anymore. He sighed, turning away from her, wondering where Manvil was.

No, he was not going to play the coward. He

forced himself to consider bold Miss Shelby and her questions. "Might I ask why you're so concerned with my sister, when it is my grandmother who has employed you?"

She hesitated. "Because Miss Wade and I will deal with each other every day. As I said before, I don't want to cause her any—"

"Distress, yes, I remember what you said. And strangely, I sense a deeper reason."

"Ah, Lord Wade, maybe you're trying to see too much into my innocent questions."

He arched a brow at her, then heard her gasp.

"I didn't mean—"

He gave her a slow smile. "I know what you meant. And I don't take offense that easily. But now you're stalling."

"You are far too perceptive."

The respect in her voice irritated him. Was she surprised that a blind man could figure her out?

"I have no hidden agenda, my lord. I simply see a girl who is confused and in need of help. And I would like to help."

"How? What do you think you can do that her family is not already doing?"

"In my last position, I worked with a young girl to prepare her for her Season, when she was quite in fear of it. Though I do not mean to imply that I was the only reason, she did well, and is now married."

But all that Simon could see was Louisa's

reputation—and Georgie being too closely associated with it. "No."

"I beg your pardon?"

"Georgie is on uncertain ground, but recovering. I feel that with her family's support, her confidence will grow again, and then she'll be ready."

"Forgive my impertinence my lord, but I don't agree with you."

"Then that is your misfortune, Miss Shelby."

"But without encouragement and assistance, she might magnify her past mistakes into something so large, she'll feel she can never recover."

He smiled. "I think I know my sister and her reactions better than you do. But I appreciate your concern for her."

She said nothing for a moment; she was so still, that all he could hear was her even breathing, as if she were trying to control her temper. He was amused and intrigued.

"I have taken up enough of your time," she said pleasantly. "Would you like me to escort you to your room?"

He came back to the reality of his situation. "No, Manvil will come when he's called."

"Then good night, my lord."

He heard her leave, and suddenly the conservatory seemed cold, as empty as any warehouse. He was a man once unaccustomed to being alone. He was used to servants and family and friends and admirers. He had always felt his best among a party of people.

But the eternal darkness separated him, and he found himself wanting to call for Manvil like a child afraid at night. Afraid of the dark.

He heard Manvil's heavy footsteps.

"I thought she'd never leave," the valet said.

Simon smiled tiredly. Thank goodness for Manvil, whose irreverence hadn't changed a bit since Simon's blindness.

"Unless you want me to bring her back," Manvil added with humor.

"No, it's time for bed."

"Then I should definitely fetch her back."

"Vulgar tonight, aren't you?" Simon said, standing up, the cane gripped in one hand as usual. He reached forward, and Manvil's shoulder slid comfortably beneath his other hand, like an anchor in a sea of darkness.

Chapter 4

When Louisa awoke in the morning, the same frustrating thoughts were running through her mind, and they all concerned Lord Wade. She'd had a hard time falling asleep, berating herself over their encounter. He made her nervous and awkward, all the things she usually never was.

She couldn't be surprised at his bitterness, nor that he hid it from his family. He didn't bother to conceal it in front of her, and she didn't know if that was an encouraging sign or not. It could mean he was beginning to deal with his emotions—or simply that he didn't care what she thought of him.

For a woman who'd decided she could help people, she'd done little of that last night.

And he'd forbidden her from doing more! Miss Wade's crisis of confidence would not disappear on its own. But at least Lord Wade had helped her to understand his sister's plight, and that was something she could focus on.

After Miss Wade's initial clumsiness in front of the queen, everything had spiraled downward. Louisa had to find a way to help her see that the past was over, and she could begin anew.

Louisa knew she was disobeying the viscount; she would have to deal with his anger eventually. She almost ... looked forward to it.

After breakfast with the ladies, Louisa had her first outing with Lady Wade, accompanying her to the home of her friend, Lady Perry.

When they arrived, Lady Perry was waiting for them on a chaise lounge in the drawing room, a blanket across her legs, but with a welcoming smile for her friend.

When she gave Louisa a curious look, Lady Wade explained with a laugh. "This is Miss Shelby, my new companion. You should hire one, Margot. She would be such a help."

Louisa was flattered by the recommendation, but she knew she hadn't yet helped Lady Wade at all. Lady Perry waved her to a chair a little away from them, and Louisa took her place, recognizing that she would not be much a part of this conversation.

But instead of being bored, she listened intently when the topic immediately turned to Lord Wade.

"How is your grandson?" Lady Perry asked in a hushed voice, as if it would cause a scandal to be overheard. "I am so sorry I wasn't here to be of comfort to you when the tragedy happened."

"He is very well, thank you," said Lady Wade a shade too brightly. "The family was all together, and able to comfort each other. Simon is as busy as ever."

"Indeed? 'Tis a shame a man with such handsome features and good bloodlines is removed from the marriage mart."

"Margot, that is not true," Lady Wade said.

Louisa had a difficult time not looking at her employer in shock. Lady Wade thought Simon should attempt to marry?

"He has only lost his sight," Lady Wade continued. "He will make a lucky young lady a fine husband."

"Is the poor man actually looking?"

Lady Wade hesitated. "The tragedy is so recent, and he is still recovering."

"My daughter and granddaughter visited him and his siblings before he left London. She claims the afternoon a disaster."

Louisa could see the rigidity in Lady Wade's posture.

"She tried talking to him, of course," Lady Perry went on quickly. "She told me that she even raised her voice, so that he could understand her better."

Louisa wanted to groan aloud at such stupidity.

Lady Wade clenched her jaw. "He's only blind, not hard of hearing," she said mildly, showing great restraint.

But Lady Perry seemed not to have understood.

She heaved a great sigh. "He was once so high in her considerations for a husband, but now . . ."

The visit didn't last much longer. Louisa found herself seated in the carriage beside a very distracted, upset Lady Wade.

For several minutes, the older woman tapped her fingers, looked blankly out the window, and gave several sighs. Louisa held her silence, having learned that a companion did not regularly initiate discussions—especially with a new employer. Some women didn't like the familiarity of that.

But Lady Wade finally gave her a determined look. "Tell me, Miss Shelby, were you as bothered by that conversation as I was?"

Caught by surprise, and uncertain about how frankly Lady Wade wanted her to speak, Louisa only said, "I don't know Lady Perry."

"I thought I did."

Louisa could only imagine what it was like to see your grandson so injured, his life changed so drastically.

"Lady Wade, some people don't know how to react to a tragedy, especially when the person is changed in some fundamental way."

"I know I can't let myself be so easily offended. But I want to defend my grandson all the time," she added softly.

"That is only natural. But it seems to me, only knowing Lord Wade casually, he would not want that."

Lady Wade studied her thoughtfully, but made no answer.

Louisa shifted uncomfortably, reminded of the dark conservatory, Lord Wade so near her, the attraction to him that had never gone away. As if any of that made her an expert on the man!

After luncheon, Lady Wade went to her morning room to work on her household accounts, leaving Louisa with the afternoon free. And she knew just whom she wanted to spend it with. She found Miss Wade in the drawing room, frowning at a blank canvas, a dry paintbrush in her hand.

"Am I disturbing you, Miss Wade?"

Miss Wade looked up with a smile, full of as much charm as her brother's. "Of course not, Miss Shelby."

"I have not had a chance to tour the park yet. I was wondering if you would walk with me? I'll be honest, I have an ulterior motive."

Miss Wade seemed relieved to put her paintbrush aside. "I confess that I'm curious. What deeper motive could there be in a casual walk?"

"I'm trying to find out if you have an archery field. I've lived in London my whole life, but whenever I was in the country, I practiced with a bow and arrow." She leaned toward Miss Wade and lowered her voice. "I'm quite good, and I'd hate to lose my skills."

"Then you'll be happy to know we do have targets and equipment, although we'll have to have someone set them up for us." Miss Wade looked toward the door, as if to be sure no one was listening. "To be honest, after a near-mishap a few years ago, I thought I should give up learning the sport."

"Nonsense." Louisa grinned and slipped her arm through Miss Wade's. "I'll teach you."

And Louisa would be teaching her the first steps to a new confidence, too.

After the targets had been set up in a field between the garden and the stables, Louisa re-taught Miss Wade the correct technique for holding the bow. Miss Wade had just taken a few practice shots—all of which had fallen short of the target—when Louisa happened to see Lord Wade and his valet walking through the garden toward the manor. She almost told Miss Wade to freeze, so that Manvil wouldn't see them.

But Manvil did, and to Louisa's dismay, he led his master toward them.

"Good afternoon, Lord Wade!" Louisa called brightly.

Miss Wade gasped, and her arrow went high into the trees. She faced her brother, guiltily hiding the bow behind her back.

"Ladies, I understand that you're attempting the dangerous sport of archery," Lord Wade said.

Louisa thought he looked suspicious.

"Georgie, did you not explain to Miss Shelby what happened the last time you tried this?"

Miss Wade blushed. "I almost put an arrow through Leo's arm."

"I'm sure that was many years ago," Louisa said smoothly. "And why ever was your brother between you and the target?"

Lord Wade cocked his head toward his sister, letting her explain.

Miss Wade sighed. "He wasn't. Leo distracted me with a frog, and I was startled. The arrow just ... slipped. But then he chased me into the woods, and Simon had to rescue me." She smiled at the memory.

Louisa thought that Lord Wade was still trying to rescue his sister, even though she was an adult. Someone else with his disability might have let others take over his responsibilities. She was glad he still had the role of protective older brother in his family.

But there was no proof that he had to rescue his sister from Louisa, so she remained quietly confident, even as Lord Wade stared in her direction, wearing a challenging smile.

Miss Wade looked between them in puzzlement. "I think I'll search for my stray arrow."

Soon they were alone but for Manvil, who stared off into the distance as if pretending he wasn't there.

"Miss Shelby, I thought I specifically asked you not to work with my sister," Lord Wade said firmly. "She is not to be your latest project."

Calmly, Louisa answered, "My lord, ladies

practice archery together to pass the time when the weather is lovely. Would you prefer that I spend each day in my room when your grandmother doesn't need me?"

He hesitated, and she thought he betrayed a hint of frustration and even uncertainty. She relaxed, confident of victory—for today.

"You know you are not a prisoner."

She waited.

"My lord," Manvil interrupted, "might I remind you that you're due at the miller's to discuss the repairs on the mill?"

Lord Wade sighed. "Well I can't go dressed like this. I'll have to change."

For the first time she noticed that he wore no cravat, and the top button of his shirt was undone. The bare skin at the hollow of his throat seemed almost indecent, but she couldn't stop staring at it. And was that perspiration making his shirt stick to his chest beneath his coat? The day wasn't even hot.

What had he been doing?

He gave Louisa a nod. "Good day, Miss Shelby."

"Good day, my lord," she answered, suddenly reluctant to see him leave.

After dinner, Louisa was invited to the drawing room for the evening. Lord Wade joined them after his private meal, and her senses sharpened into heightened awareness. He only had to walk into a room and she noticed him, from the sound of his walk to the faint odor of his cologne. He was cheerful once again.

Manvil escorted him to a chair, then stepped back into the corridor.

"Grandmama, how was your day?" Lord Wade asked easily, stretching out his legs and crossing them.

Louisa noticed how relaxed he always strove to be. His legs did not come near to hitting the coffee table, and she wondered if he knew precisely where everything was situated. Was this also something he had worked to perfect?

While Lady Wade chattered on about Lady Perry, without any of the hurtful details, Louisa tried to pay attention to her own book. She had to stop concentrating on her employer's grandson. It was embarrassing how many times she found herself watching him when no one was looking, as if he were her personal classic sculpture come to life.

Miss Wade lifted her novel from its place at her side, and after explaining to Louisa the general plot, began to read aloud. Her voice was sweet, and she gave a dramatic turn to each character, occasionally leaving her brother chuckling. It was obvious she played to his reactions, and would do anything for him. It reminded Louisa of the closeness she shared with her sisters.

When the next chapter began, Lady Wade interrupted. "Miss Shelby, will you take a turn?"

"Of course, my lady," she answered, remembering how often she'd read to Lady Ralston.

But having Lord Wade in the room made everything different, and she felt on display. No wonder he didn't like being stared at. In the past, she would never have been nervous around men! His disability didn't bother her—it was the man himself, the man whose request she was disobeying.

Though he could not see her, she had his attention. He solemnly faced her, not watching, but again focusing on her. But he did not laugh when she read an amusing line, and his sister overcompensated by laughing too loudly.

When Louisa had finished a chapter, Lady Wade smiled. "Miss Shelby, with such a lovely reading voice, your singing must surely be pleasant. Will you please do us the honor of performing for us?"

Miss Wade was obviously trying to hide her discomfort, as she kept glancing at her silent brother. Lord Wade said nothing, just continued to wear a pleasantly blank mask that made Louisa want to know what he was thinking. Was he offended that others would dare to sing when he would not?

Simon admitted to himself that he was curious. What was his grandmother up to? She had not asked him to sing, once he'd professed he would not; since then, no music had been played in the house. Though he hadn't requested a ban, it had been easier that way.

Now he listened to the rustle of Miss Shelby's

skirts as she walked past him, heard her seat herself at the piano and begin to play. She was no great musical prodigy, but she had a light, pleasant touch at the keyboard.

And then she began to sing, and the blow to his gut was unexpected and disturbing. She had a deep, husky singing voice. Couldn't everyone hear the sultriness, the way she was able to bring out the emotion of the piece? She'd flirted with dozens of men with that voice, and now it wove a spell around Simon himself. He almost wanted to send Georgie from the room so that she wouldn't try to imitate it. This wasn't how virginal women were supposed to sing.

He could imagine Miss Shelby touched by candlelight in the night, that red hair shining. Did she sing with her eyes open or closed? Did she wet her lips? Only a year ago, he would have been able to feast on the sight of her as well.

Only a year ago, he wouldn't have imagined needing to live with his grandmother, or memorizing a house by counting the paces of each room. But everything was different now, and it was a daily struggle to prove to himself that he hadn't let blindness change him.

Surely it was only a mark of his seclusion that he would read so much into a simple song. When Miss Shelby finished, his grandmother applauded enthusiastically and requested another. She would have been the first to notice something inappropriate.

It was celibate Simon, overreacting to a woman's presence. He couldn't protest; he couldn't leave. He was forced to endure the way the goose-flesh rose along his arms at the pure power of her voice. When the second song was finished, he had to stop the performance.

"Miss Shelby, you have true talent," he said, forcing a smile. "And I thought your sister, Lady Thurlow, was the musical genius in your family. Is she still composing?"

As he'd hoped, discussion of her sister brought Miss Shelby's attention to something other than singing. His grandmother seemed particularly quiet after that, and Simon felt her attention on him. He let her think what she wanted.

That night, Louisa couldn't sleep. Even Mr. Dickens's novel held no allure. In her mind she kept seeing Lord Wade's face while she sang. She'd tried to concentrate on reading music, but she'd known the piece by heart, and her gaze had kept wandering to him. Thankfully Lady Wade's eyes had been closed as she nodded in time to the music, and Miss Wade had been working on her embroidery.

Lord Wade had tried to appear pleasant, but a frown kept peeking through, furrowing his blond brows. She had not thought he considered her performance poor; in fact, he had praised her and begun a discussion about music.

Or had he been distracting her? He hadn't even

brought up the subject of the archery lesson.

He made her feel so flustered, and she wasn't used to that.

Her thoughts were scattered and restless, and after midnight, she finally donned a dressing gown. She would go down to the kitchen for some warm milk. She could have rung for a maid, but even back home, she'd hated to awaken a hard-working servant in the middle of the night. She couldn't do it here, when she was barely more than a servant herself.

She held a candle before her as she walked, and the manor stretched away into dark shadows like a cave. She could hear the faint creaks of an old house settling, and she was comforted by the sounds.

She entered the dining room, meaning to pass through on her way to the kitchen. Before she was even halfway down the table, the kitchen door ahead of her opened. She gave a start and froze, but in the gloom, the candlelight reflected off the blond hair of Lord Wade.

He was alone. To her surprise he moved confidently, straight toward the table. She was about to call out a warning, but he turned before his cane even hit the end chair, and came around the table.

She backed against the wall and remained quiet, feeling like she was intruding on the man's privacy. She knew he didn't like to be stared at. And she was stunned at how easily he moved about alone.

She held her breath as he passed, then grimaced when he paused.

"Miss Shelby?" he said.

Letting her breath out, she softly answered, "Yes, my lord?"

He turned to face her, and as was her habit, she drank in the beauty of his face, the way his dimples etched deep shadows in his cheeks by candlelight.

He frowned. "You have a distinctive perfume. We seem to keep running into each other in the night. Were you following me?"

"No, my lord. I couldn't sleep, and I came down for milk. I didn't mean to disturb you—I would have just let you walk on by—"

"Leaving me ignorant and foolish," he said, an edge to his voice.

"You're twisting my words," she said firmly. "You're walking down here alone. It is obvious you want no one to know. It wasn't my place to intrude."

"I don't care who knows."

Though mindful of her place in this household, she couldn't help her curiosity. "If you don't care, then why don't you walk alone by day?"

An ironic smile touched his face. "Because they'll want to help me, to follow me to make sure I don't hurt myself. But I don't need help—and neither does Georgie."

He protested far too much.

"It's not just concern about people helping you," she said, feeling bolder.

He cocked an eyebrow. "Reading my mind now?"

"You don't want them to see you looking unsure, or looking lost."

He scowled.

"Or you don't want people coming on you unawares when you can't see them. You care very much what people think about you."

He took a step closer to her and raised a hand, passing it slowly before her. She watched in surprise and curiosity. When he neared the heat of her candle, she almost called out a warning. But he leaned toward it and blew out the flame.

Because she was so startled, a small gasp escaped her. She knew she shouldn't have betrayed herself, because a reaction must be what he wanted. Her eyes, unaccustomed to the dark, could not see him.

"Is the candle out?" he asked.

"Yes." She whispered, as if things were too intimate in the dark with him.

In the tense silence, she remained still, knowing he was before her—or was he?

When he spoke, he was behind her, and she jumped.

"*This* is my world, Miss Shelby," he murmured.

It was her turn to feel his breath, and it bathed her neck with a heat so very foreign. She didn't

know what he meant to do; he might as well have
been a stranger—or one of the relatives of her last
employer, who had always kept trying to come
upon her alone.

But it was strangely thrilling to be sharing the
darkness with Lord Wade.

"Right now you don't know where I am," he
continued.

This time he was on her right side, a solid presence.

"Or what I'll do. This is what I live with every day. You'll have to pardon me if my behavior
doesn't suit your expectations."

She lifted her chin. "Why aren't you telling this
to your family? They want to share your feelings.
Instead you pretend that things haven't changed,
all in an attempt to keep them from being hurt.
But it's all right to make a stranger uncomfortable?"

"You're not a stranger."

He was in front of her again, closer this time.
Though she wore but a nightdress and dressing gown, her skin buzzed with awareness, and
surely the folds of the gown seemed to move, as
if something brushed against it near her feet. Her
breath was coming far too fast, but it wasn't in
fear.

She licked her lips. "I'm almost a stranger. We
had only conversed a few times."

"I still remember what you look like."

She was startled, intrigued, flattered. "Of all the

women who gathered around you everywhere you went, how could you remember me?"

"You have red hair, blue eyes, and the whitest skin that shows every blush."

She was blushing now—she was hot with it. She kept expecting him to touch her; she admitted to herself that she wanted him to. The expectation was maddening, confusing.

He made a sound she could not place. "And there were always admirers gathered around you, too," he said.

Her eyes were adjusting; faint moonlight shone through the tall windows, and she could see the outline of him dark before her, too close, as she'd known he was. A shadow man. She closed her eyes to be one with him in the darkness again.

Chapter 5

∽ ∽

Simon knew she had not moved since he'd begun to tease her. He thought he could hear her heart pounding; he could definitely hear the sound of her breath, moving rapidly in and out of her lungs. He imagined her breasts rising and falling with it.

She couldn't be wearing much. If he could see, he might be able to tell if her nipples were erect, if her lips were parted. Surely she was experiencing desire; she wasn't afraid of him.

Or was she? Was he misunderstanding this whole confrontation? He knew he should be angry with her, with her assumptions that she understood him. Instead he was powerfully aroused. Did she not feel the same? It was agonizing not to be able to tell, not to read her expressions. He had never known until he was blind how much his sight really told him about a person's thoughts.

"If you knew I had gentlemen around me," she said, "then you were aware of me—as if you were an admirer, too."

He knew she was trying to be bold, but her voice trembled. For a moment, she didn't sound like a woman who knew how to lead on a man.

He told himself she was not new to this flirtation. He could kiss her, and he would not be the first.

But something held him back, and it wasn't fear of rejection, or fear of looking foolish. Not with this woman who so bravely stood alone in the night with him.

Why did she allow this to happen? What did she hope to gain with a blind man?

But he played along with it, knowing it was dangerous, but just not to which one of them. "Every man was your admirer," he said. "Wasn't that what you wanted?"

He slowly reached forward, and his fingers touched her trembling stomach. For just a moment, he imagined he could feel the softness of it, covered so temptingly, so barely, in the silk of her nightclothes. No plain cotton for Louisa Shelby.

Then she backed up so suddenly that he could hear her hit the wall.

"I must go," she whispered.

"But you can't see."

"My eyes have adjusted to the moonlight."

"But some of the corridors have no windows."

She didn't ask him to escort her—just as he wouldn't have asked in her place.

"There's still a small fire in the kitchen," he

said. "I'll light your candle. Hand it to me."

He put his palm out, and she set the heavy candleholder in it. There was no fumbling on her part. The moonlight really must be helping her.

Once again they were on unequal ground.

"Wait here," he said.

She had been right earlier; he didn't want her to watch him. When he brought the candle back out to her, she took it from him, said good night, and hurried away.

He was left alone with his frustration.

Louisa spent the next day far too aware of Lord Wade. She could hear his voice in the great hall, or the tap of his cane down a corridor leading to his study. She didn't want him to know how he made her feel—or heaven forbid if his family should see her dilemma. She was embarrassed to be so attracted to him.

In the afternoon, as she changed clothing in preparation for the arrival of Lady Wade's guests, Louisa could not forget his words, that every man was her admirer, and wasn't it what she wanted. She wished she would have had the presence of mind to tell him that all women wanted to be admired. There was nothing wrong with that, other than a little vanity.

But when he'd said it, it sounded ... sordid.

And then he'd touched her, and she'd known she had to run. All right, she hadn't exactly run, and she was proud of that.

But not much else. She'd *wanted* him to touch her.

So much for being of help.

She took a deep breath. She had to get control of herself. She was attracted to the viscount, but she had to ignore those feelings. She was here to help. Her goal had expanded from being Lady Wade's companion, to Miss Wade's instructor, and now Lord Wade's—what? Friend? It was obvious he was in turmoil, behaving one way in front of his family and another in front of her. Perhaps he had touched her to deliberately drive her away.

Did he want to be alone in the night? In only a couple days, she'd come across him that way twice now. Maybe he couldn't sleep. Or ... was he in despair?

She sucked in a breath, and worry enveloped her. Her father had kept his despair hidden from them all until it was too late. Wouldn't grief be all the more powerful if one were never going to see again? Was Lord Wade hiding the same terrible secret her father had?

It seemed so difficult to believe. He wasn't retreating from his family, as her father had done—although he was hiding behind a genial mask when he was with them. Wasn't that a form of retreat?

Lord Wade was carrying on with his work; he had purpose, where her father somehow thought he'd lost his, and was ashamed. Family hadn't been enough purpose for her father.

But Lord Wade was definitely ashamed of his blindness. He was a man who used to live to be among people at parties and dinners. And he'd given all of it up. No conversing at dinner parties, no singing in the evenings, no card playing with his gentlemen friends. His old life was gone.

Louisa would have to keep an eye on him, putting aside her own foolish emotions and needs.

Feeling calm and full of purpose once again, she left her room and went to the drawing room to join Lady Wade before her guests arrived. She was having several women to tea, and Louisa would use this opportunity to watch Miss Wade's behavior, and come up with the next step in her plan to help the girl.

Heaven knew she couldn't imagine how she could help Lord Wade. But she could not let him give in to despair, even if it meant alerting his family to his dilemma.

Four ladies, middle aged and older, were being escorted into the drawing room by the butler when Louisa arrived. She took her place away from the main grouping of chairs and sofas. Miss Wade gave her a smile, but she looked nervous, pale, unlike her usual cheerful self.

The ladies chattered on about their neighbors, and their neighbors' children, and who was betrothed to whom. But Louisa continued to watch Miss Wade, who seldom spoke unless asked a direct question. When a teacart was wheeled into the room, her eyes went wide as if it were a monster come to attack her.

But biting her lip, she dutifully began to serve her grandmother's friends. It might have been better for all if Louisa had offered in her place.

Miss Wade spilled tea, dropped a cucumber sandwich on the floor, and in general made herself the object of pity. She was miserable in her lack of confidence.

She only brightened when the butler entered and intoned, "Mr. Paul Reyburn."

Mr. Reyburn was not a man who dominated the room with his physical presence; he wasn't excessively tall, nor could his looks rival Lord Wade's. But his personality more than made up for it.

"Lady Wade," he said laughingly, "if I would have known you were having a party, I would have come sooner."

All the ladies laughed and tittered like hens around a rooster.

"My grandson is not present, as you can see," Lady Wade said fondly. "But you are welcome to stay and visit with us."

"What grandson?" Mr. Reyburn asked, moving about the room, bowing to each of the ladies in turn. "I only came for you, my lady."

Then he saw Miss Wade, and he made an elaborate show of turning abruptly and presenting her with an exaggerated bow. "The lovely Miss Wade," he said, smiling at her from beneath laughing eyes.

Though Miss Wade blushed, she waved off his

display with amusement. "Mr. Reyburn, you're having a boring afternoon and relieving it at our expense."

"Hardly at your expense," he said, putting his hand to his chest in horror. "Surely you cannot fault a man for wanting to be entertained by your loveliness."

Louisa thought he reminded her of Lord Wade, brash and smiling and teasing. The style obviously suited Miss Wade, for she treated him almost as fondly as she treated her brother. Louisa would have to instill her with the confidence to treat everyone the same way.

"I thought I heard another male voice," said Lord Wade from the doorway. "Perhaps I'm not outnumbered after all."

He stood beside his valet, not touching him. Louisa felt a strange little shiver just looking at him, but she ignored it. He was wearing a charming grin, donned purposefully for his grandmother, Louisa suspected.

Mr. Reyburn turned to look at him. "Ah, *this* grandson, Lady Wade. He's been so reclusive that I forgot about him."

Lord Wade smoothly put a hand on Manvil's shoulder—as if it was always right where he needed it—and entered the room. Louisa watched him greet the ladies as one by one they reminded him who they were. One deliberately raised her voice—Lady Wade winced—but Lord Wade took no noticeable offense.

When Lord Wade reached Mr. Reyburn, Mr. Reyburn said something in a low voice, and Lord Wade laughed.

Louisa's whole day brightened at just the sound of his amusement.

Lord Wade said, "And have you met my grandmother's companion, Miss Shelby?"

Louisa felt all eyes turn to her, and she rose smoothly to her feet.

"Miss Shelby," Mr. Reyburn said, giving her a bow.

"Good afternoon, sir," she answered, curtsying.

"I mean no disrespect, Miss Shelby," Mr. Reyburn said, turning to the older ladies, "but Lady Wade, you are not old enough to need a companion."

Everyone laughed, including Louisa, who said, "I have thought that myself."

She felt Lord Wade's concentration on her, but she kept reminding herself that he couldn't see her. She would do her best to ignore the way her pulse fluttered, and her stomach contracted in memory of his bold touch. He was only trying to distract her from seeing him too closely.

"You young people enjoy your teasing," Lady Wade said. "Gentlemen, go on and escort the young ladies for a turn in the garden. I'll have refreshments sent to the terrace. We old ladies need time to discuss our physical complaints."

Some of the women gasped at her frankness, but Miss Wade practically jumped to her feet. "What a good idea, Grandmama. Come along, Simon." She entwined her arm with her brother's and expertly led him through the drawing room.

Mr. Reyburn held out his arm to Louisa, and although she took it, she said, "Lady Wade, are you certain you do not need me?"

"Go, Miss Shelby. It is a beautiful day."

She and Mr. Reyburn followed Miss Wade and her brother to the terrace. It was an unusually warm spring day, and the sun felt good on her face.

"Miss Shelby," Mr. Reyburn said, "if you don't mind my saying, you seem familiar to me. Are you often in London?"

"Yes, I was raised there. And you seem familiar to me," she said, as they caught up with the Wade siblings.

Lord Wade smiled. "Paul, how can you forget Miss Shelby? She was one of three sisters, and their father was a banker."

So she was unforgettable? Louisa thought, feeling pleased and flattered.

"Ah, yes," Mr. Reyburn said, looking at her with more interest. "Your sister married Lord Thurlow. I am a member of Parliament, in the House of Commons with him." He glanced back at Lord Wade. "Although someday I'll be there alone, because Lord Thurlow will have taken his father's seat in the Lords. Simon should already be there."

Lord Wade frowned good-naturedly. "Don't scare the girl off, Paul. You know how women hate politics."

Louisa arched a brow. "We hate politics? Such a shame I didn't tell my father that, instead of talking with him about the Corn Laws late into the night. In your expert opinion, what do we females like to discuss, my lord?"

Miss Wade laughed and tried to drag her brother away. "No politics! You promised I would have a walk in the sunshine, away from complaints of gout and hearing loss."

But Louisa could not miss the nervous look she cast between the men. She didn't want them to discuss politics? Or Parliament itself? Was she worried that Lord Wade would think he had to forgo his seat there?

After Miss Wade guided her brother down the stone stairs of the terrace to the gravel path below, Lord Wade turned back as if looking at Louisa.

"Accept the truth, Miss Shelby. You women like to talk about hats. An endless discussion of them."

"Hats?" she said incredulously.

Mr. Reyburn held up his arm again and she rested her hand on it. "Ignore him, Miss Shelby. He likes to think he knows the female mind."

"Then he must be displaying an astounding ignorance of it for a particular reason."

Mr. Reyburn smiled, looking uncertain of her wit, but she saw Lord Wade's shoulders shake, as if he were trying not to laugh.

She was pleasantly satisfied.

As the path widened, the two couples were able to walk abreast, and Louisa enjoyed listening to the men talk. Mr. Reyburn asked Lord Wade his opinion about a factory he was considering purchasing, and Lord Wade spoke about the poor conditions for women and children in such jobs, sounding perfectly ready to take his place in the House of Lords. He was not the featherhead he had sometimes seemed at so many of the parties she'd attended. But then she already knew how good he was at hiding part of himself.

Into a pleasant lull in the conversation, Louisa said, "You have a grasp of the practical that impresses me, Lord Wade. I never would have guessed."

Mr. Reyburn laughed, Miss Wade caught her breath, and Lord Wade came to a stop, dragging his sister with him.

"Are you calling me shallow, Miss Shelby?" he inquired pleasantly.

She grinned, enjoying bantering with this particular man. "You are very good at projecting that when you want to, my lord."

"She has you, Simon," Mr. Reyburn said, leading the way back up to the terrace.

A display of cider and cakes had been left on a wrought-iron table. Louisa watched with a frown as Miss Wade made sure to pull out a chair for her brother and guide him into it. His jaw tightened, but he said nothing; perhaps he didn't want to hurt his sister's feelings.

To Louisa's surprise, Miss Wade placed a slice of cake before him and proceeded to cut it into small pieces. Mr. Reyburn studiously ate his own cake, but Louisa was too intrigued to feign disinterest. Did Miss Wade think her brother would allow her to hand-feed him? If he could walk about an entire mansion unassisted, he could find the food on his plate with a fork. But would he?

Miss Wade was trying to do too much for him. She was trying to coax her brother back into the world, whether it was through his business dealings, or with food.

Didn't Lord Wade realize that by her constant attention to him, Miss Wade was gladly letting go of her own life?

Miss Wade lifted her chin resolutely. "Simon, I placed a piece of cake in front of you. Shall I help you eat it?"

Lord Wade smiled politely, although Louisa watched his hands clench in his lap.

"No, thank you, Georgie. I'm not hungry."

Her lips trembling, Miss Wade looked away, ignoring her own piece of cake. The ensuing silence was awkward.

Mr. Reyburn swallowed and took a sip of cider. "Simon, I rode over on that new gelding I told you about."

Louisa held her breath. Did he even like to be reminded of horses?

Lord Wade distracted them all with his charming grin. "Paul, I know you're dying to show him off. Go show the ladies. I'll wait here for you."

"Simon," his friend began.

Lord Wade gave a wry smile. "I know Georgie has longed to see him. Go, Georgie, I'll be fine."

Louisa watched Miss Wade smile hesitantly as she glanced at Mr. Reyburn. Perhaps they would need a chaperone, Louisa thought. But they had plenty of stable hands and grooms, leaving Louisa the chance to talk with Lord Wade.

"I haven't finished my cake," Louisa said. "You two go on."

Miss Wade didn't need to be encouraged. She dashed down the stairs, not bothering to wait for Mr. Reyburn, who only laughed and shook his head as he followed her.

"I think your sister likes him," Louisa said.

Lord Wade turned his head toward her. "Paul? They're just friends. He helped me keep an eye on her when we were children."

"Things change," she said.

"And once again, you're too interested in my sister, Miss Shelby."

She rested her chin on her fist and studied his reaction. He wasn't angry, just . . . concerned.

"I can't ignore her offer of friendship, my lord," she answered truthfully. "We are the only two young women in this household."

"But you're older than she is."

Louisa straightened in surprise. "She is eighteen, is she not?"

He nodded.

"There are only six years between us."

"But you've had many more experiences."

He seemed to deliberately stop himself from saying more.

"But isn't that the point, my lord?" she asked in confusion. "I have experience at managing the complexities of Society. Why should I not advise her?"

"Because she is not ready to try again, Miss Shelby."

This stubborn side to him was something she wouldn't have imagined when she'd first come to know him in London last year. But maybe no one had ever crossed him.

And she didn't want to push him too far, at least about his sister. But there were other things in his life he needed to confront. She took a deep breath and risked a personal question. "Does your response to Mr. Reyburn's horse mean you're not interested in attempting to ride again?"

"Not interested in your interference, Miss Shelby."

The mask he wore for his family was slipping, she realized, shocked and curious.

Lord Wade turned that intimidating focus back on her. "And how would I ride? Would you be the one to lead my horse around by the reins like a good companion should?"

"You're not an elderly woman, my lord," she said evenly. "You don't need me as a companion. Anyone could assist you in learning to ride again. Your family wants to help."

"You're my grandmother's companion," he continued, "and I suggest you keep to that. What I would require in a female companion is not what you're offering."

She blinked at him, startled by his vulgarity— but then intrigued by it. Had he been thinking about *her*, as she'd been thinking about him? She should encourage it—for his recovery, of course. Not for the fact that her palms had gone damp and her mouth dry.

"I thought I was offering friendship," she said. "Or pity."

"I don't pity you, my lord. I pity those children in the factory that you spoke of."

He slowly smiled. "You have me there, Miss Shelby."

"Riding again is your choice, of course. I am simply glad that you decided you could sit with me."

"You *are* alone with me on a terrace. Is that permitted?"

"Your grandmother told me to come. And it's the middle of the afternoon."

"It's always night to me," he answered softly.

She blushed, though he couldn't see it, and found herself watching his mouth. "Right now there are several elderly ladies who are probably peering through windows at us as we speak."

"I don't think they're worried about your virtue," he said dryly. "Not anymore."

She stiffened in outrage. Did he know what had befallen her at Lady Ralston's? "I beg your pardon?"

Chapter 6

Simon was surprised by the alarm he heard in her voice. Did she know about the rumors circling London about her? Or did she mean something else?

"I'm referring to the fact that I'm no longer looking to marry," he explained. "My grandmother's friends would surely think you're safe with me."

"Oh." She sounded relieved and embarrassed.

He was intrigued. "What did you think I meant?"

"The same thing, of course."

She didn't lie very convincingly.

"One of your grandmother's friends said that you were off the marriage mart," she continued. "Lady Wade assured her it wasn't so. So who was wrong?"

But he wasn't going to let her unusual reaction go. "I can tell that you're not saying what you were thinking a moment ago."

"So you've gained new abilities now that you're blind?"

It was rare that anyone mentioned his infirmity, and he found himself grudgingly respecting her for it. "You thought those ladies wouldn't be concerned with your virtue. Why?"

He heard her inhale swiftly. "You wouldn't be speaking like this were I not a servant in your home."

"You're not a servant, and I'm only trying to help."

"Not a servant? Do you know what a companion *is*, my lord?"

"I thought I did," he said with hesitation.

"What you have here at Enfield Manor is not reality. Your grandmother is a wonderful woman, and treats me with the utmost respect. Even you, in your strange way, have treated me with respect."

"Even me? I'm not sure I'd go that far," he said, remembering how he'd stalked about her in the night, breathing in her scent, wanting more than a touch.

"But at my last place of employment, when I truly had no recourse for monetary support but that position . . ." Her voice faded away.

He found himself leaning toward her, wanting to know her secrets, wanting to understand the mystery of a woman like Louisa Shelby.

"My employer's male relatives thought they could abuse my place in their household."

She spoke calmly, distantly, as if it no longer touched her.

Before he could find a question that wouldn't

further her pain, she hurried on. "Oh, I resigned before more than ugly invitations were bandied about. But I thought you meant that rumors had spread that I was unaware of."

He didn't know how to answer that. She seemed to be only referring to her work as a companion, not her time in London, when she was sought after—and whispered about—by so many men. It wasn't his place to hurt her by telling those truths.

"Is there someone I should call out?" he said lightly. "I can find dueling pistols. You only have to tell me where to aim."

She laughed.

He realized he'd eased the tension between them with humor, which used to come so naturally to him. Something about her made him relive the old days, and it wasn't such a painful thing.

The next morning, Simon found his grandmother alone in her morning room.

"Am I interrupting, Grandmama?" he asked.

"I'm only writing a letter. It can wait, I assure you. Do come sit down."

Manvil led him to a chair, and when Simon was seated, he dismissed his servant to the corridor, his usual place. He paid Manvil well to be so available to him, but Simon still felt uneasy with it. Manvil had to be his constant companion.

And that made him think of Louisa Shelby, his grandmother's companion.

"Grandmama, I want to talk about Miss Shelby."

She laughed. "I keep trying to convince you and your sister that I'm not as young as I used to be."

"And we're not convinced."

She didn't respond.

"That's not correct," he continued. "Georgie seems convinced. But I'm the one who's constantly running into Miss Shelby, who's being forced to listen to her sing, to walk the garden with her as a group of 'young people.' Wasn't that how you put it yesterday?"

"I had plenty of companionship with my friends visiting. She doesn't need to be with me every moment of the day."

"You're deliberately putting her in my way, Grandmama. I'm not going to marry—ever."

"I am not putting her in your way, Simon," she said firmly. "My actions are not always about you."

She ignored his talk of never marrying, and he let her get away with it for now. If he was supposed to feel put in his place, she'd failed. He knew she was not yet ready to back down from this new plan of hers—matchmaking. She didn't need a companion; she was finding him a bride. He was angry and uncomfortable, but consoled himself with the knowledge that at least Miss Shelby did not suspect she was being used as a pawn to draw the poor blind man out of his shell.

Unless the rumors about her had made it so difficult to find a husband that she'd lowered herself to consider him. Was trying to get close to Georgie Miss Shelby's way of getting close to him?

His anger hardened into fury, and he called for Manvil.

"Simon, you only just arrived," his grandmother said.

"I feel the need to be outdoors for awhile."

"I understand that the house can make you feel trapped," she said. "Go on and enjoy yourself."

Her voice sounded happier, as if it was a miracle that he was getting about on his own. Instead he needed a servant to get him through the garden.

"To the lake," he told his valet when they were in the corridor.

What was wrong with him? he wondered as he walked with Manvil. He had thought himself content with his life, resigned to what fate had given him, confident that he would get by.

And then Miss Shelby arrived, turning up at the wrong times, making him think about her as a woman.

He knew how to get rid of that sort of frustration.

While Lady Wade wrote letters, Louisa wandered to the drawing room to set up easel and watercolors for the afternoon's entertainment. She was trying to forget the strange conversation she'd had with Lord Wade, where she'd told him about her intimate problems with men at Lady Ralston's. What woman would talk of such a thing—to a man?

But he'd been a good listener. Perhaps it had eased some of the strain of their relationship. Surely he thought he could begin to trust her, now that she'd revealed something so personal to him.

"Miss Shelby?"

Louisa turned away from the drawing room windows, where she hadn't even realized she'd been standing. Miss Wade had entered the room.

"Since my grandmother and Simon need neither of us," Miss Wade said, "would you like to walk the garden with me?"

Louisa smiled warmly. "I would enjoy that very much."

It was a warm day, almost unseasonably so. They needed only bonnets to protect their faces from the sun. To Louisa's surprise, this time Miss Wade linked their arms together.

"Your grandmother has so many friends," Louisa began.

Miss Wade smiled, her hand on her bonnet as she lifted her face to the sun. "Surely you're not still wondering why she hired you."

"No, I accept her need to be prepared as she ages. But if you don't mind my prying, I don't see you going off to meet with friends like she does."

Her smile faded and she shrugged. "So many are going into town soon for the Season. They're busy planning wardrobes. It seems to take so much time."

"Is there a dressmaker nearby, where perhaps you've had your things made?"

Miss Wade frowned. "I haven't had anything new since before my coming out. And my mother controlled that."

Louisa sensed no bitterness, but almost ... indifference. Surely Miss Wade knew she did not look like the other girls. Did she think she couldn't? Louisa was trying to frame a subtle suggestion about a new wardrobe, when Miss Wade suddenly brightened.

"Ah, there's Simon," she said. "He had cancelled his meetings this morning."

Louisa looked around, but only saw several gardeners on their hands and knees among the flowers. "I don't see him."

"Not here," Miss Wade said, giggling. "On the lake!"

The garden sloped down subtly, to what was really an enormous pond rather than a lake. Louisa frowned and shielded her eyes, because the bonnet wasn't helping.

"Is there a path circling the lake that I don't see?"

"Well, yes, there is one, but that's not where Simon is. He's in the boat on the lake."

The small wooden boat contained only two men, one dark haired, and one light. And the light-haired man was rowing.

Lord Wade moved at an astonishing pace, all on his own strength. She could see him in his shirtsleeves, using both oars, moving rhythmically without faltering. He seemed powerful, unstoppable, and it excited her.

"Is that his valet with him?" Louisa asked, hoping her voice sounded calm and indifferent. So this was what he'd been doing before he'd come to their archery field.

Miss Wade glanced at her. "Yes. Manvil navigates for him."

"Why did he take up rowing?"

"Because he discovered that he could. I think he felt ... lost when he couldn't ride anymore." She lowered her voice. "I felt terrible yesterday after I left to see Mr. Reyburn's horse. That wasn't fair to Simon."

"He wants you to enjoy your life. Just because he can't ride doesn't mean you shouldn't." Louisa frowned as she watched Lord Wade slow the boat as he reached the far side, turn it around, and then begin rowing again at a quick pace.

"Why does he row so fast?" she asked.

Miss Wade shrugged. "I think he likes being tired afterward. He says he thinks and works out his frustrations."

He must have had a lot of frustrations, because although they spent a half-hour walking all the paths in the garden, Lord Wade continued to row.

As they were heading back to the manor, Miss

Wade said, "So you really think Simon wants me to enjoy my life?"

Louisa glanced at her in bemusement. "Of course."

"Grandmama, too?"

"Surely you know that your family loves you."

"I know. And I've done nothing but embarrass them," she said softly.

"You mustn't think that, Miss Wade."

"I just wish ... oh, I don't know what I wish."

Louisa studied the girl thoughtfully.

"Miss Shelby is watching, my lord," Manvil said suddenly.

Simon wiped his wet face on his arm, and tried to ignore his ridiculous surge of pleased satisfaction. "And you thought I'd want to know that?"

"I did. You're spending time with her, aren't you?"

Simon frowned and continued to row, picking up the pace until his muscles ached with the strain. He spoke between breaths. "She's my grandmother's companion. We're both living in the same house. I can't help but spend time with her."

"I'm living in the same house too, but I don't see her as much as you do. Not that you *see* her," Manvil added casually.

Simon splashed him.

But he had to admit that a buried part of him was glad Miss Shelby knew he rowed.

Was he so vain that he *liked* knowing that she was watching him? He didn't row to put himself on display. It was simply freedom to him. It was *his* power moving the boat, *his* ability making something happen. His life was sadly lacking in that.

Lately, it was only full of frustration. Besides the puzzle of Miss Shelby, he was in the middle of an all-out war between two of his grandmother's tenants. They were arguing over who had the rights to a tiny orchard that straddled their property line.

Just listening to them, Simon could not understand why they weren't solving the problem on their own. In times past, he would have understood from their faces, from the way their eyes looked confidently at a man, or scurried away in guilt. Later when he questioned Georgie, she simply thought they were foolish, but you couldn't tell a man that. Simon felt ... blind to a solution that would satisfy everyone.

So he rowed. And when he was exhausted, he slept better. He was able to fight off the need to roam the halls at night in the dark.

He didn't need to keep running into Miss Shelby, although he certainly wanted to. He'd only touched her stomach through clothing, and he wanted more. He imagined her hair down, reclining on his big lonely bed. He'd cover her and—

And he rowed harder.

* * *

Lord Wade did not join them that night in the drawing room, and in the morning he immediately disappeared into his study. Louisa wondered why he was avoiding his family, but couldn't very well ask him.

That afternoon, Louisa and Lady Wade were reading their novels silently in the drawing room when Miss Wade entered and sank down with a sigh next to Louisa on the sofa.

Lady Wade closed her book and smiled at her. "Did you and Simon have a productive morning, Georgie my child?"

"We did, Grandmama."

"Perhaps you can teach Manvil to assist Simon with his business dealings when we leave for the London Season."

Louisa let her book sag to her lap. There was a noticeable silence.

For a moment, Miss Wade looked hesitant, even hopeful. Then she folded her arms across her chest. "I'm not sure I should go, Grandmama. Simon needs me. I would feel so much better helping him, than standing alone in a corner in successive ballrooms."

Louisa felt even more determined as she listened to the buried pain in Miss Wade's voice. Would Lady Wade accept an offer of help, or like Simon, did she think Miss Wade would eventually solve her own problems?

"Remaining here might seem easier for you,"

Lady Wade said gently, "but how will Simon feel knowing you gave up your dreams for him?"

"I don't know if I have dreams anymore," she whispered.

Lady Wade suddenly looked at Louisa. Was this her opportunity to suggest ideas to help?

But Lady Wade said, "Before I hired Miss Shelby, I spoke at length with Lady Ralston, her last employer. Her granddaughter was frightened of her first Season. Miss Shelby worked with her, helping her become more confident. She was a success in London, and made a good marriage."

Lady Wade gave Louisa an urgent, pleading look.

Feeling relieved, Louisa suddenly understood. She and Lady Wade had had the same idea. Louisa hadn't been hired as a companion—but as someone to help Miss Wade. And since it was now Lady Wade's suggestion, surely Lord Wade would no longer object.

Filled with purpose and excitement, Louisa turned to take Miss Wade's cold hands in hers.

"Lord Wade wouldn't want you to forgo your life for him," she said firmly. Louisa was touched at how much the girl loved her brother.

Miss Wade closed her eyes. "But—"

"I had success helping Miss Ralston prepare for Society. I'd like the opportunity to work with you. You're a lovely young lady, with so much to offer. I know I could help you feel at ease. We could start with a whole new wardrobe, one that shows you off like a jewel in a crown."

Louisa glanced quickly at Lady Wade, realizing she was offering to spend a large sum of money that wasn't hers. But the viscountess was smiling with relief.

Miss Wade rolled her eyes. "There's a lot more wrong with me than clothing."

"There's nothing wrong with you, Miss Wade. I'll prove it to you. And I don't mean that you shouldn't help your brother, too. Perhaps you can help him in the mornings, and spend your afternoons with me?"

Miss Wade glanced at her grandmother with hope. "You would not mind if I continue to help Simon?"

"Of course not, Georgie my child," the old woman said gently.

Miss Wade looked back at Louisa. "I would like to work with you, Miss Shelby. But you might be disappointed by the results."

Louisa smiled with confidence. "I believe you'll be pleasantly surprised."

Lady Wade rose and came forward to kiss her granddaughter's cheek. "Thank you, my dear. You've made an old woman happy."

Miss Wade smiled uncertainly. "I hope you'll keep thinking so, Grandmama. Louisa—you don't mind if I call you that? I'm just Georgie."

"That would please me immensely, Georgie," Louisa said, filling with happiness and purpose.

"Come to my room after luncheon. I have some beautiful sketches to show you of the latest London fashions."

"You came prepared," Georgie said with admiration.

"I'm always prepared. It gave me such joy to help Miss Ralston. Knowing that I can work with you, too, has showed me my true purpose, to help young girls prepare for their coming out."

Georgie studied her. "But don't you want the same thing you're helping me to achieve? Don't you want everyone to admire you, to find a man who loves you?"

Louisa hesitated, not wanting to dissuade the girl. "Honestly, I loved every moment of the Season. I loved the excitement of every ball, dancing with men, and even wondering whom I would sit next to at dinner parties. But I've done it for several years now, and I find myself wanting something new. Thank you for allowing me to help you."

Georgie nodded and left, presumably to join her brother.

Lady Wade stood beside Louisa and watched her go. "You have exceeded my expectations, Miss Shelby."

"Call me Louisa, my lady. We'll be working together, after all. And this was why you hired me?"

Lady Wade smiled. "Partially. I do like knowing I have company even when my grandchildren

are busy. And they won't live here with me forever, I know." Her smile faded. "Though Georgie seems like she has everything, hers has been
a difficult life, even before Simon's accident. I'm
so disappointed in my son, God rest his soul. He
allowed his wife her way in everything. Some
women can only focus on men, Louisa, and she is
one of them."

Louisa suddenly remembered Simon's words
about Louisa having admirers; had he been com-
paring her to his mother?

Lady Wade sighed. "To my daughter by marriage, Georgie barely existed. Simon and Leo
were the lights of her life, and it was always easy
for them to charm her. She considered them a success. Although she certainly ignores Leo's many
problems." She lowered her voice, glancing at the
door. "I think she gave up on Georgie, because
the girl would never be today's ideal of beauty.
And Georgie, being no fool, took that to heart,
and thought she herself was the problem. What
little girl wants to believe ill of her mother?"

"I'm glad you told me this, Lady Wade. Do you
have suggestions on where we might start?"

"Her wardrobe. Her mother insisted on what
she has now." She shuddered. "If I didn't know
better, I would have thought my daughter-in-law
wanted Georgie to look bad. But certainly it is only
negligence. I would never tell Georgie that."

"I understand. If you don't mind, my lady, I
need to go find those sketches. Could we take a

trip into London sometime in the next few days? We have dressmakers to see."

Lady Wade grinned. "I would be thrilled to accompany you."

Louisa practically bounced up the stairs on her way to her bedroom, startling a maid who was dusting.

Finally, she knew what she wanted, what her true purpose was! Though there might not be many young ladies of the *ton* who needed her services, there were certainly girls among the families of the newly rich industrialists who had not been raised to enter Society. Louisa's world, though not of the *ton*, had its own strict rules and arrogance. There would be many families who would pay for her help.

As she turned into the ladies' wing, she suddenly came to a stop and faced the gentlemen's wing. What about Lord Wade? If Georgie blossomed into a confident young woman, as Louisa was certain she would, the girl would head off to London. Lord Wade would be alone, since he had vowed he would never marry. Could Georgie persuade him to accompany her?

Chapter 7

After eating dinner in his study, Lord Wade joined them in the drawing room. During their afternoon going over sketches, Georgie had told Louisa she would tell Simon their plan this evening, and Louisa found herself nervous, though she was still confident. After all, formal instruction was now Lady Wade's idea.

Lord Wade was not the kind of man who would explode in anger; he was very good at hiding his true emotions from his family—like her father. She would have to watch him carefully.

She admitted to herself that she watched him all the time, even when she didn't have to. She melted at the way he tried to protect his grandmother from the depths of his emotions. Lady Wade was obviously more a true mother to him than his own.

Louisa liked the way he walked, and now that she'd seen him rowing, she understood why there was an athleticism to his every movement. Even the aid of a cane and his valet couldn't disguise that.

When Simon was seated, and Manvil had departed, he said, "So Georgie, what is the big secret you wanted me to be here for?"

Louisa glanced nervously between Georgie and Lady Wade.

Georgie cleared her throat. "I'm sorry to call you in tonight, Simon. I know you had more work to do."

Work in the evening? Louisa thought suspiciously.

"Georgie, anytime you need me, I'll come running."

Lady Wade smiled. "That I would like to see."

Simon grinned. "Poor Manvil would have a hard time keeping up with me."

Georgie took his hand. "I wanted you to know that for the next few weeks, I'll only be able to work with you in the mornings."

Lord Wade smiled. "Ah, so who is more important than I am in the afternoons?" he teased.

"Louisa," Georgie answered.

He looked puzzled.

There was an excitement in Georgie's manner that made Louisa feel relieved.

"I guess I should say that I'm working on *me* in the afternoons with Louisa," Georgie continued. "She seems to think I'm not hopeless where the Season is concerned."

"Of course you're not hopeless," he said. "I

always told you that. You just needed more practice."

"She's going to teach me."

Louisa saw the briefest stiffening of his shoulders, but Georgie continued speaking.

"Grandmama says Louisa helped another girl before me, and she's even married now. The first thing we're going to do is plan a new wardrobe."

Louisa knew that Lord Wade could not miss the hope in Georgie's voice. Didn't he see that this could be a good thing? It was obvious his sister was relieved to have help.

Simon gave his sister a smile. "If you're happy, then I'm happy, Georgie."

But there was something off about his reaction, as if he were performing. Louisa exchanged glances with Lady Wade, but neither of them would say anything to dim Georgie's happiness.

"Is that all you need me for tonight?" Lord Wade asked, his hands resting on his knees as if he were about to stand.

"Yes, Simon," Georgie answered.

He stood. "Then I think I shall go back to work. Manvil?" he called.

The valet came through the door. But something felt wrong to Louisa. She wanted to ask Lord Wade to stay, but it wasn't her place. Lady Wade and Georgie were already starting to discuss a problem in Georgie's embroidered handkerchief as he left the room.

Without stopping to think, Louisa rose. "Lady Wade, might I be excused for a moment?"

The viscountess glanced at Louisa, then at the open door. But all she said was, "Of course, Louisa."

Louisa hurried into the corridor. Lord Wade and Manvil weren't far ahead of her. "Lord Wade?"

They both stopped and turned.

Louisa swallowed and said, "Might I speak with you a moment?"

He hesitated. "Manvil, would you mind waiting by the stairs for me?"

The servant left them to stand farther down the corridor. Lord Wade waited, his head inclined as Louisa came toward him. Maybe this had been a terrible idea, but it was too late to back down now.

She stopped in front of him. Oil lamps lit the long corridor, and he was cast in their shadows. His blond hair gleamed, his eyes shone, and his smile was faint, mysterious. Did he know what she was going to say?

"My lord," she began. But her mouth was so dry, she had to swallow and lick her lips. "My lord—"

"Nervous, Miss Shelby?" he inquired pleasantly. "Perhaps there is a reason for you to feel this way."

She stiffened. "I want you to know that I did not go behind your back and enlist your grandmother so that I could work with Georgie. Lady

Wade asked me for my help. She admitted that that was her purpose in hiring me."

"She has so many reasons, doesn't she," he said dryly.

She took a step nearer. "Pardon me?"

"Never mind. I'm just rambling." He took a step back.

"I did not tell her that you objected," Louisa continued. "Why didn't you do so tonight?"

"What would be the point?" he asked. "Georgie seemed excited by your help. I'm forced to give you the benefit of the doubt."

"Forced?"

"That's a good enough word. Now if you'll excuse me—Manvil?"

Confused, Louisa opened her mouth, but the servant was there before she could think of a reply. Lord Wade let himself be led away, leaving her frustrated.

When Louisa retired to her room that evening, she didn't even try to sleep. Warm milk wasn't going to help. She should start letters to her sisters telling them all about her new purpose in life.

But she was worried about Lord Wade, and he was all she could think about. Louisa knew that Georgie was doing the right thing, but did he?

Biting her lip, she went back out into the dark corridor, carrying a candle. The other ladies had gone to their beds, but was Lord Wade still in his study all alone?

As Louisa entered the central portion of the house, where the two wings met at the top of the dual staircases, she heard male voices. She ducked back the way she'd come, blowing out her candle. Lord Wade and his valet came up the stairs and turned into the gentlemen's wing. She crept behind them until they reached his bedchamber and disappeared inside. Then she hid in a recessed doorway until her legs grew cramped and her back began to ache. Finally the valet left, turning toward the servants' staircase at the far end of the wing.

She went to Lord Wade's door and laid her ear against it. There was no sound, not even footsteps. She told herself he was already abed, peacefully asleep, but she couldn't believe it.

Suddenly the door was flung wide and he was standing there glaring at her as if he knew everything. He was in shirtsleeves, and his cravat and collar were gone, leaving his throat bare.

"Why are you following me?" he demanded.

"I—I—"

"Louisa, I could hear every step you took."

Then he reached forward. She gave a little squeak as he found her arm and dragged her inside. When the door slammed shut, he let her go, and she put her back against it.

He folded his arms across his broad chest. "I want an answer."

She lifted her chin. "I was worried about you."

Whatever he had thought of her motives, that

wasn't it, because he gaped at her. "What are you talking about?"

"Well ... you have benefited greatly from Georgie's help, and now I'm taking her away from you. I know you've been avoiding your family the last day or two, but Simon—"

"I haven't been avoiding my family," he said with disbelief. "I've been avoiding you!"

"Me?" she whispered. "I thought you were close to despair, that you might do something desperate!"

"Despair? Why would you think that?"

"I—well, there's a whole list! You won't go to London to visit your friends, you won't eat with your family, and you refuse to marry. And now I've taken Georgie away from you."

"You helping Georgie isn't taking her away. And I visit with my friends," he added defiantly. "And if I don't want to make a fool of myself in London, that's my business."

"But Simon—"

He suddenly put his hands on the door over her head, and she sucked in a breath. She was surrounded by him, though they didn't touch. His wide chest filled her vision; his face was just above hers.

She had always respected the warnings never to be alone with a man, assuming it was so the man couldn't take advantage.

She had never understood that *she* might want to take advantage of the man.

Especially this man. He smelled divinely, and she could feel the warmth of his body so close to hers.

She shouldn't be here. She couldn't breathe.

"I'm avoiding *you*, Louisa," he said again, his voice gruff, deeper. "Because all I can think about is kissing you."

She had spent days studying his beauty, her nights thinking about every brief moment alone with him. He made her feel more alive than any man ever had. They were alone now, and no one knew—no one would know.

She stood on tiptoes and kissed him. For one electric moment, it was a gentle thing, the softness of his lips, the warmth of the contact. Then he leaned into her, pressing her body hard to the door, his arms trembling where they were still braced against the wood. His mouth slanted over hers as he groaned.

It was a kiss every girl dreamed of, full of passion and temptation. It was everything her sisters claimed it could be.

And then she felt his tongue slide along her lips, and a jolt of something even more sinful shuddered through her. She hadn't imagined—

She opened to him, and the kiss became so much more. It was dark and wild and forbidden, their mouths joined, their bodies straining against each other. He led and she followed, learning quickly. When his arms came around her, she clung to him tightly, as if her bones had disappeared, and she would sink to the floor.

Beneath him.

She gasped and boldly licked inside his mouth, tasting the warm rasp of his tongue. Her hands wandered across his back, feeling the differences between them; he was hard muscle, broad and strong.

His hands wandered too, lower and lower until they slid over her backside, cupping her. He pressed her against himself with an urgency that made her head spin. She wanted to feel everything, but there were far too many clothes between them.

And then suddenly he was gone, backing away from her, his mouth wet. She leaned against the door, trembling.

"You have to go," he said hoarsely. "Don't come here again, or I'll prove I'm not a gentleman."

She didn't like the anger she saw on his face—it was directed at himself, not her. And this was all her fault. "Simon—"

"Just go, Louisa."

When she was gone, Simon pushed the door closed and rested his head against it. Everything inside him raged at the loss of her. It had been so many months since he'd lain with a woman. His body was so eager he'd almost forgotten everything but burying himself inside her. A few more seconds and he would have lost all control.

He walked toward the hearth, feeling the

warmth of the grate. His fingers skimmed along his bed, ran over the desk at the foot of it. In five steps he reached the wingback chair and sank into it.

Though it had been close, it was over, and he would not let it happen again. Who knew how many men she'd kissed like that? She'd tried to play innocent at first, but she could not keep up the pretense long. She might have done more than kiss those men. A beautiful woman like her should have had a husband by now. Why would no one marry her?

And was she so desperate that she'd come to him wanting to be compromised? She'd kissed him when any smart woman would have fled.

He'd stopped in time, thank God, and he'd never have to learn Louisa's real motivations.

He remembered the excuse she'd used to follow him—that she'd thought him in despair. She'd sounded so convincing, so frightened for him. She'd said she was worried he'd do something desperate. Like hurt himself? It seemed so preposterous.

Yet there were nights, right after he'd lost his sight, that the world seemed such a bleak place that he could imagine the relief of not having to face another day again.

Was that what she was talking about?

He was over that self-pity. He'd proved that he was all right. He knew his family was worth overcoming his depression. But of course, he had not begun to eat with them, although he'd been practicing for that day long enough. It was time he do so, to ease his grandmother's worry.

She had hired Louisa, obviously with Georgie in mind—and maybe Simon, too. Though he'd been suspicious at first, he didn't believe that Louisa would have tried to enlist his grandmother against him. Grandmama thought she could heal her family, instead of letting time take care of it.

He understood and loved the old girl, but surely she didn't know about the rumors that followed Louisa. And how could he tell his grandmother, spreading the rumors even farther? Yet Georgie was the one who could be hurt by association with Louisa. When Louisa had first broached the subject of helping Georgie to him, he should have explained why he refused.

But even now, he could not imagine telling a young woman about her reputation. Though tonight's kiss seemed like a confirmation of it, he couldn't be certain. All he could do was bide his time and see exactly what Louisa planned to teach his sister. He would be ready to step in when necessary. Georgie had to be protected.

But damn, he would have to spend even more time with Louisa. He would sit across a table from her at dinner every night, imagining how the candles gleamed on her skin, hearing her sultry voice. Over and over he would relive the memories of the warmth of her mouth, the softness of her body, the nagging certainty that she would have let him do more.

He wouldn't allow himself such a weakness.

Louisa lay alone in bed and trembled. She didn't know what to do with herself, with these sensations that only Simon had ever inspired.

She longed for him; she longed for more than just that kiss.

But she had made him angry—angry with himself. As if he needed another reason for that.

He was a man, and men always enjoyed the company of women. She was no fool—she knew men could allow themselves more intimacy than a virginal woman could. But Simon had locked himself away from society for so many months now. He wouldn't let people watch him eat, let alone allow himself to ... have a woman.

And she had just flaunted that in his face by kissing him. She felt embarrassed and angry with herself.

She suddenly wondered if she should ask for his forgiveness, promise that it would never happen again. She would have to find him alone, of course.

But when something inside her unfurled in pleasure at just the thought of being alone with him again, she knew there would be no apologizing. She no longer trusted herself not to act on these base impulses.

She would have to pretend nothing had happened. Even though she could not stop touching her lips in wonder. She smoothed her hands down her body, feeling restless and aware. Her nipples were hard and sensitive, and she pulled her hands away in shock.

Heaven help her.

Simon began his day in the normal way—breakfast early, alone, then getting started on paperwork with his secretary. When Georgie joined them, he worked another hour, but she was fidgety and nervous, and she knocked over his pens twice. He sent his secretary on an errand.

"All right, Georgie, just tell me," he said, exasperated.

"Louisa and I are going shopping in Enfield this afternoon. She says we have ribbons to buy and lace to compare. And she's never seen the village of course, so we—"

"Then why are you acting so nervous? You know everyone in the village."

"Well, yes, but ... she doesn't, and I'll have to introduce her, and what if I make a mess of everything?"

"Georgie, give me your hand." When she did, he felt it trembling. "If you don't want to be with Louisa, you have to tell Grandmama."

"Oh, it's not that. Louisa is very nice. But she thinks she can help me, and I don't want to ... disappoint her."

Simon was the disappointed one. He had been

hoping that Georgie was being forced to go along with this plan, but it was obvious she'd made up her mind.

"You won't disappoint her," he said firmly. "And since she wants to help you, she expects you to *need* her help, correct?"

"Oh." Her voice sounded relieved. "I hadn't thought of it that way. If I were perfect, she'd have nothing to do."

Simon sighed. "I don't have any meetings this morning, so you can leave early."

He felt her swift kiss.

"Thank you, Simon!"

When she was gone, he imagined the two women in the carriage on their way into the village. But in his mind, it was he alone with Louisa, and he knew what he'd do during the short journey.

He groaned and covered his face. Louisa's kiss had somehow unleashed him—unleashed everything he thought he'd buried because he was a blind man now.

He reminded himself that he had to worry about Louisa, and not just for his own peace of mind. There was Georgie to protect. But what trouble could they get into during a visit to Enfield?

He found out late in the afternoon, when the parish vicar came to visit. Once a week, the elderly man did his duty visiting the parish sick, and though Simon had tried to protest months before that he was no longer "sick," the vicar would not hear it. So Simon tolerated the man each week, making promises to pray more, to let God into his life and heal him.

He wasn't going to be healed, but maybe he could say a silent prayer or two to help his control where Louisa was concerned.

But for once, the discussion of the state of Simon's soul was relatively brief. Then there was an awkward silence. The elderly gentleman sipped his tea rather loudly, tapped his foot on the floor, and seemed not to know where to begin.

"Mr. Baylen?" Simon said. "Is there something specific you need to talk to me about?" He was beginning to wish he'd called for his grandmother. Maybe she'd know what was going on. He was feeling more blind than usual.

"Lord Wade, it is ... about your sister." There was a wealth of reluctance and hesitation in his voice.

"Go on," Simon encouraged.

"I did not know if I should say anything ... your sister has always been such a perfect young lady, so modest and shy."

Simon's stomach clenched. "You know that she is, Mr. Baylen."

"Of course," the man said quickly. "But ... today I saw her in the village with a strange woman."

Simon told himself to relax. "That is simply my grandmother's companion, Miss Louisa Shelby."

"Oh. Oh, well then, I am relieved on one score."

But obviously not about something else. Simon waited impatiently.

"I saw your sister and Miss Shelby on a public street, laughing quite loudly with two gentlemen—two soldiers."

The disapproval in his voice spoke volumes. Simon didn't have to read his face. "Was that all?" he asked.

"Yes, my lord."

"They did not sneak off alone somewhere?" he continued dryly.

"My lord! Your sister is a lady. I stood nearby to protect her, but they left the gentlemen, and I did not have to intervene."

"I'm glad to hear that." Simon knew the vicar was only trying to help, but he found himself angry that the man would feel the need to spy on Georgie.

Simon called the visit short by saying he had to work. He was alone with his thoughts for only a short while, when he heard footsteps.

"My lord," said Manvil, coming closer. He lowered his voice. "Glad the old snoop is gone."

"So you heard?"

"His righteous indignation was loud enough."

Simon winced.

"You aren't going to listen to him, are you? Miss Georgie is young, and it's good to hear she can have fun."

Manvil was right—yet the valet didn't know about Louisa's reputation. Simon was going to have to speak with her. Alone.

But first he would have to row—even though it was raining. Maybe he'd be too tired to think about her as more than simply a threat to Georgie.

Chapter 8

After an enjoyable afternoon shopping, Louisa was just sitting down to dinner with Lady Wade and Georgie when Simon was led into the dining room by his valet. Georgie's eyes went wide, and Lady Wade went utterly still, her face a study in hope.

A tightness enclosed Louisa's throat as he sat down at the head of the table, his rightful place. She was still too raw where her strange feelings for Simon were concerned. She was glad to be here on such a momentous occasion, but how could she watch him speak, remembering what his lips had done to her, or watch him eat, remembering how his hands had felt on her body?

Simon smiled. "It's very quiet in here. When ladies have just finished shopping, they usually have much to discuss."

Georgie cleared her throat and dabbed her eyes. But she spoke cheerfully. "I bought a beautiful new hat. Louisa says it will be perfect with the new hairstyle she's going to show my maid tonight."

As Georgie went on to describe the decorations on the hat, the first course, oxtail soup, was announced and served. Everyone tried not to watch Simon as he picked up his spoon, found the edge of the bowl with a tap and began to eat.

It took several minutes for the three ladies to join in.

Simon knew every eye was on him, and now he understood how an actor must feel. He mustn't forget his lines—or his responses to Georgie's chattering, in this case.

He was concentrating too hard on eating, but for him this was like the first dining exam of many. He'd been "studying" for months now, practicing until he felt he wouldn't make a fool of himself.

Eating the soup was almost easy. He didn't think he'd spilled any on himself. When he was served brill with shrimp sauce, however, he hesitated. But just by moving his fork about the plate, he realized that the fish had already been cut for him. One step at a time, he thought with relief. One item of food per plate, but he'd already told the cook that.

"So did you meet up with anyone in Enfield?" Simon asked, remembering the vicar's comments.

"Two soldiers from the militia," Georgie answered promptly. "Louisa had met them at a dinner party last year, but they even remembered me."

"You're memorable," Simon said. "And not because of any accident-prone duke's son."

She giggled. "No, they weren't in London when my public mistakes occurred."

"Did you enjoy talking to them?"

"Not at first. I didn't know what to say. Louisa asked them about people we had in common, and before I knew it, we were conversing."

"She did very well," Louisa said, "once she forgot to be nervous."

Simon found himself startled. Just the sound of her voice made him remember the feel of her in his arms, the way her soft curves had formed to him. He tried to act like nothing was wrong, but when he brought the fork to his mouth, it was empty. He hoped he'd dropped the food on the plate.

He would still have to talk to her about what the vicar said. She would have to be warned about taking care of Georgie's reputation.

But he couldn't hurt her by telling her about the other rumors. He found himself dreading the private talk with her—and anticipating it for a baser reason. How could he be worried about Louisa's reputation, and so willing to add to it at the same time?

Later that evening, he walked down the corridor alone, knowing most of the servants would be preparing for bed. It was easy enough to find her room because she'd been given the blue bedchamber, and it was the last door. He hesitated before knocking, and then was glad he had.

He could hear two women laughing. He recognized his sister's voice immediately, but it was the sound of Louisa's pleasure that had him enthralled. Her laughter was as deep and husky as her singing voice, and it made him weak with longing to imagine how she would express a more intimate pleasure.

Feeling ridiculous, hoping no one was silently observing him, he waited in the corridor, listening. They were discussing hairstyles for Georgie, and from their happy exclamations, they apparently approved of whatever experimenting they were doing.

How could he interrupt a blossoming friendship? He remembered Georgie's friends as being more interested in him than in her. And although Louisa had kissed him, he didn't believe she would ignore Georgie or treat her badly. Their own mother had never paid this much attention to her.

He couldn't hurt Louisa by warning her to be careful with his sister's reputation. He would just have to stay closer to his sister, even if that meant spending time with Louisa. He owed Georgie far more than he could ever repay. She had been his lifeline in the dark days when he'd first been blinded. And he would make her happy, even if it meant suffering through this unwelcome desire for Louisa.

When Simon was expecting Georgie in his study the next morning, the door opened. But it only took a current of air before he knew who it was. And he came to attention in more ways than one.

"Miss Shelby," he said, then cursed himself for how husky his voice sounded.

"Lord Wade."

"To what do I owe the pleasure of your visit?"

When there was a moment's hesitation, Manvil suddenly said, "I'll return later, my lord."

Simon gritted his teeth. He really hated not being able to see what was going on.

When they were alone, he said, "So you frightened away my servant?"

"You know I didn't, Simon," she said coolly. "He simply looked between us and left."

"Why are you here?"

"Not so polite when we're alone?"

He gripped the arms of his chair, then forced his fingers to relax. "Louisa, you would try the patience of a saint. And I'm not a saint."

"I'm sorry." She whispered the words.

He groaned and closed his eyes. "I didn't mean—God this is awkward."

"I know. And it's all my fault. I wouldn't have intruded, except that Georgie left with your grandmother to visit several invalids of the parish. I'm certain there will be other girls her age accompanying their mothers. Georgie didn't want to leave you, because she knew how much you depended on her assistance. So I volunteered to take her place."

Their awkward silence was gradually suffused with a passionate tension that he didn't know how to combat.

"Do you feel this?" she suddenly whispered. "It's like there's something in the air whenever I'm with you. Is this ... normal?"

So he wasn't alone in this rising desire. He wanted to pretend he didn't understand, but he couldn't embarrass her like that. "It's my fault."

"You didn't do anything. You haven't even looked at me, and yet I feel . . ."

"I don't need to *look* at you. I still feel you, taste you. This is ... a special awareness between a man and a woman."

She moaned, and the sound only drove his need higher.

"Oh, Simon, what have I done? I shouldn't have kissed you."

"Do you truly regret it?" he asked, hoping he would know the truth when he heard it.

"I—" She sighed. "God help me, I don't. I've never felt that way before. But I promise that it won't happen again."

He didn't know if he believed her.

Before he could say anything, they were interrupted by his steward, Oscar Edgeworth, who ushered in the two tenants who'd been fighting over the proceeds of a shared orchard.

How the hell was he supposed to concentrate when Louisa Shelby smelled so good?

Louisa rose to her feet as the three gentlemen entered the study. Instead of feeling nervous and wondering how she could help Simon, she was far too interested in watching him. Before his accident, his reputation had named him charming and carefree; then she'd seen firsthand his kindness and compassion when he'd helped her sister Victoria find her place in Society. But now she knew him better, saw the depth of emotions he hid to keep his family from worrying. But what kind of businessman was he?

She had already met Mr. Edgeworth, the steward of the estate, a tall man with a brisk, efficient manner.

"Miss Shelby," he said, giving her a brief bow.

"Miss Shelby will be taking my sister's place assisting me today, Edgeworth," Simon said from behind his desk.

Mr. Edgeworth nodded. "Of course, my lord. Miss Shelby, allow me to introduce Mr. Harrison and Mr. Plum, two of Lord Wade's tenants."

Both men bowed to her, and she curtsied. Mr. Harrison, sporting a gray mustache and bushy sideburns, frowned at her but was polite. Mr. Plum, florid of complexion, was as round as his name suggested. Both were well dressed for farmers.

Simon sat back in his chair. "To begin, let us summarize the situation, gentlemen. You have been arguing over who has the rights to an orchard that straddles the property line between your farms. Tell me again why you cannot divide the proceeds evenly."

Mr. Harrison gave an exaggerated sigh. "Lord Wade, dividing the profit doesn't work. My men do a larger amount of work throughout the year, so how is that fair?"

"That is not true!" Mr. Plum's face grew even redder. "I cannot help it if you have your workers there at dawn. Mine have cows to milk before they can see to the orchard."

"I have my workers milking cows *before* dawn. I can't help it if your son does not oversee your farm properly."

"Son?" Simon interjected. "What does Mr. Plum's son have to do with your argument?"

Both farmers glared at each other and said nothing.

"There is more anger here than is necessary for a simple property dispute," Simon said.

"It's not so simple," Mr. Harrison said, sitting forward on the edge of his chair. "We are talkin' about a lot of money!"

Louisa realized that in his anger, his accent was beginning to coarsen.

"Of course it's over money," Mr. Plum said. "If my son weren't being distracted—"

Mr. Harrison rose swiftly to his feet. "Distracted! And who would you be accusin' of that!"

Mr. Plum pushed himself up out of his chair to meet the other man's glare.

"Gentlemen, please," Simon said in a soft, firm voice. "It seems to me that there is more here than a dispute over an orchard. What else comes between you?"

They said nothing; one stared at the floor, the other stared out the window. Louisa saw guilt in both men, and a stubbornness that resisted compromise.

Simon folded his hands on his desk. "You have spent years as amicable neighbors; something had to have happened recently. Something to do with young Tom Plum? Is he bothering you, Mr. Harrison?"

Louisa was surprised that Simon knew the boy's name.

"He's not botherin' *me*," the man said grimly.

"Ah, then he's bothering someone else in your family."

"Tom's not bothering her!" Mr. Plum finally exploded. "She's too damn—excuse me, Miss Shelby—too darn forward. What's a boy supposed to do?"

Simon gave a faint smile. "Mr. Harrison, are we referring to your daughter, Emma?"

"She's not forward!" Mr. Harrison insisted, glaring at Mr. Plum. "She's a good girl. It's your son who—"

Mr. Plum opened his mouth to respond, glanced at Simon, and then sank back in his chair heaving a sad sigh. "He loves her. I've tried to talk sense into him, tried to tell him he could marry the miller's daughter—even the vicar's daughter."

Mr. Harrison narrowed his eyes. "Are you tryin' to say he could do better than my daughter?"

"I've met Emma," Simon interjected. "She's a fine young lady. And Mr. Plum, your son Tom is smart and ambitious. So why are the two of you so upset about their courtship? Are either of them engaged?"

Mr. Plum shook his head, as Mr. Harrison said, "No."

"Mr. Plum, we're nearing an agreement for you to purchase your farm."

Mr. Plum nodded and glanced at his neighbor, who looked at him with reluctant interest.

"And Mr. Harrison," Simon continued, "I understand that Emma has a dowry."

"Of course she does," Mr. Harrison said proudly.

"With Mr. Plum's son, she would own land."

Mr. Harrison and Mr. Plum both nodded in resignation.

"So can you settle the profits of the orchard?"

They nodded again, forgetting that Simon couldn't see them.

"We won't be taking any more of your time, Lord Wade," Mr. Plum said.

Mr. Harrison reached for his hat. "We'll send word of our agreement. Good day, Miss Shelby."

Mr. Edgeworth followed them to the door. "I'll see them out, my lord."

Louisa watched Simon, who seemed to stare at the door the men had left through. "So will their children marry?" she asked.

"It seems to be inevitable," he said, smiling.

"And that was the only source of their disagreement?"

"Every man wants his children to do better than he did. They just needed to realize they'd already accomplished that goal."

Softly, she said, "Georgie told me she acts as your eyes in these meetings, telling you what people's expressions conveyed to her."

"Yes."

"It seems to me that you understood what was going on all by yourself."

"That was a fluke."

"I don't think so. I always admired your easy way with people."

He seemed bothered by the topic. "So what are your plans for Georgie?"

First she'd kissed him, now she was admiring him. How much more obvious could she be? She was glad to think about something else—anything else but how drawn she was to him. This—awareness—between them was almost frightening, when one had never experienced it before. She was confused and worried. What were they supposed to do now? How could they go back to a simple friendship? Because she knew he didn't want more than that.

She told herself that as a friend, she could be grateful for his triumphs; he'd begun to eat in front of his family, even in front of her. And he ate like the gentleman he was, although with slow caution. He did eat one item of food at a time, and she noticed that someone had cut his meat before it was served to him. But if he eventually learned to do that himself, he would surely have more confidence.

But she had to remember to keep Georgie between them. "My plans for Georgie are quite simple, my lord. If you had bothered to ask me when I first proposed this to you—"

Frowning, he interrupted her. "That's in the past. Much has happened—and you know my name."

"That is far too intimate. If we are to ignore this—"

"But—"

She waited, but he said nothing more. She was terribly curious, but once again the pleasant mask had come down over his face.

"Your grandmother will be escorting Georgie and me to London in a few days to order your sister a new wardrobe."

"Good. She needs one."

"And is a wardrobe so important to you, my lord?"

A smile eased across his face, and she relaxed.

"Obviously not," he said. "You could wear sackcloth, and I wouldn't know the difference."

She blushed, uncertain if he were complimenting her or stating a simple fact.

"But it's important for my sister to feel good about herself," he continued.

"I'm glad you feel that way. I've also worked with her lady's maid to change her hairstyle."

He only nodded.

"I'm going to work on her musical abilities."

"She doesn't sing well."

"But she can play. We'll make her so accomplished that everyone will want to be accompanied by her. As a hostess she can learn to master serving her guests. As a dancer . . ."

He visibly winced.

"You've told me the dancing didn't go well," she said, smiling. "I can remedy that. I am an excellent dancer."

"Modest, too," he said with amusement.

"Lord Wade, this is not a situation that calls for modesty. My talents can help your sister."

When he said nothing, she couldn't read his face.

"Do you doubt me, my lord?"

"No, but don't be surprised if I decide to make sure you know what you're doing."

The challenge should have bothered her—instead she shivered with anticipation.

* * *

The next afternoon, Louisa realized that Simon was making good on his threat. She and Georgie were in the drawing room going through sheet music, when Manvil escorted him into the room and helped him find a chair near the door.

She knew Simon wasn't watching her, but once again she noticed how much his attention could capture her. She forced him from her mind as she sat on the piano bench and instructed Georgie in the best way to accompany various types of singers—hesitant, loud, too fast, too slow.

"Now you need to practice," Louisa said, raising her voice. "I wonder if there is someone biding his time in boredom who might want to sing."

"Very funny," Simon said dryly from behind them.

Georgie exchanged a glance with Louisa then looked over her shoulder at her brother. "If you're not going to sing, why are you here? Surely there is business to work on, or boats that need to be rowed."

Louisa laughed. She watched Simon fold his arms over his chest.

"So if I want to hear my sister play an instrument, that is poorly done of me?" he said with a wounded air. "I can't pass a quiet moment in peace, receiving pleasure from sound, one of the only senses I have left?"

Louisa and Georgie both groaned.

"All right, all right," Louisa said with resignation. "I'll sing. Georgie, get ready."

She preceded to sing at every possible pace imaginable, until they were both breathless with laughter, and she could sing no more. Simon wore a smile, though he never approached them.

Quietly, Louisa said, "Keep playing, Georgie. I'm going to see if your brother will actually join us."

"Regardless, you should be impressed with yourself, Louisa. He hasn't come near a piano at all until you arrived."

Louisa frowned. "You should know that he's practically challenged me to make sure I do a decent job by you. That's probably why he's here."

Georgie hit a wrong note. "What? That is the silliest things I ever—I'll just have to talk to him."

"No, please let me handle this. I don't want him to think I'm betraying his confidence."

"If you insist," she said reluctantly.

"Keep playing," Louisa whispered, then left Georgie to walk to Simon. She made sure her footsteps were loud.

"You don't have to pound the floor," Simon said as she approached.

"Pound the floor?" she asked innocently, sitting down beside him.

"I heard you before you started walking heavily."

"Such incredible hearing you have—but it *is* one of your only senses left."

"You're very good at turning my words around."

"Because it's so easy to do," she said sweetly.

He smiled and shook his head, and she felt some of her nervousness leave. He was a man, and she had always thought she understood men. But then she'd never dealt so personally with her gentlemen callers. She let herself admire his fair hair, and those masculine dimples that were made for laughter. When pleasure tensed and curled inside her, she tried to put it aside. Was she making everything worse?

"So are you really going to sit here and just listen?" she asked, wondering at his true motives.

"Why not? My sister plays well. And how can you be upset that I'm here? I'm not hiding from my family, as you feared."

She winced at his sarcasm. "You could sing."

"She doesn't need me to. In fact, she doesn't need you singing either."

Frowning at him, she wished she could read the expression in his eyes. But there was none. She hadn't realized how much she understood people by that alone—and how much he must miss the ability.

"And why shouldn't I sing?" she asked.

"Because you sing quite … passionately." His voice had deepened. "And I don't mean with emotion."

She was relieved that he couldn't see her shock. "Passionately? My lord, that song was about a shepherd girl tending her flock!"

"It doesn't matter what you sing—your voice gives the song an edge. I don't know," he added with a shrug. "Maybe only men can hear it."

She sat back, stunned, and watched Georgie continue to play. "So when I sing about shepherds, men hear something else?"

"I'm sorry I said anything," he said, rising to his feet. "I'm sure I'm mistaken."

"No, you don't think you're wrong."

He didn't call for Manvil, so he stood still, with obvious indecision.

So he thought she sang … suggestively? It made her feel strange and uncertain, something she usually never was.

"Simon?" Georgie called. "Can I escort you somewhere?"

"No, trusty Manvil will have heard you," Simon said.

The valet appeared in the doorway. "My lord?"

Simon left, Georgie played on, and Louisa sank back in the chair. She should take offense at Simon's words, but she couldn't. This was a man who'd kissed her passionately, had said he couldn't stop thinking about her. Of course he could hear things in her voice—because his thoughts put them there. She was the first single woman he'd been near in many months. She shouldn't even be flattered in his interest, when of course he was desperate. And he was fighting it.

He at least recognized their flirtation as only that. She wasn't so certain what she thought of it. She only knew that something had to be done, or he'd sit in this house obsessing about her for no other reason than that she was all that was available.

And that wasn't very flattering.

Chapter 9

$\sim\!\!\!\infty\!\!\!\sim$

Simon rowed harder and harder. He could hear the slap of the oars hitting the water, the rush of the waves he created with his own power. Sweat ran down his face, stinging his eyes, and his tired muscles ached.

"You're going to break the oars," Manvil said casually.

"Then we swim."

They were silent for several more minutes.

"Your sister plays well."

Between grunts, Simon said, "Thank you."

"Miss Shelby sings well."

One oar went too deep, out of rhythm with the other. Simon caught it and continued rowing. "She does."

He still couldn't believe he'd told her she sang passionately. What the hell had he been thinking? He didn't know if he'd made her feel badly—or revealed too much about himself.

She knew he was attracted to her. He'd already

admitted it, and proved it with his hands and mouth.

His big mouth.

"Why didn't you sing with her?" Manvil asked.

"I didn't know the song."

"But even if you did, you wouldn't have sung with her."

"Probably not."

"Can't trust yourself, huh?"

Simon frowned. "Manvil, isn't there a line between employer and servant that you're crossing?"

"I passed that a long time ago. So why couldn't you sing with her?"

"Be quiet," Simon said tiredly.

"Then I shouldn't tell you we're about to hit the shore?"

Simon quickly reversed his rowing until they slowed down. He felt a gentle grind along the keel. "Were you just going to let me beach the boat?"

"Might have been good for you."

Simon sighed and used an oar to push away from the shore. "I wish you'd find that line and cross back over it."

"And let you be bored?"

Simon harrumphed.

Simon thought he was quite subtle the following morning when he questioned Georgie about the day's lesson with Louisa. It would be dancing, another thing he could not help his sister with. He remembered Georgie writing him letters about her dancing masters whining over their injured toes. She'd made it all into a joke, and he'd been so busy with his own life, that he'd accepted it.

Not anymore. Dancing was a sensitive topic for her since she'd tripped the duke's son. He didn't remember her dancing at all after that, unless he himself dragged her onto the floor. How would Louisa handle such a delicate thing?

Georgie invited him to attend, confessing her nerves, giving Simon a way in without making it look like his idea.

After luncheon, Simon had Manvil escort him to the far end of the manor, where the ballroom occupied a corner of the ground floor, and opened up onto the terrace.

"The ladies are going to dance?" Manvil said doubtfully.

"Are they here?"

"Yes, in the far corner where the housekeeper is seated at the piano."

"I wondered who was going to play for them."

"I was impressed with how you managed to get yourself invited."

Simon gave an exaggerated sigh. "It's a shame I must keep you around all day."

Manvil didn't answer, only guided him into

the room. Simon imagined it all as he walked. He could see the tall windows in his mind, see the sun shining in them rather than moonlight. And there would be Louisa, that red hair shining. He remembered other ballrooms, where he'd watched her through the crowd. She'd been almost a queen among subjects then.

As always, he wondered why she wanted to help Georgie more than returning to be the toast of London.

"Simon, you came!" Georgie cried.

Manvil retreated to the corridor as usual. Simon heard the sound of her soft slippers running toward him, then lowered his cheek for her quick kiss.

"I don't mind being moral support," he said mildly.

"Moral support?" Louisa said. "Dancing is that frightening, Georgie?"

"The memories are not good," Georgie said. "Do you ... know what happened, Louisa? How I embarrassed myself?"

Simon began, "You did not embarrass yourself—"

Then he felt a soft touch on his arm and stopped. He knew who touched him like that, full of hesitancy, yet lingering a bit too long. Louisa.

"Georgie," she said, "your brother told me a little. You must feel terrible that people witnessed your mistakes in so public a place."

After a pause, Georgie said, "It was dreadful.

I don't even think the duke's son would have asked me, but Grandmama knew his mother and … I'm sure he felt obliged. And then I put him on his face on the floor."

"Oh dear," Louisa said.

"His nose bled," Georgie continued grimly. "There were spatters of blood on his white waistcoat. I can still see it when I close my eyes."

"What did he do?" Louisa asked.

"The bastard walked away," Simon said in a low voice. "I saw it all."

"He sounds like a fool." Louisa spoke dismissively. "What man would treat a young girl that way? He probably deserved a good bloodying. He shouldn't have left you standing there."

"He needed to clean himself," Georgie said weakly.

"But he didn't return." Simon cocked his head toward his sister. "And you refused to dance after that."

"That night only you asked me!"

"Other men did at later events."

"Brave ones. I would have tripped them, too."

"It sounds to me like you just need practice," Louisa said. "Mrs. Calbert will play a quadrille, and you and I will begin."

"Will you be the man, Louisa?" Georgie asked.

Simon relaxed at the returning sound of laughter beneath her words.

"I make a very good man," Louisa said.

He almost snorted at that one. "There would

be a lot of padding and binding involved to make you look even remotely like a man."

"I think that was a compliment!" Georgie cried.

"Nonsense," Louisa said.

He liked the practicality in her tone.

"He's just trying to make excuses for why I won't be able to dance like one," Louisa continued. "There are a lot of steps in the quadrille, and I'm sure I will be able to recreate the man's part."

But it was harder than it seemed. Georgie guided Simon over to the piano, where he listened to Mrs. Calbert keep up a running commentary on the dancing while she played.

In the middle of the dance, Louisa would curtsy when she was supposed to bow, step on Georgie's feet when she moved during the lady's steps.

"Oh, dear," Mrs. Calbert said, ending the song on a discordant note. "They've both fallen to their knees."

The laughter went on so long that Simon thought their stomachs would be aching. It was good to hear Georgie enjoying herself.

"So much for my playing the part of a man," Louisa said shakily. "Later we'll just keep doing the women's steps ourselves, side by side. But for now, while we have a man available, I suggest we waltz."

Simon tensed as neither of the other two women answered. She was actually challenging him. Was he going to sit here and not try? Georgie needed him, and the least he could do was partner her.

He rose to his feet and took a deep breath. "I know a dare when I hear one."

For a moment, Louisa said nothing, and he realized he'd rendered her speechless.

"You did waltz well, my lord," she finally said. "I saw you once at a ball."

"You noticed Simon in a crush of people?" Georgie asked.

He frowned at how amazed she sounded. Women often used to notice him, he wanted to say. But it wasn't exactly appropriate to confide that to his eighteen-year-old sister.

"Of course I noticed him," Louisa said. "He has all that blond hair. And the lady I was talking to was quite mad for him."

"And who would that be?" Simon asked.

"Ladies never tell."

For a moment, he thought of other things ladies never told. When Louisa touched his arm, and her perfume enveloped him, he barely kept from flinching. What had seemed like an acceptable challenge now seemed like a dreadful risk.

"I'll watch you two dance," Georgie said.

Simon frowned. "But I thought you and I were going to—"

"Oh it's been many months since I waltzed."

"Me, too," he said dryly.

"But you waltzed for years. You'll remember with Louisa, and then you'll dance with me. Go ahead."

Simon heard the first flow of music, and he stood frozen, feeling self-conscious and ridiculous. There was nothing but air all around him, and he was adrift. And then he felt the brush of Louisa's skirt against his legs, felt her hand coming to rest on his shoulder. It was natural to slide his hand around her waist, to take her other hand in his.

She wasn't wearing gloves. Her skin was warm and dry, and suddenly he wondered if his palms were sweaty. And then he took a step and she was with him, twirling lightly in his arms. He didn't know where he was on the dance floor, but she did, and with subtle pressure, led him as he once would have led her. The rhythm of the dance caught him, and his feet moved effortlessly. If he could see, he would be looking down into her eyes. He didn't even know what his expression looked like to her.

This was too serious, too ... on display.

"Do you see, Georgie?" Louisa called.

Simon thought she sounded breathless, and he imagined how breathless he could make her in bed. He found himself tightening his hold. He could feel the muscles in her back as she moved, and their thighs brushed as he whirled her ever closer.

"Simon is displaying the correct dancing posture for the man," Louisa continued. "You can use that to help you remember your own form."

Her voice sounded ever fainter. Her hand clutched at his shoulder.

He had to put a stop to this before their attraction to each other was obvious to everyone. He let his arm go limp, and hers did, too. She stumbled against him, her shoulder hitting his chest, before she righted herself.

"Now you see why you each must hold yourselves erect," Simon said. "Your arms should be taut, not as collapsible as a string."

"What else should I look for?" Georgie called.

Long ago, from across ballrooms Louisa had watched Simon waltz and had longed to be in his arms, the recipient of his playful smile and his single-minded attention. She hadn't known his name then, had only caught glimpses of him in the crush at parties. But she'd envied the other ladies who'd known him well enough to be asked to dance.

But in this private dance he wasn't smiling. And he wasn't seeing her of course, but oh how she'd come to bask in the focus that was all his. They'd moved together like he'd never stopped dancing, like his lack of sight didn't matter. It was all body to body, taking cues from each other. And he'd allowed her to lead him about the ballroom floor without complaint.

But it was too dangerous. He was wise to change this lesson into a demonstration. His hand crept up her back until she was forced to lift her elbow higher and higher.

"A bad waltz partner will leave you flapping your arm like a bird," Simon told his sister.

"But how can I stop him?" Georgie asked.

Louisa pushed his forearm down. "Like this. It will be better to embarrass him for a moment."

Then Simon pulled her right up against him, and with a squeak she tried to push away. His thigh dipped hard between hers, and she was shocked by the surge of pleasure. It was sinful, and far too embarrassing with Georgie in the room. And Louisa wanted desperately to be alone with him.

Georgie laughed. "Louisa is trying to move you back, Simon. What do I do if my partner won't?"

"You stop dancing," Louisa said, dropping her arms and giving a final push. Simon stepped away. "A gentleman will understand that he took liberties with you which he must not. You should conclude that he is a rake, and must be avoided."

Was she trying to convince herself?

"Simon, you never danced like that," Georgie said, shaking her head.

He put a hand to his heart. "Never."

Georgie rushed forward. "My turn!"

Louisa gladly backed away and let her pupil dance with Simon. He was all smiles and decorum for his sister.

"Now, Georgie," he said patiently, "the men you'll dance with will lead you. But with me, you're going to have to lead. Otherwise we'll ram into a wall or go through a window."

"Oh." She controlled her giggle. "I don't know how to lead."

"It's all done with pressure. I'll show you."

Louisa sat down beside the piano and exchanged smiles with Mrs. Calbert as the woman began to play another waltz. Louisa reminded herself that it was good to see Simon instructing Georgie, to see him taking a risk by dancing. Maybe it was one step closer to seeing him attend a ball again. Although it would be much riskier for him to dance with dozens of couples at once. But this was a good start.

Though she wanted to see him thrive, she didn't want to be the woman he turned to because she was the only one available.

Chapter 10

In the morning, all three ladies left for London, and Simon remained at home. Georgie had tried to talk him into joining them for the day, but he claimed visiting dressmakers was a woman's duty, not a man's. Louisa and Georgie would be well chaperoned by his grandmother, who loved to shop.

When they had gone, the house seemed empty. Oh, there were servants bustling about, and a bailiff from a nearby estate who needed to speak with him.

But Simon accepted the fact that he was lonely. He reminded himself that his grandmother and sister brought him happiness with their conversations and their caring.

But somehow Louisa Shelby had become important to him. Her no-nonsense compassion moved him, rather than making him feel beholden to her.

And he didn't know what to do about it.

How could he be worried about her reputation

one minute, and wanting to ruin it himself the next?

The women were home in time for dinner, and Simon joined them. He liked listening to the sound of their voices talking about the coffeehouse they'd stopped at for luncheon, or the old friends they'd met on the street. Louisa had praised Georgie's new wardrobe, until he could practically hear his sister's pleased embarrassment. Whatever he might think of Louisa's effect on Georgie's acceptance in society, her cheerful, helpful company was doing Georgie a world of good.

He was her brother; he should be helping as much as he could. When they retired to the drawing room, he listened to her plink the piano keys, as if her thoughts were turning sad. He wanted her happy.

"Are you going to play a real song?" he asked. "I can't make myself sing to *that*."

There, he'd said it; he couldn't take it back now. And the audience was only his family—and Louisa. Once upon a time, dozens of young ladies had stared enraptured as he sang. Surely this couldn't be too difficult.

"You'll sing with me?" Georgie said, her delight returning.

"Only if we sing a duet—one I know."

Lady Wade gave a loud sigh. "My favorite way to spend an evening. You children are so good to me."

When Simon rose to his feet, Manvil was there to guide him to the piano. He could hear Georgie paging through sheet music, and at the opening chords, he knew the song immediately. She had a musical ear, but a weak singing voice that she could never seem to make louder. He had the lungs to belt out anything he sang. He concentrated on her voice, trying to drown out his doubts and insecurities.

Why did he feel on display? Louisa was a woman he'd kissed, for God's sake. But he'd come to hate being the focus of attention.

And Georgie had been so thrilled to accompany him, just as she'd done her whole life.

When the song ended, the butler announced Paul Reyburn, and Simon was relieved.

"Don't stop on my account," Paul said. "It's good to hear you sing."

Louisa tried not to show her disappointment at the arrival of Simon's friend. She'd been enjoying the opportunity to stare freely at Simon. He kept his eyes closed while he sang, and she wondered if he was seeing the music in his head.

Or if again, he didn't like to think of people staring at his blank eyes. Didn't he understand that he was so easy to look at—and it had nothing to do with his eyes.

Georgie closed up the piano and escorted Simon over to sit near Mr. Reyburn.

"So how are the lessons going, Miss Wade?" Mr. Reyburn asked.

Louisa stared at the girl in surprise.

Georgie blushed. "I told him about them. He was sympathetic." She turned and beamed at Mr. Reyburn. "We've ordered a new wardrobe. And I'm working on my dancing—I even danced with Simon."

Mr. Reyburn glanced at Simon in surprise.

Simon shrugged. "Little sisters are such an annoyance."

"Simon!" Georgie said.

"You know," Louisa began slowly, "we were going to work on Miss Wade's conversation skills. Mr. Reyburn, would you like to assist us?"

She saw Simon give her a small frown, but she ignored him. She didn't want to demonstrate her skills with Simon. It would be too revealing of her feelings.

They treated it like a play, with Louisa and Georgie taking turns. Even Lady Wade got involved, contributing suggestions as to where Georgie should stand when she was first "introduced" to Mr. Reyburn. Simon didn't say much, and Louisa found herself occasionally glancing at him. He had an amused expression on his face, but she knew how well he hid his feelings when he wanted to.

Louisa made the introductions, and Mr. Reyburn said all the polite things about the weather and the evening. When Georgie wasn't trying to stop laughing, she answered well enough, but Louisa knew the true test would be with a stranger, when Georgie wasn't relaxing at home with her family. They would have to begin accepting invitations when the first gowns of Georgie's new wardrobe arrived. It was the only way she was going to put to use what they'd been practicing.

After Mr. Reyburn left, Georgie and Lady Wade stood up to retire. When Louisa was going to join them, Simon said, "Could you wait, Miss Shelby? I have something I want to discuss."

Louisa's uneasiness rose to the surface, along with a thread of anticipation that she couldn't deny.

Lady Wade gave them a curious glance, but all she said was, "We'll leave the door open."

"I promise not to compromise her, Grandmama," Simon said dryly.

"Simon!" his grandmother said sternly.

But finally Louisa was alone with Simon. She was seated on the sofa, and he was in a chair to her right.

Far too close.

"What do you wish to discuss, Simon?"

"Your conversational skills have always been formidable," he said slowly.

She blinked at him. "Well, thank you. I always think it's best to have many interests, to read books. A man appreciates that a woman can converse about something other than the weather. I'm working on that with your sister."

"So now you're a governess, too?"

"Of course not."

"Forgive me, my own conversational abilities are lacking tonight. I can't help wondering if these interested men you're talking about were interested in what you were actually saying."

She bristled. "Speak plainly, Simon."

"A man doesn't always say plainly what he's implying."

"I don't know what you mean."

"Surely you know that there are some men who delight in teasing a woman."

"And a woman should know how to deflect such a thing, even walk away."

"But what if she doesn't realize what is going on? What if he's doing this for the amusement of his nearby friends?"

"Simon, what are you trying to say? I can't prepare Georgie unless you speak plainly."

He took a deep breath. "All right, let me give you a mild example. We're introduced at a dance."

Suddenly he leaned toward her and smiled so charmingly that she caught her breath.

"Miss Shelby, you are a wonderful dancer." His voice was smooth and flowing, and did things to her insides that she had no name for.

Trying to remember her skepticism, she said, "Thank you, my lord."

"I hear you're a woman of many talents."

"I do play the piano." She didn't understand what he was trying to say. It all sounded so normal—although said in his most elegant, charming way.

"Do you play the flute?"

"No, but I've always wanted to learn."

"Then I'll have to make sure you do." With a sigh, he leaned back in his chair and folded his arms across his chest.

It took her a moment to get over the spell of his attention. "What?" she demanded.

"There are some men, when they say they've heard that you're a woman of many talents, are implying something ... sordid."

She gaped at him. "Talents as in . . ."

"In the bedroom."

She felt her face flame. "That can't be so."

"And talking about making sure you learn to use a flute?"

"Yes?" She tensed.

"That can be an allusion to a man's genitalia."

She inhaled swiftly, and didn't seem to know what to do with her hands. Thank God he couldn't see her. "Really?" she whispered.

"Really. I've seen groups of men employ this technique just to amuse themselves for the evening."

"Such scandalous men aren't worth knowing," she said primly.

"My point exactly. And in conversation, a woman needs to learn how to tell the difference. So often it's in his expressions, in the way he holds his mouth, or glances to the side at his friends."

"Or by reputation?"

Simon hesitated. "There is that. One can never be too careful." He rose to his feet, picking up his cane. "Manvil?"

His valet entered and came to his side.

"Think on what I've said, Louisa." Simon put his hand on Manvil's shoulder.

"How can I disillusion her?" she said, standing up to block his way. "She's frightened enough. If I give her such knowledge, she'll only speak to old ladies. I was never told such things, and I was just fine."

He shrugged. "Were you? Or maybe you didn't know what was going on. Good night, Louisa."

She watched him leave, and inside, her nerves made her stomach ache. Had she had conversations where she didn't understand the real meaning? She didn't like how that could twist her memories. It just couldn't be true.

Late that night, Simon couldn't stay in his room any longer. He took to walking the corridors in frustration. He shouldn't have explained the innuendoes to Louisa. She'd sounded genuinely horrified. How could someone acquire such a fast reputation and not know the intricacies of flirting with a rake?

He still hadn't deciphered her motives for teaching Georgie. How could she simply want to help people? So she'd lost some friends when she'd come down in the world—hell, he knew all about that. But why give up London Society if one didn't have to? Other women found ways to entertain themselves. Did she need someone to do it for her? Those kinds of women used to appeal to him. He'd always loved to entertain, and had enjoyed their attentions in return. But now he found that sort of helpless woman needy. He was no longer "the entertainer," a position he'd so valued his entire life. From childhood, he was the one who could make his parents laugh, and it took him many years to realize that it was the only time they seemed happy together.

Louisa had never struck him as the sort of woman who needed someone else to make her feel complete. Why was he so drawn to her? All right, he enjoyed the husky sound of her voice. He was grateful for the compassion she showed his grandmother and sister. And that perfume that lingered everywhere she'd been was enough to drive him wild.

Suddenly his cane hit something hard and he came to a stop. With all his ruminating, he'd forgotten to count his steps when he'd turned down the hall. And had he turned to the right or left? He wasn't sure if he was in the gentlemen's or ladies' wing of the manor. He squelched his instantaneous embarrassment. For several minutes he stumbled down the corridor, feeling more and more foolish. Door after door, he would knock, listen for silence, then step inside, each time hoping he could find a piece of furniture that would give him an idea which room he was in.

Suddenly, he heard a door open behind him, and he froze.

"Simon?"

It was Louisa, the one person he didn't want seeing him like this, fumbling around helplessly like the blind man he was.

"Is everything all right?" she asked, and her voice was closer now.

"Everything's fine," he said briskly. "You can go back to bed."

"But why are you opening doors?"

"I simply forgot to count my paces, and I lost my sense of direction. I was hoping I'd recognize a room to reorient myself."

"Ah, I always wondered how you found your way around at night."

His skin was hot with embarrassment. He was back to the beginning again, wondering how she looked at him, how she pitied him. His muscles were stiff; his jaw ached from clenching his teeth. Every time he was convinced he was getting by, that he was all right, something happened to make him realize how helpless he was. He was so tired of feeling alone, something he still wasn't used to.

He walked toward her voice. "I can't sleep. Mind if I come in?"

He heard her gasp, knew how scandalous he was being. She'd send him on his way any moment.

Then he felt her arm slide into his, and she led him inside. The entire room smelled of her; he could imagine lazy mornings waking up surrounded by the essence of her.

"I didn't have a chance to light a candle," she said. "I think there's a chair right here."

"Ah, so you're in the dark tonight, too." His tension began to subside.

With his cane he found the chair, then he bent until he could feel the seat. He sat down, then gave her a half smile. "I know I shouldn't be here."

"Stay a little while. I was writing letters earlier, and it always makes me miss my sisters. Your company is appreciated."

"I don't think so. This is a good excuse for you to pick my brain and try to see what I'm thinking."

"Me?"

"Yes. I told you before, I'm not in despair—although my foolishness tonight probably has you wondering."

"I didn't think—"

"Then what were you thinking when you came to my room? There aren't many women who would immediately assume that I wanted to kill myself, not when I have my family and my faculties. Well, most of them."

She was silent for a long minute, and he began to wonder if he'd touched on something too deep for her to discuss.

"My father had those things, too," she said

softly, hesitantly. "And it didn't matter. He killed himself."

His mouth fell open, and he had to cover his shock as he said, "I never heard that. I'm so sorry, Louisa."

"We hid it. I shouldn't even be telling you. I vowed to my sisters and mother that I'd never tell a soul, and here I've just ... blurted it out."

"Maybe you needed to tell someone. I promise you that no one will ever hear about it from me."

"Thank you. You see, I never recognized *his* despair. Of all my sisters, I was closest to him and I never saw his problems, never realized he needed help."

"He hid them from you?"

"Oh yes. Several business investments had gone bad, and he was finally out of money."

Simon inhaled sharply. "You mean he left his family alone to deal with his mistakes?"

"Surely you can see that he was not in his right mind."

He could see that the man had been a coward, but she didn't need to hear that.

"My mother was ... not herself. She didn't want their old friends and business acquaintances to know. And she wanted him buried in the church graveyard."

"So you took the burden of hiding a suicide." He imagined three young women seeing their father's body, hearing their mother's hysteria. They'd become the adults in their family.

"It wasn't that difficult," she said distantly. "He'd hanged himself. We didn't let anyone see the body."

"My God." No one had comforted her, and he couldn't now, though he wanted to take her into his arms.

She took a deep breath. "So forgive me for jumping to conclusions about your mental state."

"I do. It's understandable."

In the dark, in their companionable silence, he felt a closeness to her that had been rare with anyone these many months. It made him sad and uneasy that he'd somehow lost the ability. Had he changed so much? He didn't want to think so.

"Your situation makes my parents seem quite ... normal," he said.

"You didn't think so before?"

"They were not exactly selfless. My mother is a very beautiful woman, and I think she was disappointed that Georgie doesn't look like her. That doesn't say much for my mother, does it."

Bitterness crept into his voice, but Louisa said nothing.

"And Leo took up so much of their time—constantly having to be told to study, and rescued from his various schemes."

"Your brother doesn't sound much like you."

"Oh, he's a charming scoundrel, believe me. He's very good at making one want to help him. I've probably done too much for him myself. For my parents, Georgie was too easy to raise—a hard worker and very dutiful. When my mother neglected to take her under her wing, to teach her of the feminine arts involved in the *ton*, Georgie seemed glad to be free of it all. Her inferior governess tried to seduce me more than teach Georgie."

"And your mother didn't do anything about her?" Louisa asked in outrage.

"Well I didn't exactly share that last part," he said wryly. "And as I said before, my mother—"

"Was more concerned about herself. It's amazing you—and Georgie, of course—ended up such decent people."

"You think I'm decent?" he said. "You wouldn't think that of me if you knew what I was thinking when alone in the dark with you."

Chapter 11

Louisa found herself shivering, although she was terribly warm. She was seated close to him, their knees almost touching. Her eyes were constantly drawn to the loose buttons undone at his neck, leaving his skin bare. The moonlight sculpted him, shadowed him, made him remote and yet so touchable. Every time she was with him, her own skin seemed alive with sensation. She reminded herself that he was lonely, and a romance was not the way to help him. He needed a friend more than a lover, and she wanted to be that for him—though a dark part of her longed to be the other.

"You should go, Simon," she whispered, although she made no move to see him to the door.

She watched his face. Shadows hid his eyes, but she basked in the way he always focused on her. She'd felt so drawn to him that she'd told him about her father, broken vows she'd sworn to her family. What more would she do in the name of this ... awareness between them?

And how could she know if sympathy were driving her emotions, and if he were just reacting to that? She sensed that his selfish mother had worked her cruelty on him as well. How would a woman like that tolerate a blind son?

He rose to his feet, and when she did, too, she took his arm. She felt him stiffen, saw the way his head swung to look down at her.

"When you touch me," he said in a low, tense voice, "it's hard to remember that you're only helping a blind man to the door."

"I'm a friend helping a friend. Why can't you accept anyone's help? It doesn't always have to be about pity or lust."

"I'd prefer lust."

But he let her help him toward the door.

"You know, Simon, you've walked so much at night that you know your way about."

"And you got that from tonight?"

"Tonight was an aberration. But if you'd walk around even more—say, by day—you'd become more proficient at it."

"I hate not knowing who's in a room."

"Then tell everyone that. When you enter a room, they should know to tell you they're there. You're not imposing on anyone that way. Everyone here cares about you. Look how much you pleased them by simply sharing your meals."

For a silent moment, she regarded him, trying to find the emotions he hid behind his expressionless face.

"I'll think about it," he finally said.

But there was a quirk to his lips that made her think she had won this point.

She opened the door, checked the corridor to make sure it was empty, and then guided his hand to the doorframe. "Good night."

The next day, while the ladies were just sitting down to luncheon, deep in conversation about their next London trip, Simon came into the dining room—alone.

Louisa understood the significance immediately, and her heart lifted with gladness. Simon let his fingers trail along the chairs as he walked toward his place at the head of the table. Louisa almost called out a warning, because Lady Wade's chair was several inches farther out than the empty ones next to her.

But Simon's cane tapped the leg of the chair, and with his fingers he found his way around it. Startled, Lady Wade frowned up at him, then understanding flooded her face, and her eyes moistened with tears. She stared hard at Georgie, who gaped at Simon, then put a finger to her lips.

Simon pulled out his chair, sat down, and gave them all a smile. "This silence among you three is rather obvious. No, Manvil did not accompany me. Yes, it's a miracle. Can we eat?"

"Oh, Simon," his grandmother said fondly. "I knew you could do it."

"I'm trying, Grandmama. But you'll have to

promise that when I enter a room, someone tells me who's there."

"Oh, of course. And right now, it's Georgie, Louisa, and I."

He grinned. "Thank you."

Louisa took a chance. "You know, my lord, I have been thinking about the way to serve you food. I know you usually have only one item on your plate."

"Makes things simpler," he said dryly. "But do you plan to change that, too?"

Lady Wade and Georgie looked between them with obvious curiosity.

Louisa blushed. "What if we try four items, and tell you where they are? Like top, bottom, left, right."

"I don't wish to unduly burden the servants," he said, putting his napkin in his lap.

Georgie flashed a worried look at Louisa.

But Louisa struggled on. "They're already preparing several plates now. I don't think it's any more of a burden to place the food on one plate in a certain position."

He sighed. "Don't you feel you're burdening the poor blind man with too many new things in one day?"

"Simon," Lady Wade scolded. "I haven't noticed any self-pity, so you can't start now."

Louisa held her breath, exchanging glances with Georgie.

Simon hesitated. "Grandmama, just because

I don't display my every feeling, doesn't mean I haven't experienced them. Self pity, especially. But I'm doing better. And I'll think about what Miss Shelby said regarding my food."

"That's all anyone can ask," Lady Wade said.

They ate in companionable silence until Simon was served a plate of ham, and Georgie tried to cut it for him.

"Georgie," he said, "if you don't want me to pity myself, then I need to start cutting my meat so I feel older than five."

"Oh," she said, straightening up and setting down his knife. "I knew that Cook would—I never meant—"

"Of course you didn't," he said gently. "You have been my source of strength through this, Georgie, and I wouldn't have come this far without you."

Lady Wade dabbed at her eyes again, and even Louisa felt a tightening in her throat. Before making fools of themselves crying in front of Simon, they went on talking about Georgie's wardrobe fittings. They all pretended not to watch Simon, who was the center of attention, whether he wanted to be or not. He cut his meat slowly, felt purposefully for the meat, speared it, and put it into his mouth. He showed no triumph at doing something so little, but Louisa felt it for him.

Had she truly helped him? She'd encouraged him to walk alone, but hadn't imagined he'd be ready to take two new "steps" on the same day.

She was filled with a sense of happiness that she'd made a difference. There weren't many men who would so graciously accept her help, especially when she and Simon were … distracted by each other, feeling things they shouldn't be feeling. She closed her eyes and tried to forget how just her touch had made him react. She well understood that. He did the same thing to her.

As if he could sense her staring at him, he looked toward her, and she blushed and took another bite of her eggs. She tried to let him eat in peace by turning to Georgie. "Though we're only going for fittings, I'm sure we can persuade the dressmaker to give you a few gowns that day. Then we can begin the next phase of your education."

Georgie sat back in her chair, looking nervous but determined. "What do you have in mind?"

"It's time to accept invitations from local families, perhaps a small dinner party or musicale. You'll feel like a different person with a new hairstyle and wardrobe."

Georgie nodded, but Louisa sensed that the bravery wasn't coming easily.

"Everything we've been working on will start coming naturally, Georgie, I promise. Even the dancing. We'll practice the quadrille again this afternoon."

While Lady Wade discussed Enfield's imminent—but minor—social calendar, Simon appeared almost too thoughtful. Louisa knew he was worried about Georgie being hurt again.

She wanted to reassure him, but not in front of his sister.

Simon tried to concentrate on the delicate task of cutting his meat, but his thoughts wouldn't leave the image of Georgie walking into a dinner party beside Louisa. God help him, he knew Louisa would never purposefully harm anyone, but just by being at Georgie's side, harm might result. There were men with no scruples, who would lead on a naïve young woman, and have her alone before she realized what was happening. Had Louisa been such a victim?

In his mind he saw Louisa, beautiful, confident, unaware of the ugliness in some men's minds when they looked at her. She would be crushed if she knew the truth.

But Georgie could lose the opportunity to attract her own callers. Simon considered accompanying them, but what good would he be to them? Georgie would feel like she had to take care of him, rather than giving herself the chance to be available to talk to future suitors. Simon would be forced to imagine what people were thinking or doing. It would be a terrible way to spend an evening, and with no redeeming value to Georgie at all.

Then he thought of Louisa, naïve in some ways about how she affected men. She, too, would be vulnerable. But Simon would have to rely on his grandmother, or maybe Paul, to tell him what happened.

His plan to guard Georgie from what Louisa might teach her hadn't really worked yet—because so far there was nothing to guard against. Louisa was helping.

For several days, Louisa was busy, going on calls with Lady Wade and working with Georgie in the afternoons. Her life felt almost fulfilling—especially since she was watching her other "secret" student blossom. Simon was moving cautiously about the manor, and it lifted everyone's spirits. Whenever Louisa had free time, she followed him just to see how he was doing—what he was doing. When she wasn't with him, she was wondering about him. Once she saw him trip on the legs of a table that had been moved. She almost went to him, but stopped herself in time. He wouldn't want her to know she'd witnessed what he probably thought was a humiliation. She only saw bravery and determination in everything he did.

This obsession with Simon wasn't good for her, because the lingering temptation of him was only slumbering, waiting, feeding on itself and growing larger, so that at night she lay awake and ached for him. She played the kiss over and over in her mind, and imagined he'd come to talk to her again, this time of his own volition.

She kept reminding herself that he had virtually trapped himself in the house, that she was the only lady here not related to him. Of course he would be distracted by her.

The day after returning from the London dress fittings, Louisa and Georgie were practicing their quadrille in the afternoon when Lady Wade entered and sat down to watch them. Louisa was doing well in the man's steps of the dance. When they were finished, they curtsied dramatically as Lady Wade clapped her enthusiasm.

"Oh, girls, that was marvelous," the old woman said. "Georgie my child, with that lovely hairstyle and that beautiful gown and such grace, everyone will admire you."

As Georgie blushed, Louisa looked at her with pride. She almost felt like a mother.

"But there's someone to see you in the drawing room," Lady Wade continued.

"Who?" Georgie asked. "Is Mr. Reyburn visiting?"

"Yes."

Louisa had thought she detected a curious, momentary hesitation in Lady Wade's manner, but Georgie was already patting the curls of her hair where they brushed her neck.

"Do I look all right?"

Louisa smiled. "You look beautiful."

And that wasn't a lie. With a flattering hairstyle and an elegant green gown that matched her eyes, Georgie could turn many a head. But maybe Mr. Reyburn's head was all she wanted to turn. Louisa thoughtfully watched her walk to the door.

"You, too, Louisa," Lady Wade said, waving her away.

"Of course," Louisa answered, smiling. "Georgie needs a chaperone."

She caught up to Georgie in the corridor and said, "So Mr. Reyburn has caught your eye."

Georgie shot her a startled look, and although she blushed, she said, "We're simply friends."

But when they entered the drawing room, although Mr. Reyburn was there with Simon, so were two other gentlemen. They all rose when the women entered, and it was like being ringed by a tower of trees. Georgie almost skidded to a stop, and as Louisa came up beside her, Louisa gave her an encouraging look. Simon, who was still seated on the sofa, cocked his head.

Georgie cleared her throat. "Good afternoon, Simon. I'm sorry we interrupted. It is Miss Shelby and I."

As Simon rose to his feet, the other three men bowed almost in unison. Louisa, who was used to the attention, curtsied back, but it took Georgie a moment to do the same. The girl was flushed, but it made her prettier.

There was a different air in the drawing room, of horses and the outdoors. Not many things could compare with a man's admiring gaze. And there were three of them to admire Georgie.

"Ladies," Simon said. "Do join us."

Two gentlemen slid more chairs near the sofa, and Georgie and Louisa sat down.

"Some of you might have met my sister, Miss Wade," Simon said. "Her friend is Miss Shelby."

Louisa blushed at the interested glances cast her way, but she was determined to let Georgie do all the talking. If she could have pushed her chair back into a corner, she would have.

Simon introduced Mr. Tilden, a redhead who blushed when his name was spoken, and Lord Keane, an elegant man who leisurely looked Georgie up and down since her brother could not see him.

Lord Keane said, "I haven't had the good fortune to meet you, Miss Wade. It is lucky we rode out from London to cheer up your brother."

Georgie mumbled a reply, and Louisa withheld a wince. She saw Mr. Reyburn do it for her. She wanted to speak up, to guide Georgie into a conversation that the girl could be a part of, but unlike the discussion with the soldiers, this time Louisa had to remain in the background and let her student try alone.

"I told them I don't need cheering up," Simon said. "But they refused to believe me."

"Now, Simon," Mr. Reyburn said, "when Tilden and Keane came by to recruit me this morning, I thought it might be an interesting afternoon. You have to admit that you've enjoyed hearing what our London friends are up to."

Lord Keane was still watching Georgie with narrowed eyes. He suddenly brightened. "I know where I've seen you before. We all had a good laugh when you caused Wallingford's whelp to plant his face before the *ton*. Brilliant."

Louisa held her breath, Simon angrily opened his mouth, but Georgie took a deep breath and beat him to it.

"Yes, Lord Keane, I did it quite deliberately," she said conspiratorially, batting her eyelashes at him. "How else to make a splash in my debut?"

The tentative thread of sarcasm made the others smile and Lord Keane look uncomfortable—and angry about it. Louisa was wondering how Georgie would forestall another sly comment.

"But Lord Keane," Georgie continued innocently, "were you there when I spilled my drink on Lady May?" She shook her head and sighed. "It caused a scandal I haven't recovered from yet."

Except for Lord Keane and Simon, the other two men rushed to assure her it was just an accident, that it had all been forgotten. Louisa wished she could share a satisfied glance with Simon. She was happy to see that he'd relaxed, that he hadn't immediately rushed to defend his sister.

"Well, Wade," Lord Keane boomed, as if he had to dominate any gathering, "your sister seems to be blossoming, along with so many other ladies."

He glanced at Louisa, then gave her a grin he must have thought charming, but she only thought of as sly.

"It's a shame you have to watch from the sidelines, Wade." Lord Keane paused. "Forgive me—you can't exactly watch."

Simon smiled benignly. "No, but I have ways of knowing what's going on."

Lord Keane grinned, while the other men glanced at each other uneasily.

Louisa fumed in silence. How dare the man make insinuations in Simon's own house! And right to his face, as if he couldn't do anything about it.

Mr. Reyburn awkwardly distracted the men with the topic of a coming horse race. Georgie gave Louisa a worried glance. As a maid entered the room, pushing a cart loaded with tea and sandwiches, Louisa surreptitiously motioned Georgie toward it. The two women met, turned their backs to the men, and after the maid had been dismissed, began randomly moving the sandwiches from plate to plate.

Bending her head to Georgie, Louisa whispered, "I cannot stand how Lord Keane is treating your brother, as if his blindness makes him unattractive to women."

"But what can we do?" Georgie whispered back.

"I'm the only available woman here, but if I fawn all over Lord Wade, it will seem like I'm a servant currying favor."

"What if you simply talk to him," Georgie said with excitement, "showing interest in a favorite subject of his? You will seem interested in his mind, which of course is as sound as ever."

"I'm not sure Lord Keane would care about

that, but it's all we have. So what is a favorite subject of his?"

They looked at each other in a panic, and Louisa's mind went blank.

"Rowing?" Georgie squeaked.

"That's a sport!"

"But ... he's designing modifications on his boat."

"Really?" Louisa said, so intrigued she almost forgot to whisper. "What are they?"

"I don't really know," Georgie said. "Something about an oarlock and how the oar fits into it."

"Ladies," called Simon, "do you need help with the tea?"

Louisa gave Georgie a determined smile. "Wish me luck."

They turned and began to ask the gentlemen how they preferred their tea. When all had been served, Louisa sat back down across from Simon.

Taking a deep breath, she said into the silence, "Lord Wade, of course your friends know about your rowing, but I understand from your sister that you're working on a new design for an oarlock."

He lifted his head as if looking at her. She could read nothing in his eyes, of course, but she knew him well enough to sense his skepticism. Then his mouth turned up in a half smile, as if he suddenly knew what she was doing.

"Rowing?" Lord Keane said.

Mr. Tilden cleared his throat and blushed. "You row, Lord Wade?"

"Oh, he does," Louisa said. "I am amazed by the speed at which he flies across the lake." Trying to look serious and contemplative, she added, "This oarlock design sounds—"

"You should think of competing," Mr. Tilden said. "At my club, we—"

"Thank you for the suggestion, Tilden," Simon said, "but I'm afraid I would lose terribly, because the weight of my navigator would slow me down."

"And without a navigator, you'd end up in the reeds," Lord Keane said.

Louisa and Georgie exchanged wide-eyed looks. This wasn't the direction they'd meant the conversation to take.

Chapter 12

Simon listened to Georgie try to steer the conversation to someone's upcoming ball. He was proud of how she had made light of her own mistakes, how she seemed to be holding her own in a room full of men.

Until she'd begun to conspire with Louisa Shelby to defend him against Keane's barbs. He knew damn well what they were doing. He would make sure they understood how unnecessary it was.

"Wade," Keane said, "I can't help but admire that you try to row in your condition."

Back to this topic, Simon thought in frustration. What had Louisa been thinking? "I like being out in the fresh air," he said mildly.

"Although of course you can't race with Tilden's club," Keane continued. "What do you say to a little rowing wager right now?"

Simon didn't need to see, not when he could hear the low mumbling of angry voices. This wasn't worth starting a fight over.

"Keane, leave off it," Paul said stiffly.

He could hear skirts rustling loudly, as if Louisa and Georgie were about to burst to their feet in outrage.

Simon tilted his head. "What do you have in mind?"

The reaction was silence, except for Keane's chuckle. "I'll challenge you to a race across your little lake."

"Across and back?" Simon said softly.

He heard Louisa's indrawn breath.

"Agreed," Keane responded.

"But Lord Wade needs a navigator," Tilden interrupted hesitantly.

"Then I'll have one, as well. We'll wager nothing too extravagant—fifty quid?"

Simon nodded. "Done."

As everyone started to rise, Keane spoke again. "Let's make it even more interesting. The ladies can navigate."

Georgie's was the first voice he could understand above the excited chatter. "But I don't know how."

"Then you'll ride with me," Keane said smoothly. "I don't need much help. Wade, you may have the lovely Miss Shelby."

Simon felt her arm slide through his as she whispered, "I think he meant something sordid by that."

"Hmm."

She paused. "May I escort you?"

"I enjoy being displayed on the arm of a beautiful woman."

He felt her arm tighten in his, but all she did was laugh, that husky laugh that made him yearn to hear it in private.

She was patient and cautious as they walked, speaking softly of every obstacle in the way. He was the one who couldn't concentrate, with her soft breast pressed into his upper arm. He stumbled once when they reached the terrace, and she hugged his arm even tighter. He could have groaned.

The voices in front of them faded away as they were outdistanced.

"So what are they all doing?" Simon asked.

"The big bully is already down by the lake, pulling off his coat." She hesitated. "Do you think you can win?"

"I've spent months doing this several times a day. I don't have any doubts."

"Do you forgive me for instigating this? That Lord Keane is so infuriating."

He grinned. "I forgive you."

"He looks in fine physical condition," she added.

"He fences. A little boxing, too."

"Oh."

"Do I hear doubts?"

"Well—"

"And what would it matter anyway?" Simon asked lightly, slowing as the gravel beneath his feet sloped away toward the lake. "So he defeats a blind man. Can you imagine the gossip headlines? 'Keane Outrows Blind Viscount.' If I can't win, I'll enjoy that."

"But you'll win."

"Of course. Even better would be 'Blind Viscount Routs Keane.'"

"Simon, how evil of you." She playfully swatted his arm.

He gave her a smile. "Have the servants brought a second boat?" he asked.

"They just launched it and are tying it up to the pier. Manvil is there."

"He'll be upset that he isn't with me. This is what he's been waiting for."

"Oh, dear. Should I withdraw?"

Simon laughed. "Trust me, he wouldn't want that. Would you mind putting my coat somewhere?" He stripped it off and handed it to her, along with his cravat.

"Ah," Keane said, "a serious opponent. I'll enjoy that."

"Then I hope you enjoy the spray from my boat hitting you in the back of your head."

As everyone hooted with laughter, Simon was surprised at how much he was relishing this challenge. He would have to thank Louisa for instigating it, and even pompous Keane for suggesting it.

"Georgie?" Simon called.

"I'm here," she said.

"Now you help Keane. He's going to need it."

He felt a hand on his arm and a soft kiss on his cheek. "Good luck, Simon," Georgie said. •

"He'll be the one who needs it," Keane said, his voice not quite so jovial.

Louisa led Simon down to the pier. "How should I help you in?"

Manvil spoke at his side. "I'm here, my lord. I'll hold the boat for you both to get in."

When he and Louisa were seated, he said, "Manvil, bring both of the boats to the end of the pier, you hold onto one, and have Robert the gardener hold the other. I assume all the outdoor servants are gathered?"

"Of course, my lord. There are wagers to be had."

Simon grinned. "The two of you will let go when you give the signal to start. Don't worry, Keane," he called. "Unlike me, you'll be able to see if anyone is tempted to cheat. But then Georgie will be watching you."

"I do not cheat," Keane said darkly.

Louisa sat in the stern of the boat and clutched both sides, not because she was worried. She was so thrilled to be a part of this race that she could barely control herself. She wanted to raise her fists in the air defiantly at that scoundrel, Lord Keane. The day was sunny with an endless blue sky. The grassy bank where the gathering spectators stood was so green as to make a desert weep. Everything was perfect.

And there was Lord Keane in the other boat; he was lean but powerful, his expression a grimace of concentration. Though Georgie was seated in the stern facing him, Louisa sensed he didn't really see her. Georgie gave Louisa a smile, but Louisa knew her well enough by now to see her nerves. She was holding her own with the men, so she should be enjoying the day.

Georgie held an umbrella over her head, and Louisa reluctantly opened the one a maid had handed her. It wouldn't do for every freckle on her face to pop out.

Robert the gardener helped Manvil guide both boats to the end of the pier. The boat rocked gently beneath her, and she was wondering how much it would really rock once Simon was rowing. She'd seen how hard he worked, how fast the boat went. She prayed that she was not the type to get seasick.

"The course is such, gentlemen," Manvil said. "Row straight across the lake from this pier. Begin turning back after your bow passes the large boulder off the far shore. Remember to turn to the outside. Ladies, do make sure they don't hit anything, including each other. The first one whose bow passes the end of this pier wins. You should have sufficient time to slow before you scrape bottom near the shore. I will count to three, and then call 'start.' Are we ready?"

Simon gripped the oars, his head bent in obvious concentration. She could see the tense line of muscles in his arms, the taut skin over his knuckles.

"What should I do, Simon?" she asked.

"Just tell me if I veer off this straight line. And watch your fingers."

Puzzled, she clasped her hands together. To her shock, he spread his legs and braced them on her seat on either side of her. Her skirt was caught on one side, but she said nothing. She just watched his tense expression in fascination. Who would have guessed that such a casual, easygoing man would be so competitive?

As Manvil started his slow count, Simon leaned toward her, his oars behind him in the water. At "Start!" he pulled straight back, the oars moving powerfully. The boat surged forward, and Louisa swayed backward. She gripped the seat between his boot and her hips.

He didn't need much correction from her, whereas within twenty yards, she heard Georgie shout, "To the left. I mean *my* left!"

Keane was glancing constantly over his shoulder to the far side of the lake, obviously not trusting Georgie. Simon did not have that distraction. He was totally focused on moving the oars as swiftly and evenly as possible. His arms moved like a machine, and they began to pull ahead of Lord Keane.

"He's falling behind, Simon," Louisa called. "Veer a little to your right."

As he corrected his course, he gave her a grimace that was part smile. Sweat broke out on his forehead. As they neared the far side, his shirt began to stick to his body. To her surprise it was a sheer garment, and the wetter it became, the more she could see. Whenever he leaned back, she could see the dark shadow of his nipples. And always, there was the spread of his legs right before her, and the interesting way his trousers fit him.

She wished she'd brought a fan to flutter in her hot face.

"We're approaching the boulder!" she called. "It's between the two boats, but we don't look like we're going to hit it."

"How far back ... is he?" Simon asked between grunts.

"Maybe five yards?"

"Not ... enough."

"Our bow has passed the boulder!"

She found herself falling to the side as Simon abruptly began to row each oar in opposite directions, turning in a tight circle.

"Stop turning!" she cried, impressed, as he reversed the rowing to steady the boat. "You can go straight."

For two full strokes of the oars, they were moving in the opposite direction from Keane. Louisa saw his shocked expression, then watched with satisfaction as he began to turn. Apparently he wasn't used to rowing, because he only used one oar, and they turned in a wide circle. But she saw the surge in his shoulders when he began to chase them once more.

Louisa looked over her shoulder. "He's done turning." Facing the pier again, she said, "Veer a little to your right!"

"How far ... is he behind?"

"Maybe twenty yards?"

"I want ... more."

She didn't think that he could go any faster, but he did. The wind tossed her hair back, and several curls finally escaped their pins. She laughed with the sheer exuberance of feeling like she was flying.

"Oh, Simon, this is wonderful!"

But his face was grimacing with the strain, his muscles heaving and bunching, and still he continued to row at this punishing pace. Louisa turned back to see that Lord Keane had fallen even farther behind.

As they reached the pier, Manvil shouted, "The winner!"

Simon immediately rowed in the opposite direction and she fell forward, catching herself with a hand on his thigh. She pulled back quickly, but not before she got the impression of damp wool and hot, hard muscle. Simon rowed slower and slower, then finally pulled in his oars. She didn't know where to look as he took in great gulps of air, his chest heaving, his body slumped tiredly as he propped his arms on his thighs. The boat bumped gently on the bottom, with barely a scraping sound.

Out of the corner of her eye she saw Lord Keane pass the pier. His boat soon crunched along the bottom, and Georgie, too, almost fell forward. Her umbrella tipped over the side and floated like a miniature boat.

"He just finished," Louisa said softly.

Simon lifted his head and grinned at her, sweat running down his cheeks from his damp hair. "Ah, victory is sweet." He lifted his head. "Manvil, are we near enough for you to grab the oar?"

"Yes, my lord."

Soon the valet was pulling them to the pier, then helping both of them out. On the other side, Lord Keane climbed onto the pier, and to his credit, he turned to help Georgie.

Damp and bedraggled, Lord Keane gave Simon a reluctant nod. "A good race, Wade. I'm impressed."

Simon put his hand out and Lord Keane shook it. "Thank you, Keane. Why don't you all stay for dinner. I'm sure Cook has been preparing for it all afternoon. You can even stay the night if you don't want to get started too late for London."

"I've got to return to Town early, so I can't spend the night. But I appreciate the offer. I'll send you your winnings."

"I'm not worried," Simon said with a grin. "You will let me know if this makes the papers."

Lord Keane stiffened, then gave a tight smile and shook his head. "Tilden would never tell." He looked at the other man. "Would you."

Mr. Tilden blushed.

* * *

After the guests had left, Louisa watched Simon head down a corridor, assuming he was going to change. She ducked away from Georgie, who was relating the exciting story to Lady Wade. Louisa wanted to make sure that in his jubilant state, Simon didn't lose his way. To her surprise, after he moved into the depths of the house, he opened the door to the billiards room and went inside. Cautiously, she approached and peered in.

And there was Simon, waiting. She gave a gasp that revealed her. He caught her waist, pulling her inside and shutting the door. He pushed her back several steps until she came up against the billiards table. As he loomed over her, his lower body held her in place, and the pressure was exhilarating. His damp shirt clung to him, revealing more than it concealed. His hair hung in short, wet curls that almost reached his vivid green eyes.

He put his hands on the table on either side of her. "You've been following me. Do you know how that makes you look?"

She swallowed, trying to control her breathing. "Like I'm a smitten woman."

He closed his eyes. "Are you smitten?"

He seemed to be having just as much trouble breathing as she was, and it was a heady feeling.

"I've been worried about you, in your first days walking about alone." She moistened her lips. "And you know I feel … something for you."

He pushed his hips harder against her, almost a slow roll, and then she really felt something—it was hard and long, and made her want to shiver deep inside.

"You called this feeling an awareness," he said in a deep voice.

She couldn't make herself push him away.

"You know I've experienced it, too." He tilted his head, as if he would bring their mouths together. "So why do you continue to follow me? You had to know that I could practically feel you—"

He pressed even closer to her, his chest coming into contact with hers. She whimpered softly.

"And I can always smell you."

His hands slid up her arms, across her shoulders to her neck. His face brushed against the side of hers, then behind her ear. As he inhaled deeply, her nipples became taut points that began to ache.

"The scent of you lingers everywhere," he murmured.

As he talked, she could feel his lips moving against her skin, making her quiver. She gasped when he licked her, a long, slow swipe that circled the rim of her ear. He pressed kisses along the line of her jaw until once again his mouth was just above hers.

"I assume there's no one in this room," he said, his breath a soft, warm puff on her lips.

"No one," she whispered.

"I can think of other uses for this billiards table."

She tried to make sense of her thoughts. "Are you … are you implying something you aren't saying?"

"Oh, yes."

Her mind flashed with images of them lying in each other's arms on the table, and she shuddered.

He slid his hands to her waist. She felt his thumbs feather across her ribs, just beneath her breasts. Biting her lip kept her from groaning. She wanted him to touch her in ways no innocent woman should.

"It's been many days since you kissed me." He kissed the tip of her nose. "Surely you don't want me to be out of practice." He lightly pressed his lips to hers. "Am I in the right place?"

With a moan she slid her arms around him, and he held her tightly. Their kiss was sudden and passionate, no sweetness, only heat and frantic need. She knew what to expect this time, even reveled in the hot thrust of his tongue. She explored his mouth as he did hers, tasting the essence of him, breathing in his scent.

He slid his hands up the front of her, and to her shock he cupped her breasts. Why did she have to be wearing so many clothes? She wanted to feel each caress against her skin, but her corset and dress muted every feeling. She moaned in frustration.

"Wait," he whispered against her lips.

His deft fingers found the buttons on the front of her bodice, and with practiced ease he undid them and spread her bodice wide. She shouldn't, she mustn't—but when his fingers slipped gently between her breasts, she sighed with pleasure.

"Ah, a low corset," he said triumphantly.

He gave a single push down, and the corset spilled her breasts free. They were still covered in her chemise, but he pushed that off her shoulders and suddenly her breasts were exposed to air.

But not his regard. He did not touch them. Frustration crossed his face, and he murmured, "With hair so red, you must have the whitest breasts, their tips as pink as a summer rose."

Her nipples hardened like blooms that closed into tight buds when darkness fell. She should cover herself—what if someone came in?—but she stood there, bare, wishing he could see her, her hands clutching his upper arms as if he might let her go.

His hands skimmed up her sides, his thumbs brushing the sides of her breasts. She shivered, suddenly glad for the feel of him so tightly pressed against her hips. It answered a need, but aroused in her so much more. His fingers trailed across her collarbones, then slid slowly downward, riding the slopes of her breasts. She held her breath, her very skin afire wherever he touched. In passing he skimmed over her nipples, and she found herself shuddering hard against him.

"Oh, Simon," she whispered, but what could she ask for? She only knew that her body craved more of this, that she needed to be so much closer to him. She found herself moving against his hips, seeking something. "Oh, please."

Then his hands closed around both breasts, and she bit her lip to keep from crying out loud. She dropped her head back, pressing into his palms. He kneaded and caressed, then swirled the tips of his fingers against her nipples. He bent and took one in his mouth.

The shock of his hot, wet tongue caressing her was like nothing she'd ever imagined. Each tug evoked an answering ripple deep in her belly. She pressed against him frantically, holding his head to her. When her hips wriggled against his, he caught her knee in his hand and lifted. He was able to press deeper against her, more intimately. Even through all of her clothes, she knew that this was right, that this would stoke all these wild feelings building inside her.

He groaned and moved to her other breast, sucking her nipple deep into his mouth. With every pull of suction, every moist rasp of his tongue, it was harder and harder to keep her cries silent.

His questing hand found the hem of her skirt, and then he was beneath, sliding up her stocking-covered leg, then over her garters and knee to her outer thigh. After skimming over her drawers, his hand cupped her behind and ground her even tighter against him. Another whimper escaped, as she felt his fingers slide along her bottom, then find the open slit of her garment. For one moment his fingers touched her bare flesh, and it was wet.

With a gasp she suddenly pushed at his chest.

"We shouldn't—we mustn't—" She tried to gather her bodice together, but her hands were trembling. What had she been thinking, to let him take such liberties?

Chapter 13

Simon shook with the effort of getting himself under control. His body, so long denied, burned to finish what it had started—what *he* had started.

He could hear the rustle of her clothing, knew she was covering herself again, when all he wanted to do was taste her, to bury himself inside the tight heat of her.

"Louisa," he began, then stopped, clearing his throat to ease the huskiness.

"You said you didn't want to be out of practice," she said in a low, trembling voice.

"I was teasing you."

She went on as if she hadn't heard him. "Am I just a woman to practice on, conveniently available?"

"No!"

"Then what am I? I am a terrible role model for my student, and if your grandmother found out—" She heaved a shaky breath. "I've never done anything like this before, never knew there were feelings such as these. Now I realize that *this* is what those men at my last position wanted to do with me, but I always managed to elude them. And now I'm here with you. Except for a few meetings in public, we've only known each other for a few weeks. And yet I've let you . . ."

She trailed off, and he heard the anguish in her voice.

"Forgive me, Louisa," he said softly. "I never meant to let this go so far. You've been following me, and it's made me think of you, and that kiss in my room—"

"Oh, I know it's my fault. I have . . . led you on, as women have always been warned not to do."

"No!" He rubbed his hands down his cheeks. "It's not your fault. I was trying to say that it's mine. I should have known better. In my experience—"

"And you have had so much more than I," she said tiredly. "When you hold me, I don't even know what to do with my hands, and yet you touch me so . . ." He heard her sigh. "I have to go. Will you be able to find your way—"

"Yes, yes, don't worry about me. Have you forgiven me?"

"How can I not, when I was so complicit?"

He felt the swirl of sweet-smelling air as she passed by, heard the door open, and then she was gone.

Was she right? Was he attempting to seduce her because he thought she was easily available to him? That couldn't be true—most women didn't inspire him to uncontrollable passion.

But did he succumb because he thought she was more experienced than she was? Every rumor had said she'd been kissed, and the common consensus was that she was ready to take intimacy further. But nothing said she had—not until he had tried to seduce her. Her innocent reactions made him know for certain that no one had ever taken such liberties before.

Or she'd never let anyone.

Then why him? Did it still go back to her needing to find a husband? God, he wished he could find some way to ask her the truth.

He found his coat in a heap near the door and folded it over his arm. How did he look? He smoothed his hands through his hair. He had to fool anyone he ran into—especially his grandmother. He would not allow Louisa to be hurt by new rumors.

Louisa came down to dinner and treated Simon civilly, pleasantly. But he felt the wall she'd put up between them as if it were a physical thing. The next day she avoided him, and he found himself missing her company, missing the way she put him at ease. She and Georgie went riding in the afternoon, and Georgie hesitantly asked his permission. As if people couldn't ride horses around him anymore!

He was in a frustrated, ugly temper.

That night, he found himself on the balcony, standing at the balustrade, feeling the cool wind in his face. The sounds of the night were haunting, soothing, but his restlessness wouldn't go away.

And then he remembered that the balcony ran the width of the rear of the manor. Louisa's room was at the far end. He went back to the manor until his hand could touch it, and then he started walking. When he reached the end of the building, he turned back one door. Her room.

He leaned his head against the glass pane, not knowing if she were awake or asleep. He just knew that he couldn't leave things as they were yesterday. Though tempted to knock, he didn't want to disturb her if she'd already fallen asleep.

Testing the handle, he discovered it unlocked, so he slipped inside. The room was warmer than the night, and smelled powerfully of Louisa. He kept his back against the glass door and waited. If she didn't notice him, he would leave, assuming she slept.

"I think there's a viscount in my bedroom."

At the reluctant humor in her voice, he smiled with relief.

"Could he be here for nefarious purposes?" she asked. "Because I could have bashed him on the head with a heavy candlestick."

"No, no evil purposes. I just ... didn't like the way we parted yesterday."

"You've seen me—been with me several times since then."

He wondered if she was sitting up in bed. When his mind began to imagine what she was wearing, he forcefully thrust that image aside.

"I may have *been with* you," he said, "but you were only … pleasant."

"I'm always pleasant."

"Too pleasant. You usually tease me about something."

At that, she remained silent for a minute. He let her take her time.

Then she sighed. "What do you want from me, Simon?"

"I don't really know. I've apologized about … the second kiss—"

"Kiss?" she echoed dryly.

"Passionate kiss, then. The last time I talked to you, you thought I was treating you as a convenience, and I want you to know that is far from the truth."

She said nothing.

"But I have no excuse for my behavior. I will try to make sure it doesn't happen again."

"Try?"

"I can't make guarantees, Louisa. As you've said before, there's an awareness between us, and sometimes it's too powerful."

"Is that why you're here tonight?" Her voice sounded cool.

"No. I simply enjoyed talking to you the other night in this room, and I thought we could … talk again." God, he sounded like an idiot, even to himself. "And make things better," he added.

She gave another sigh, and when she spoke, her voice was gentler. "I don't have a candle lit, but I think you're only about three paces from the chair you used the last time. Straight ahead of you."

Putting his hand out, he walked slowly, then found it easily enough. He heard the sound of clothing being donned, felt her footsteps as she neared him and sat down beside him. They were both in darkness, their common ground, and he was a little embarrassed by how comfortable he felt like that.

"So what do you want to talk about?" she asked.

He hesitated. "Perhaps why you felt the need to prove to Keane that I'm still a man—an intelligent man, anyway."

"That's not what I was proving, Simon, and you know it."

He liked her defensiveness, liked the prickly way she reacted when he'd aroused her anger. He was used to women wanting to behave as they thought *he* wanted them to. But Louisa had a mind of her own. She was certainly not needy.

"Lord Keane is a—a boar," she continued, as if that was the worst insult she could find.

He chuckled. "He's not so bad."

"To slur you like that, because he thought he could get away with it now."

"He's always slurred me like that. Frankly, I was glad he hadn't changed."

"Oh." She sounded shocked and puzzled. "Still, it was unforgivably rude to taunt you about women, when you certainly have no problem—" She stuttered to a stop.

He chuckled again, feeling warm and content. "I have no problem talking to women?" he said to help her out.

"Of course." She choked on the words.

Regardless of her guilt, she'd enjoyed what they had done together. He felt foolishly glad about that.

"Being among those men," she began in a more serious voice. "It reminded me too much of my old life."

He frowned. "I don't understand. I thought you said you enjoyed Society."

"Yes, and I have many happy memories. But ... I guess some of those memories are linked with having money, and I had no idea how much it made me equate money with happiness."

He said nothing, unsure if she wanted a response, or just needed someone to listen.

"When my father died, I realized that he obviously equated the two. When he didn't have money, he didn't want to live."

"Or maybe he didn't want to live with the shame of everyone knowing the mistakes he'd made."

"Perhaps. But when my circumstances were reduced, part of me thought that maybe I'd equated money with happiness, too. I loved those parties and balls and dinners. I was at ease in that world, confident of who I was. But when I no longer had that life, I eventually realized that I needed to find another, better way to be happy."

"And you thought you could achieve that by being in someone's employ?" he asked doubtfully.

"No, as I told you from the beginning—by helping someone. Specifically young girls like your sister. I thought that when I left here—"

He felt a strange pain in his stomach at the thought.

"—I might be able to hire myself out to the families who are newly rich, whose daughters have no idea how to behave in Society. I don't mean amongst the *ton*, of course, but amongst my Society."

"You say that as if it's a class below."

"You know it is, even though you have always moved freely between the two. So what do you think about my plan?" she asked brightly.

He didn't like the thought of her hiring herself out to families who might not appreciate her. But she didn't want to hear that. "You'd be excellent at whatever you did."

"Now you're being patronizing," she said with a huff.

"I am not. But you told me how you were treated at your last position. I just worry that you might run into the same situation—someone who would force you into something that you didn't want."

When she didn't say anything, he felt tension grip his stomach. She hadn't felt ... forced by him, had she?

"Well, you needn't worry," she said primly. "I plan to do some of my own interviewing before I accept any position."

"So the employers have to give *you* their references," he said with amusement.

"Correct."

They sat quietly for several minutes, and he realized how peaceful he found her company. He was still driven crazy with lust at just the smell of her, of course, but when he could subdue that, he simply ... enjoyed her for the person she was.

"I should leave," he finally said. "You must be tired."

"I haven't been riding in a long time, and muscles I had forgotten I had are sore." She hesitated. "Georgie felt quite guilty riding."

"And I told her not to. She actually asked my permission. Just because I'm afraid, doesn't mean she has to ..." His words died away.

She said nothing to change the topic, so he was forced to continue. "I wouldn't be able to see where I'm going, and I would have to be led around like a child learning to ride."

"That's not such a bad thing, especially if you're with people you enjoy."

He took a deep breath. "I'm worried I'll be thrown again."

"You have every right to be worried," she said.

"When I *could* control the animal, I was thrown onto my head. A horse knows if you're tentative, and tries to get away with what it can."

"But a gentle mare . . ."

"Now you're the one threatening my manliness."

She giggled. "Well, think about it. I would be glad to take you somewhere in private and ride with you."

With her innocent words, it all came rushing back, the taste of her skin, the heat between her thighs when he'd pressed himself there. He imagined her on top, riding him. Gripping the arms of his chair, he tried to sound mild as he said, "You're getting good at saying one thing and implying another."

"Oh!" She sounded shocked and puzzled at the same time. "You just assume everything has a hidden meaning. Now you really need to go. The door is to your left."

He rose to his feet. "I know. So will our friendship survive?"

He heard her stand. "Is that what we have—a friendship?"

"I'd like to think so."

"I'll agree to that. As a friend, we could have a serious discussion about oarlocks."

He laughed. "There's not much to tell. I'm just rethinking the design. Good thing no one pressed me on the concept. That will teach me to confide in Georgie."

He reached the door and opened it, letting in the cool wind and the smells of the garden. "Sleep well, Louisa."

"Good night."

When he had gone, Louisa collapsed back on her bed, arms thrown wide, confused and happy and worried all at the same time. She was glad he considered himself her friend, and worried because she didn't know if it was a good idea for him to feel free to wander into her room in the name of that friendship. If she forbade it, he would acquiesce. But telling him not to return seemed impossible. She wondered if this friendship was another convenience for him, but she was willing to give him the benefit of the doubt.

Obviously she missed her sisters terribly, because she was telling her secrets to a man she wasn't even sure could be a friend. And he was telling her his. She ached with sympathy over his inability to ride. She knew how important such a thing was to a man.

And being intimate with women was even more important.

Simon was enjoying a pleasant dinner with the three ladies the next night, when the door opened fast enough to bang against the wall. He waited for a servant to make an announcement, but instead heard, "Hello, everyone!"

It was his younger brother, Leo. Simon folded his arms over his chest and shook his head as Leo, slapping him jovially on the shoulder, greeted their sister and grandmother.

"Well, Georgie," Leo said, "I was ready to find you wearing spectacles this time around. You have been more and more a bluestocking each time I see you."

"Leo, as usual, you don't know anything," Georgie said sweetly.

"Well you do look rather grand today. What's the occasion?"

After a curious pause, Leo called, "Hey, no need to hit me! I'll just stay on this side of the table with sympathetic people. Grandmama, you look as lovely as ever."

Simon could hear the smacking kiss from across the table.

"It's about time you visited us again," Grandmama scolded. "Your brother and sister have been worked to death trying to keep me entertained. I actually had to hire a companion!"

"Ah, a newcomer. Let me get a good look at—Miss Shelby."

Simon frowned. Leo's voice had actually softened. Was that a hint of uneasiness he heard?

"Mr. Wade," Louisa answered coolly.

So they knew each other as more than just gossip.

Georgie asked, "How do you know my brother, Louisa?"

"We have met at several events," she answered diplomatically.

"She allowed me to step on her toes once or twice on the dance floor," Leo added. "Miss Shelby, so you have to put up with my grandmother now? You have my heartfelt condolences."

Simon was reluctantly impressed by Leo's tact in not questioning why Louisa had come down in the world. Maybe there was hope for his brother after all. Now if only Simon could persuade him to tell no one of Louisa's reputation.

"So why have you arrived so late in the day?" Grandmama asked. "Surely your horse could have hurt itself in the dark."

"Or thrown me? Oh, sorry, Simon," he added, sounding contrite for Leo. "Not still a sore subject, is it?"

"Of course not," Simon answered mildly.

"I went to Reyburn's first this afternoon. Shot some quail, ran a few hounds into the ground, you know, the sort of thing one can't do in London. The start of the real Season is almost upon us, so I can't stay long. You're coming again this year, Georgie?"

"Perhaps," she answered cautiously.

Leo sighed loudly. "No one cares, sister dear. I told them all you were hopelessly clumsy as a child. No one thinks you did anything deliberately. Ow! No need to fling a fork at me, Georgie. I'm just teasing."

Simon grinned. "Did you hit him in the face? I would love to see tine marks in his skin."

"You must be joking," Leo said in mock horror.

"Scar this lovely face that the ladies swoon over?"

The evening was vintage Leo, and Simon enjoyed himself. But he couldn't help noticing that Leo never flirted with Louisa, as was his habit with a beautiful woman.

After dinner, when the ladies rose to leave for the drawing room, Simon called Leo back.

"Simon, I can have my port with the ladies. Grandmama might even let me smoke a cheroot in front of her."

"I need to talk to you," Simon said. "Are we alone?"

The doors closed.

"Now we are. A brandy?"

"Thank you."

Leo sat down beside him and said, "You're scaring me, Simon. I feel like I used to when Father needed to have a discussion with me."

"I'm not here to punish you, Leo."

"Good, then I'm glad we're alone. I need some advice. There is this actress—"

"Later, this is important." Simon took a sip of brandy. "It's about Louisa."

"You mean Miss Shelby?" Leo said a bit too thoughtfully. "Already calling her by her Christian name? Why Simon, you devil. Even blind you can still sway the ladies."

Simon sighed loudly. "I just want to warn you to say nothing to anyone about Louisa's reputation."

Leo hesitated, and when he spoke, he sounded more subdued. "I never spread unsubstantiated rumors."

"You're one of the ones who told me! You and several other fools."

"Well, yes, but I was in my cups and—"

"Then don't drink. I don't want the ladies hurt—especially Louisa. I don't think she knows what's been said. She is having difficulties right now."

"Obviously, since she's hired herself out as a companion."

"That's only part of it."

"Gossip? Tell me more."

"Leo," Simon said through clenched teeth. "I need your promise first."

"Well of course I promise. I would never harm a lady by spreading such rumors."

"Except to all the men you told."

"Actually, I told no one but you."

He sounded sincere, which made Simon suspicious. But he let it go. "Grandmama brought Louisa here to help Georgie, too."

"I did notice the new gown. Not something Mother would have chosen."

"Exactly. Louisa enjoys helping girls prepare for their Season."

"Oh."

Simon didn't know what that meant, and for the hundredth time wished he could see his brother. Leo's face was always open to him. But he was finally beginning to learn that sound could carry much meaning. "So there's Georgie to consider. I know she's going to start attending parties, and I somehow have to minimize the effect of Louisa's presence."

"Surely you are overreacting," Leo said.

"So I'm supposed to take the chance that Georgie's reputation could suffer?"

"I see," Leo answered softly. "But only a few men know, and surely no one was crass enough to tell the ladies."

"But we don't know that. Don't worry, I'll handle everything. I just want you to keep your mouth shut."

"You always do like to take over and control things," Leo said with amusement. "It's good to have that Simon back."

Chapter 14

Louisa bent her head over her embroidery and listened as Lady Wade and Georgie speculated about the motives for Mr. Wade's visit, as if he regularly avoided them.

She wouldn't put anything past Mr. Wade. She remembered him as a forward young man who used to try to maneuver her alone at parties. She had thought him charming and reckless, and had laughed off his advances. But he had been only her first experience at that sort of man. Later, at Lady Ralston's, she had really understood how cruel some men could be, and how little they respected her.

She had never given Mr. Wade the opportunity to harm her, and she told herself that everything would be all right. He'd seemed surprised to see her, but he was civil and kind. Perhaps he regretted his behavior now that he was several years older. She would give him the benefit of the doubt—but she would never allow herself to be alone with him.

They heard the gentlemen long before they arrived.

"Well, look at you, Simon!" Mr. Wade said boisterously. "Walking all alone. Where's Manvil? Is he sad he's been demoted?"

"He's satisfied to return to his real position," Simon said, his voice echoing ahead of him.

"A valet has too much time alone in a bedroom. There's only one reason to do that—"

Mr. Wade broke off as they rounded the corner and entered the room. He smiled, and Louisa couldn't help smiling back, even as she shook her head. The Wade brothers oozed charm out of every pore. Mr. Wade was as blond as his brother, with hair even curlier. He wore mutton-chop sideburns that drew attention to his legendary family dimples. He was taller and leaner than Simon, almost gangly in a boyishly endearing way. Louisa had been swept up in his presence as much as every other girl. When members of the *ton* graced a party hosted by a wealthy factory owner, eligible ladies took notice.

She looked between the two brothers, alike and yet so different. There was a maturity and responsibility and kindness about Simon that his brother couldn't match.

Perhaps the fact that she was "smitten" impeded her judgment, but she didn't think so. Most women would think that it was the title that made Simon more alluring. But they didn't know him like she did.

Or was she foolish to imagine that she understood him?

For an hour, the family discussed the latest London gossip, and Louisa listened with interest, since she recognized so many of the names. She was glad Georgie showed an interest, although she thought it was mostly because she enjoyed bantering with her brothers.

Mr. Wade finally turned to Georgie and gave her a raised eyebrow. "So Simon tells me you're being tutored."

Georgie tilted her chin. "I'm enjoying working with Louisa."

"I like the gown," Mr. Wade said. "Miss Shelby, is that due to you?"

Louisa set her embroidery in her lap. "Lady Wade helped greatly."

Lady Wade waved a hand. "I did not. I let the two girls have their heads and they took the London dressmakers by storm."

"So what is Georgie wearing?" Simon asked.

"A lovely green gown."

"Ah, matches her eyes," Simon said, nodding.

Georgie giggled and rose to her feet, holding her arms out as she turned a circle.

"The waist is cinched a bit tight," Mr. Wade said. "Can you breathe?"

She threw a pillow at him.

Mr. Wade ducked. "Tight sleeves, a little lace here and there, square neckline."

"Suitably modest, I hope," Simon said.

"Of course. But she's blushing now," Mr. Wade added.

Simon smiled at his sister. "It sounds lovely. But then I'm not surprised."

Mr. Wade turned his critical gaze upon Louisa, and she found herself straightening uncomfortably.

"Ah, the teacher does not want to be criticized," Mr. Wade said.

"Louisa?" Simon asked, turning toward her.

She had often imagined what Simon would think if he could see her—would he approve of her hairstyle, her choice in gowns? Of course he seemed to want to remove the latter.

"She's quite red in the face now," Mr. Wade said. "Goes well with the rose-colored gown. Modest neckline, too."

Lady Wade gasped. "Boys! Miss Shelby is a guest in our home."

Louisa looked fondly at the older woman. She knew that she was an employee, but was never treated as such. She often felt part of the family—which was too seductive a thought.

"Lady Wade, I am quite used to being scrutinized," Louisa said. "After all, that is what a ball is held for."

"To be on display," Georgie added ruefully. "A marriage mart."

"You don't think we gentlemen are on display?" Simon asked.

"Of course you are," Louisa said. "But you

don't have to wait worriedly to be asked to dance. You control a poor lady's evening."

Mr. Wade smiled at her. He seemed almost … nervous, as if she would tell his family how he'd pursued her.

"I don't think you ever waited long to dance, Miss Shelby," Mr. Wade said.

Louisa wondered why he would say such a thing in front of shy Georgie, when he knew the girl had lacked suitors.

"Sir," Louisa said, tilting her head, "sometimes it is not the honorable men who ask a woman to dance."

Now it was his turn to blush, but she believed he hid it by sipping his drink.

Simon cocked his head, looking interested. "And what do you do when that happens, Miss Shelby?"

"We attempt to avoid it by signaling our friends or sisters."

He grinned. "Signaling?"

The way he was focused on her was distracting as usual. It was hard to even think, when she remembered how he'd focused on other parts of her so intimately. He had an amazing ability to make a woman think she was the one thing he cared about—at that particular moment.

She looked down at her lap and took a deep breath. "My sisters and I had worked out a system to help each other."

"Really?" Georgie said with admiration.

"Oh, it was more for fun, really, but once or twice it did come in handy. Let's see," she said thoughtfully, looking up at the ceiling to concentrate. "I was never standing alone when a man approached; usually at least one of my sisters was with me. So if we didn't like the gentleman, we linked elbows."

Simon nodded. "And this meant . . ."

"'Please invent a reason that I can't dance right now, even though my dance card is not full.'"

Lady Wade and Georgie burst into peals of laughter, while the men looked bemused.

"The excuse was always something innocent," she hurriedly said, "like claiming that my mother just told us she needs us. Or my sister would say she felt ill, and I had to escort her out for some cool air."

"But what if the gentleman was persistent?" Simon asked.

"Then there wasn't much to be done but accept," Louisa admitted.

"I think you used that on me," Mr. Wade said, his eyes narrowed with amused skepticism.

Louisa blinked with innocence. "Never, Mr. Wade! Why wouldn't I wish to dance with you?"

Again, he sipped his drink, and Georgie gave him a curious stare. She turned to Louisa. "To celebrate Leo's homecoming, I'll play the piano, and you and Simon should sing."

Louisa felt her skin flush, and she deliberately avoided looking at Simon. "Georgie, I'm certain that Mr. Wade would rather sing with you two."

Mr. Wade sat back, relaxed once again. "Oh, no, I'd rather hear the three of you. Simon, do show me how it's done."

Louisa risked a glance at Simon, who gave his brother an annoyed expression.

"And besides," Mr. Wade added, "I have a request I need to discuss with Grandmama."

"Tell me now before the singing starts," Lady Wade said. "After that I'll be too distracted."

As Georgie went to the piano and began to look through sheet music, Mr. Wade gave his grandmother a winning smile.

"I haven't seen the locals in ages. Might we have a dinner party?"

Louisa saw the tension in Simon's shoulders, but he said nothing.

Lady Wade simply shook her head. "Not right now, Leo."

Mr. Wade stiffened, but to his credit he didn't look at Simon. "Surely enough time has passed—"

Simon opened his mouth, but Lady Wade spoke first. "Leo, you misunderstood me. You'll see everyone tomorrow night. There's a dinner party at Lord Strickland's and the entire family has been invited. I'll send word that you're coming, too."

Simon smiled at his grandmother. "I'll have to decline, I'm afraid."

Lady Wade looked exasperated. "As you wish, Simon."

"I'll go," Mr. Wade said cheerfully.

To distract everyone, Louisa rose and approached the piano. "What shall we sing?"

Georgie brightened. "I've found a lovely duet that will compliment your voices perfectly."

"Do sing for us, Simon," his grandmother said softly.

Simon obediently came to the piano, and Louisa guessed that he could not refuse her a second time this evening.

Louisa looked only at the sheet music as Georgie played the introduction. She found herself terribly nervous, not because she was singing before the family, but because she was singing with Simon. Lady Wade and Mr. Wade were intelligent people, who would very easily see her feelings for Simon if she wasn't careful.

When they began the song, she once again felt a chill at how beautifully their voices melded together. She never once looked at him, but it was as if he sang just for her. She was embarrassed—but also so caught up in the pleasure his voice gave her.

"Well," Mr. Wade said when they were done.

Louisa bit her lip.

"I certainly couldn't have done that song justice," Mr. Wade continued. "Good to see you singing again, Simon."

Louisa let out her breath in relief.

* * *

The next evening after everyone had gone to Lord Strickland's, Simon found himself prowling the lonely house from end to end. Manvil caught up with him in the library.

"You should have gone to the dinner," Manvil said. "Mr. Wade will have the advantage."

"The advantage in what?" Simon asked crossly. He ran his fingers along the wall of books as he paced.

"With Miss Shelby. Strange room for you to be in, by the way."

"Manvil," Simon said almost with a growl.

"I'll go prepare your bath."

Simon wasn't a fool—he knew that Leo had every advantage over him. But it was obvious that Louisa had not taken to Leo when they'd last met.

He reminded himself that this had not turned into a competition for Louisa's affections. She had agreed to be his friend.

A friend he wanted in his bed.

With a groan, he stalked out of the library and went up to his room.

But of course he couldn't sleep. When he heard the family returning, he waited an hour, then walked carefully down the balcony, relieved that Leo's room faced the front of the house.

He knocked softly on Louisa's door, and after a moment, it opened.

"So you're knocking now," she said softly.

"May I come in?"

"You just can't wait to hear about the dinner?"

"Something like that."

"Very well."

He entered and heard her shut the door behind him. Though he knew she was near, felt her warmth and the brush of her arm as he passed, he made himself go to his usual seat before the hearth. Maybe visiting her wasn't such a good idea.

But Simon needed to know how things had gone with Georgie. Leo had promised that he would watch over their sister, but Simon wasn't going to get a full accounting from Leo.

"How did Leo's triumphant return go?" he asked when Louisa had sat down beside him.

"If you're so curious, why didn't you attend?"

He said nothing, and for the first time he felt more like a coward for refusing, rather than a man who understood that he would be the main attraction.

She sighed. "Never mind, I understand."

And she really did, which made him feel worse.

"Your brother was well received by his old friends," she said. "In fact, right after dinner several of them monopolized him in a card game, so he didn't get into any trouble—if that's what you were worried about."

Damn, when Leo played cards, nothing else mattered—including their sister. So much for Simon being able to count on Leo's help.

"Why are you so worried about him?" Louisa asked.

"I've always had to be concerned about Leo." He couldn't very well tell her that it was Louisa and Georgie he was worried about—lately, Louisa most of all. That realization startled him. "I know how close you are to your sisters, but Leo and I aren't like that. I've sort of ... taken care of Leo, probably too much."

"What do you mean?"

Once again he heard the interest in her voice. She was always so compassionate, so ready to be of help. And he found himself wanting to tell her things that he'd never confided in anyone.

"If you haven't guessed by now, our parents were usually too busy to be bothered with us when we were young. But Leo always managed to need their attention the most, whether it was being reminded to study when he received a poor review from our governess, or when they had to rescue him from the schemes he concocted."

"Schemes?" she asked with amusement.

"Foolish things like organizing wrestling matches among the grooms, and then losing the pool of betting money."

"But you weren't like that."

"I was too busy being the dutiful son. I was the one who did everything for Leo, from teaching him to cut his meat to overseeing his schoolwork so my parents wouldn't have to be bothered. He could make you want to help him. Maybe I did too much for him, which is why he's so carefree now."

"But he also wasn't the heir, so he wasn't burdened as you were."

"Making excuses for Leo now?"

"Oh no," she said quickly.

"Then you're trying to make me feel better for my role in Leo's irresponsibility. It's generous of you, Louisa, but unnecessary."

"I could say it's your parents' fault. Would you prefer that?"

He found himself hesitating.

"Because it's really the truth," she continued. "I can't imagine that your mother reacted to your accident well."

"No, but even there, I might be to blame." He continued before she could erupt with her usual indignation on his behalf. "Oh, not about becoming blind, of course. But I had a role in the family. I used to think of myself as 'the entertainer.'" He sighed. "I can't believe I said that aloud."

"Maybe you needed to. Go on."

Louisa stared hard at Simon, who was lit by the candle she'd been reading by. He wore a rueful expression as he tried to make everything into a joke. But she could see the hurt inside him.

"So you want to hear all the sordid details about my past," he said, wearing a grin.

"Yes. I want to see how you can be positive about people who treated Georgie poorly—if you aren't offended that I said that."

"You don't need to apologize. It's ridiculous, really. But I was very good at making everybody laugh."

"I've noticed that about you."

"When I was younger, I organized Leo and later Georgie into acting in plays and singing songs. I could keep our parents amused for hours in the evening. I was a lot older by the time I realized it was the only time they seemed happy together."

"It sounds like you did a good thing for your brother and sister."

"Maybe. Maybe not."

"So how could you blame yourself for your mother's reaction to your accident?"

"She didn't know how to handle it, of course. I kept trying to show her that I would be fine, but she seemed uneasy. When she went off to visit her sister, it was actually a relief."

Louisa saw him as a man who tried to please everybody. "The entertainer" was a designation that seemed shallow to her, as if he could never have any quieter, more difficult emotions. But when it was his turn to need help, his mother had abandoned him. She was probably used to him as a sought-after member of the *ton*, and when he couldn't be . . .

Louisa hid her anger on his behalf and tried to be practical, which he'd appreciate. "I could understand why your mother's departure was a relief. Your grandmother seems much easier to get along with."

"Oh, she is. And I think we're good for her, too. It's terrible to lose a son."

To distract him, Louisa said, "I know this discussion has turned from your brother to your mother, but let's return to the subject of Georgie. I'm worried that my teaching is not having enough effect."

She saw his immediate concern. "Did something happen?"

"I still cannot seem to ease her from this shyness. Around you and old friends and even other ladies, she does well, but with men ... she seems tongue-tied. I've taught her things of interest to men, and it's begun to help. And then Lord Keane, who was seated next to her at dinner, made it a point to sit beside her when the men came to the drawing room."

Simon straightened in his chair. "Keane?"

"Well, you said you didn't mind him."

"But not chasing after my sister!"

"He asked her for a dance at the ball this coming Saturday night, and she didn't refuse him. She later said she wished I were nearby so she could signal."

"Damn. Well, I'll just have to attend to protect her."

Louisa's mouth dropped open. "You'll attend? Your grandmother will be so thrilled."

"Georgie needs me."

She promised herself that she would help him realize that an evening with friends could still be enjoyable.

"I should let you sleep," he said.

At the reluctance in his voice, she wondered what these nights meant to him. To her, they were a way to be with him, to understand him, to pretend that they could be friends when beneath all their words lurked a passionate intensity that colored everything between them. The more she was with him, the more she regretted that there could not be more.

She followed him to the door, and when he stopped suddenly, she ran into his back. He turned, catching her arm, focusing on her in that Simon way that never failed to thrill her. And for a moment, she was on the verge of asking him to stay. The stranger she was becoming frightened her.

His hand slid up her arm, barely touching, until he could cup her face in one hand. Her heart beat loudly when he leaned down and kissed her cheek. At the last moment, she almost turned her face so their lips would meet as if by accident.

They hovered there for a silent moment, their mouths close, their breathing loud.

Then Simon straightened. "Good night," he whispered.

When the door closed behind him, Louisa put her face against its cool surface and prayed for strength. Giving in to her desires would only lead to worse loneliness for herself when she had to leave him. Because he was not courting her, and she knew he did not want to marry.

And she wouldn't let herself imagine being a wife to him.

Chapter 15

***

On the night of the ball, Simon and Leo waited in the drawing room for the ladies. Simon tossed back a drink, and by his brother's silence, knew he was being watched.

"What?" Simon finally asked. "Does my coat look all right? It's been a while since I wore it, and it feels tight in the shoulders. Manvil insists it's because I've been rowing—"

When Leo started to laugh, Simon stopping rambling and put his hands on his hips.

"Look at you," Leo said, "as nervous as a girl fresh from the schoolroom."

"Not very flattering."

"Sorry. You don't need to be nervous. Just the fact that you're attending has the family beyond excitement. If I wasn't so secure about my place, I'd be jealous at all the attention you're receiving."

"Believe me, I don't appreciate the attention. Luckily, I won't know when I'm being stared at."

That wasn't true. He could feel people staring—

or was he imagining it? After all, they were bound to be curious, since he'd been holed up here for months.

"Tell me what I look like," he suddenly said.

Leo sighed loudly. "Manvil did an excellent job."

"No, I mean—"

"You look so natural, sometimes I forget you aren't really looking at me." Leo's sober voice became playful. "But then I remember that I can get away with things."

Simon hit him in the arm.

"Hey, how did you know where I—"

"I can *hear* where you are," Simon said dryly. "You might want to remember that."

"Hmm," Leo answered. "For a man who can't see, you seem to pay a lot of attention to Miss Louisa Shelby."

Simon tensed. "She's our grandmother's companion, and she's helping our sister. Am I supposed to ignore her?"

"No, but she likes watching you as much as you 'listen' to her." Leo chuckled. "That's pretty good, if I say so myself."

"Promise me that you will not be pushing women on me tonight. I don't plan to marry."

"That is the most ridiculous thing you've ever said," Leo scoffed.

His carefree brother was actually angry?

"Leo—"

"No, you listen to me. Maybe not every woman

would be able to deal with your moods, but you would have no problem finding a bride. You're a viscount, for God's sake."

"That and money would be the only reason a woman would marry me. Sooner or later she would realize her mistake, and it would be too late. No, thank you. I'll let you and your eventual son carry on the title."

Before Leo could respond, they heard the ladies coming down the main staircase. Leo walked past him.

"This discussion isn't over." Leo paused. "I'm impressed."

"What?"

"The women are on the landing above—some ribbon in Georgie's hair came loose."

"You're impressed by that?"

"No, by how she looks. I never thought our little mouse could look stunning."

Simon warmed with pride. "I never doubted it. Her old wardrobe did not flatter her."

"Oh this one does. Even the neckline." Leo cleared his throat. "Guess she really does look like a girl."

Simon frowned. Had Louisa allowed a dress that was a bit too daring for a young lady? Surely his grandmother would have objected if necessary. And he knew Louisa had Georgie's best interests at heart.

"And then there's Miss Shelby," Leo said in a soft voice.

At Leo's admiration, Simon felt uneasy. Was he actually *jealous* that his brother could appreciate Louisa's stunning beauty? It wasn't Simon's place to be jealous—he had no hold on Louisa.

"Her dress is golden," Leo continued.

Simon really didn't want to know, although it would appear suspect if he told his brother to stop.

"And if you think Georgie looks like a woman—"

Simon closed his eyes. He might not be able to see her, but he remembered exactly how her breasts felt in his hands, the sweet taste of her skin.

"Boys, you look splendid," their grandmother called. "Are we ready to go?"

And then Simon realized something he'd forgotten—Manvil. Should he take his loyal valet and lean on him as he'd done for so many months?

"Hello, Simon," said Georgie, putting her arm through his. "I'm so glad you're attending with me. We'll have fun together, I promise."

Together? he thought. He was not going to allow Georgie to spend her evening taking care of him. He shouldn't even be going—but Keane was sniffing around her.

He smiled at his sister. "I have plenty of people to be with, Georgie. You will dance and have fun and not worry about me, do you understand?"

"But Simon—"

"We'll take turns," Leo said. "There's always a

card game I could drag him to. Simon, I'll position you on my opponent's side of the table, and since he won't know who you are, he'll get nervous, thinking you're reading his cards. I'll win easily."

"Leo!" their grandmother said, taking Simon's other arm. "How terrible to use your brother like that."

But Simon found himself laughing, and his tensions eased.

"And Simon will know everyone there," Grandmama added. "It is a country ball, not a London crush."

Simon's smile faded. He wondered what Louisa was thinking. Did she look forward to this, or would she be too preoccupied about Georgie, as he was? And he worried for Louisa, too. If these men had heard the London rumors, she would be vulnerable, and he could do nothing to help her. He wouldn't even be able to see what was going on. He wanted to tell his grandmother to keep an eye on Louisa, too, but he never got the chance.

How did he think he was going to protect either woman?

He was stuffed into the family carriage with everyone else, where he listened to Louisa's last-minute instructions to Georgie, and Leo's opposite advice.

After they arrived, and the footman had helped Simon down, Lady Wade said, "Simon, as my eldest handsome grandson, you must escort me inside. Louisa, you can remain with us, while Leo escorts Georgie."

"Georgiana," his sister hissed.

Simon smiled as Grandmama put her arm through his.

"There are only two steps up to the ground floor right here," she said.

He felt them with his cane. He knew he'd been at Lady Perry's home before, but he couldn't remember the layout. He was used to his grandmother's home, but now he was entering a giant blank, and he felt adrift.

"We're in the entrance hall," Grandmama continued, "and we're going to follow stairs that circle here to the right, up to the second floor. Do you remember this two-story entrance hall? It is quite stunning."

He didn't remember, and he kept reminding himself not to squeeze her frail arm. He concentrated on every step, and to his relief, his cane found the top stair before his grandmother could even speak.

"Oh dear," Grandmama said, "that silly Margot is having everyone introduced like this is London. Try not to think too poorly of her, Simon."

A moment later, he understood her concern.

"The Dowager Viscountess Wade and Viscount Wade."

The room fell to complete silence.

Simon didn't have to wonder who was looking

at him, because they all were. Mumbled voices
rose like the buzzing of insects.

"So how many people are here?" he asked
softly, keeping a pleasant expression on his face.

"Perhaps forty," she answered. "I am so
sorry."

They waited while Georgie and Leo were introduced.

"You have nothing to apologize for, Grandmama," Simon continued. "Just guide me to the
receiving line."

"Lady Wade, where would you like me to wait
until you need me?"

He was startled by Louisa's voice. He'd been so
caught up in his own misery, he'd forgotten she
was right behind him.

"I can stay with you, Grandmama," Georgie
said.

"Oh no you don't," Leo said. "I'll take my little
sister off your hands, Grandmama. Come along,
Georgie."

"Georgiana!" she said with a groan.

"Leo," Simon began in a warning voice.

"Don't worry, big brother," Leo said. "I'll never
let *Georgiana* out of my sight."

"Leo!" Georgie said, exasperated.

They continued to exchange heated whispers
until their voices faded away.

His grandmother said, "Miss Shelby, I could
use your help right now. After we say hello to
Margot—and it will take all I have not to berate

her for her foolish announcements—I need to speak with another of my friends. You and Simon can wander the party for refreshments, if you don't mind."

Softly, Louisa said, "If Lord Wade doesn't mind."

He smothered the last of his self-pity and remembered that Louisa needed his help tonight, too. If she weren't with him, she would sit in a corner with the companions and chaperones and old ladies, where lascivious men would look her over. She deserved more than that.

Their hostess greeted Simon cheerfully, if a bit forcefully. She made sure to tell him that her granddaughter was almost engaged. He got the impression he was supposed to stay away from her, which was fine with him. He might forget houses, but he remembered women. When the granddaughter had visited him in London after his accident, she had shouted every answer, and had made it plain that she was only visiting because she'd been forced.

When Louisa took over for his grandmother, there was an awkward silence as they began to move into the room. People greeted him in passing—some shouting, some sounding hesitant, as if he might not want to talk.

Most of the time, conversations were awkward: the women didn't seem to know what to say, and the men laughed too forcefully at any word out of Simon's mouth. But Louisa was able to turn every conversation to something pleasant, and he found himself appreciating her thoughtfulness.

When they left a couple behind, Simon leaned close to Louisa and whispered, "Find me a glass of anything, and then let's stand in the corner somewhere—or even better, behind a palm."

She laughed softly, and soon there was a glass of champagne in his hand. They retreated to a corner of the ballroom, where the air was cooler and the voices softer.

"It will get better, Lord Wade," she said. "People are just not used to you yet. Another party or two, and they'll be back to normal."

"I'm not sure I'll make it through another party or two."

"Shall I tell you about your sister?"

He tensed. "Is something wrong?"

"I don't think so. She's attached to your brother, which means she's meeting people. I saw her dance a quadrille, although I do wish she wouldn't look like she's concentrating so hard." She paused. "She's seen us and is coming over."

Simon heard his sister breathing hard as she approached. "Georgie, have you even rested this evening?"

She laughed. "Of course I have. I am not as popular as some of the ladies here, although maybe this is a little more enjoyable than I thought it would be."

Louisa squeezed his arm, but Georgie's words weren't exactly a ringing endorsement for success.

"My dance card is almost full," Georgie said dubiously.

"You can't be surprised by that," Louisa said. "You're a lovely, eligible lady."

"Perhaps, but some of these men are strangers to me, recently arrived from London. When one of them heard that I was acquainted with you, Louisa, he signed my card right away. I thought that was nice of him, though I can't seem to remember his name just now."

As Simon listened to his innocent sister, his smile faded. Men from London who knew Louisa?

"You'll have to point him out to me," Louisa said.

"When I see him again, I will. Simon, even Lord Keane wants to dance with me—and a waltz, yet. Oh, the music is starting. I have to go!"

"Damn, of course he chose the waltz," Simon said grimly after his sister left. He was so upset that he spoke without thinking. "Louisa, this is what I've been worried about from the moment of your arrival."

When Louisa said nothing, he realized what had come out of his mouth.

"You know what I mean," he blundered on. "She would meet a rake and then—"

"You equated that to my arrival," she interrupted. "Why is that?"

"I just meant that your London ways might be too much for Georgie."

"My London ways? Wasn't that what your grandmother hired me for?"

His face felt hot. He hadn't imagined what it would be like to say such a terrible thing to her.

"My lord, talk to me," she said softly. "Surely it doesn't need to be the dark of night for us to tell each other the truth. Since my arrival, you've managed to be with Georgie and me during every lesson, when a busy man such as yourself must have other duties to occupy him."

He took a fortifying sip of champagne. "Nothing is more important than my sister."

She waited.

"Grandmama hired you for a good reason, but she didn't know—" He broke off. If only he could see her face. "Louisa," he murmured. "God, this is hard. Can anyone overhear us?"

"No," she whispered faintly. "It's so loud and there are so many people and—Simon, *please*."

"Louisa, you have a certain reputation among some men of my acquaintance."

Were her eyes swimming with tears? Was she so pale she might faint? He wanted to hold her, needed to hold her.

"Reputation?" She sounded shocked and full of disbelief.

"As someone who is fast, who is willing to kiss, and maybe more."

She gasped. "But Simon, I never—you *know* I would never—before you—"

"I know that now, believe me." He wanted to

touch her, thought her arm would be safe, but he missed and reached her hip covered in layers of skirts and petticoats. If they were seen, his blunder could only make everything worse. He pulled back. "It's all lies but—"

"But you ... you thought that I would ... that's why you were ... with me," she finished in a hoarse whisper.

Did she actually think he had kissed her *because* of those rumors, because he thought he could?

"No, Louisa!" he said forcefully. He winced, wondering how loud he'd sounded. "We can't discuss this here. I can't even see who's looking at us."

"No one, my lord." Her voice didn't sound like her own, so distant, so bitter. "Everyone is surely assuming that you are with me because of what you can get."

"That's not true!"

"I can't talk, I can't—"

He felt her brush by him, and then she was gone.

"Louisa?" he said her name, but already knew she wouldn't be answering.

He was alone.

"Simon?"

He was almost ashamed by how relieved he felt hearing his sister. "Georgie, thank God you're here."

"Louisa didn't even talk to me when she walked by. And I think she was trying not to cry."

"It's all my fault. It slipped out and I—"

"What slipped out?"

"I ... heard something about Louisa a long time ago. Now that I know her, I don't believe it, but—"

"Just stop," Georgie said. "Tell me what you're talking about, or I won't be able to help."

"There's a rumor that Louisa is ... fast."

When Georgie said nothing for a minute, Simon said, "Georgie?"

"I'm just trying to think what name I can call you in public."

"I get the idea."

"How could you think such a thing about Louisa?" she demanded.

"I heard it from more than one source. I was worried that you being seen with her might ... tarnish you as well."

"You treated her like this because of *me*?" she hissed.

"Now that I know her, I don't believe it anymore, but that doesn't mean that others won't. I was just trying to protect you."

"That's why you're here tonight, isn't it," she said angrily. "And now she knows. I didn't think you were this much a fool, Simon. I have to go find her."

Simon said nothing when his sister left, even though he was now alone. For a minute he waited, hoping his grandmother or brother were looking for him, but nothing happened. Conversations swirled around him; someone he didn't recognize called a greeting in passing.

From the moment he'd become blind, this was what he had dreaded the most. Words were stuck in his throat; perspiration broke out on his forehead. How could he ask for help like a child? He didn't even know if he was truly near a wall, which at least he could follow to a door and get the hell away from this mob of curious people.

He was just about to risk stumbling toward where he thought the wall was, when he heard his name called again, and this time he recognized the voice.

"Paul," he said, knowing he sounded warm with relief.

"I'm glad to see you here tonight," Paul said. "I'm surprised none of your family is with you."

"Oh, they're here," Simon said. "But there's a minor crisis, and Georgie had to take care of it."

"And she didn't take you—I mean, you didn't go with her?"

Simon smiled grimly. "We're still not used to the logistics of my needing a constant companion."

"Well, you have one now. Shall I take you to your sister? If you don't mind my saying, I had a dance with her earlier, and she looks lovely this evening."

"Thank you for telling me, but much as I would like to be of help to her right now, it's best I stay away. I'm at your disposal, Paul, and you have my thanks."

"There's a card game in the library. Would you like to come?"

"As long as you don't need me as a partner."

Paul chuckled. "No, but as usual, they're talking politics, and you're more well versed than I am."

"Then lead on. I need something else to think about."

Chapter 16

❦

Louisa ran across the shadowed terrace, not stopping until she reached the balustrade. She hit it hard, and her hips ached and her breath came in gasps, but at least that pain was preferable to the one that soaked clear into her soul.

She had a fast reputation.

Everything seemed starkly clear now. What she had thought of as a good rapport with men, was only because they thought that she was easily ... seduced. The rumors must have spread to the family of her first employer, because once she didn't have the protection of her own wealthy family, they had treated her like she was fair game for anything.

Her stomach twisted with bitterness, and she was glad she had eaten nothing so far, or it might have crept up her throat.

Every memory of her happy life as a popular woman of Society was tainted. Every meaning, every motive was suspect now, and memories flashed in her head at a dizzying pace. She had thought herself so happy, so popular, so at ease, and instead, everything was a lie.

And since nothing had happened with any man—not even a kiss, until Simon!—she couldn't tell herself that even memories from an earlier time were all right. She had to disbelieve it all.

No wonder Simon didn't want to leave her alone with his sister. No wonder he questioned his grandmother's motives. Louisa shuddered. Lady Wade couldn't possibly know … could she? But no, Louisa would have been let go if the dear lady had thought she could harm her granddaughter.

Her newest dreams for the future were dead now. She could not in good conscience ask innocent families to hire her to help their daughters. She let out a hoarse laugh. As if she even trusted herself to have anything worth teaching. Simon had said he heard these rumors from a few men, but might they not have told women, too? She hugged herself forlornly.

Simon had known the truth about her reputation, and said nothing. He'd obviously meant to protect Georgie—that was his reason for being here tonight, Louisa thought bitterly. He wasn't recovering, as she'd hoped; he was desperate. Now she understood why he'd questioned Leo's protection of Georgie at the dinner party a few days ago, and why he'd had to take over himself.

Had Simon allowed Louisa to remain at Enfield Manor for a different purpose? Her stomach convulsed with nausea, and she grasped the balustrade for support even as her tears continued to flow unchecked. Was she truly even more *convenient* than she'd thought? Had he considered her an easy way for a blind man to—

She couldn't even think the words.

She found herself questioning everything anyone had said to her these last weeks.

"Louisa!"

Hastily, she wiped the wetness from her face and hoped the torches that lit the terrace hid much. Struggling for calm, she turned to face her student. With a shiver, she realized she shouldn't even call Georgie that anymore.

Louisa put on a smile. "Are you enjoying yourself, Georgie?"

Georgie studied her with worry, and Louisa realized that she wasn't hiding her own emotions well.

Georgie briefly touched her arm. "I was doing fine until I saw your face when you left Simon."

"Left—" And then she realized that she'd left him alone. "Oh, Georgie, is he all right?"

"I can't believe you're worried about him after what he said to you. He's not helpless."

Louisa looked away. "He shouldn't have told you," she said in a hollow voice.

"I forced him to. I hope you don't judge us all on his idiocy."

Louisa gave her a faint smile. "He only wants you safe, Georgie. None of this is his fault."

"Hurting you is. He certainly didn't have to tell you about these foolish lies."

"He didn't mean to."

"That's no excuse."

"And I can't even call them lies, not anymore." The words shuddered out of Louisa.

"You're talking about you and Simon," Georgie said flatly.

Louisa closed her eyes. "Am I that obvious?"

"He can't keep himself from being near you. I've thought it was wonderful."

"And now you know that there was a darker reason. He must have thought that I—"

"Louisa, I've known my brother a lot longer than you. Even if he believed those lies, he would never treat you like that."

"Maybe we don't understand what it's like to be trapped in the dark forever, feeling desperate."

"He can be a fool, but I won't let you think the worst of him. Whatever you two have together, it is not a sordid, ugly thing. I've been hoping," she lowered her voice, "that you might someday be a sister to me."

Louisa choked back a sob. "That won't happen, Georgie. He does not want to marry."

"He'll get over that."

"I don't think so. And after tonight, now that I know the truth ... how could you think

I would inflict myself on your family? I've always known that my Society is below yours, but *this*—"

"Don't talk like that! You're not leaving us. I don't give a fig what some ignorant men say to one another. Anyone who knows you understands the goodness in you."

Louisa gripped Georgie's hand. "You are a sweet girl, Georgie, but you're naïve."

"Then naivete is a strength. Trust me, Louisa. Don't make any hasty decisions. Let us go on as we have been. I've been making real strides tonight. But now we should go back inside."

"They can't think any worse of me, but if you're with me—"

"Stop worrying so much!"

"I just need a few minutes to compose myself, please. I'll be inside soon, I promise."

"I can't leave you like this."

"I'm done pitying myself, and the tears have truly stopped. I just need a moment for my red, puffy face to look somewhat normal."

"All right, but you come find me so that I know you're back."

"I will, I promise."

When Georgie kissed her cheek, Louisa almost started crying again. But she forced a smile and a wave, and then she was alone.

But not for long. She was taking deep breaths, dragging her thoughts away from sadness, when she heard footsteps behind her. She turned around and found herself too close to Lord Keane. He was wearing a smile as he looked down at her, and he didn't bother to conceal the fact that he wasn't just looking at her face. Wishing she could yank her gown higher, she settled for a cool nod.

"Good evening, Lord Keane. If you don't mind, I came out here to be alone."

"Yes, it is rather private," he said in his smooth voice, "but surely you don't mean *all* alone. Haven't you been waiting for a lucky man to join you?"

She started to tremble. There was no one on the terrace but the two of them. And she had nothing left of her reputation or family to protect her.

"No, my lord. Have a good evening."

As she swept by him, he caught her arm. She stared down at his fingers for a moment, then up into his amused eyes.

"This is not a game," she said with a calmness she didn't feel.

Just as he opened his mouth, Louisa heard her name called. She looked up to see Mr. Wade standing in the open doorway.

"Miss Shelby, are you all right? My grandmother is calling for you, but if you need my assistance—"

"No, Mr. Wade!" She hoped this scene did not escalate into something she could never recover from.

Lord Keane let her go. "Another time," he said softly.

"There will not be another time, I assure you. For the sake of us both, please wait several minutes before you go back inside."

When she reached the door, she gave Mr. Wade a grateful smile and slipped past him.

"Where is your grandmother?" she asked.

"I lied," he said.

They both looked out through the glass doors at Lord Keane, who leaned against the balustrade and gave them a little wave.

Mr. Wade blocked her view of the terrace. "I would have come out there to defend you, but I didn't want him to think . . ."

"That I was waiting for you?" she said dryly.

He shrugged. There was a waltz going on across the ballroom floor, and their corner of the ballroom was almost deserted. Mr. Wade looked down at her, and she was rather surprised by how much he resembled Simon when he was attempting to be serious.

"Are you all right?" he asked softly.

It was her turn to shrug. "He was only attempting what other men have attempted before him."

His face went red, and he swallowed. "I'm sorry."

"It's not your fault. I know it's not even my fault, but I'm the one who will have to live with it. Simon must have told you about the rumors."

Mr. Wade's face blanched. "You know?"

She sighed. "I was hoping you didn't, but I guess that was too much to hope for."

"Miss Shelby—"

"No, it's all right. At least now I know, and can protect myself from further scandal. Tell your grandmother that I will be with the companions and chaperones, where I belong. Oh, and Mr. Wade, please make sure your brother is all right. I left him rather abruptly."

"I saw him with Paul."

She sighed with relief. "Go protect your sister from the attentions of Lord Keane."

"That I can do," he said.

Simon sat in a wingback chair in Lady Perry's library and forced a laugh at someone's joke. If it weren't for his worries about Louisa, he would have been enjoying this evening. He was surprised at how much he had missed the company of a group of men.

But he couldn't relax, because he'd caused Louisa terrible pain. He didn't know what to do for her, how to make amends. She didn't want his help, and he was frustrated with the need to do something.

"There you are, Simon!"

It was Leo, and Simon gladly stood up, bringing his cane with him. "Ah, just the person I needed to talk to," Simon said. "Excuse me, gentlemen, while I have a word with my brother."

Where once it bothered him to have to put his

hand on another man's arm for guidance, now he gladly used Leo. He was relieved to do something other than brood about Louisa.

When he heard a door close behind him, and the sounds of voices became muted, he said, "Leo, are we alone?"

"For the moment."

"Did Georgie dance with Keane?"

Was Leo's arm tense under his?

"I think so. Why?"

"He's a blackguard where women are concerned. I warned you about him, didn't I?"

"Well, yes, but short of making a scene—"

"Take me to him."

"Simon—"

"It's all right, I don't mean to call him out. I just want to have a pleasant word with him."

"Good, because I don't think he'd appreciate my aiming your pistol for you." Leo paused. "All right, we're going back down the corridor into the ballroom. Don't run into the door."

"I won't as long as you open it for me."

Inside the ballroom, the heat hit them like a wave. The music crashed, people laughed and talked.

"Do you see him?" Simon asked.

"Give me a moment. It *is* a ball."

"But a country one. There aren't that many people."

"I see him," Leo finally said.

"You sound grim. Is he with Georgie?"

"No, but—"

"Just take me to him, and let me know when we're near."

Leo made their excuses as they pushed their way through throngs of guests.

"All right," Leo said, "we're about five feet away, and he's talking to a girl I've seen with Georgie, but I can't remember her name."

"Then let's go."

A minute later, Leo cleared his throat. "Good evening, Miss Perry."

"Good evening, Mr. Wade." Then she raised her voice. "Good evening, Lord Wade!"

Simon sighed, but he managed to greet her civilly. When he said nothing else, she excused herself.

Keane laughed. "Well, the Wade brothers certainly know how to send the ladies fleeing."

Simon focused on where his voice was coming from. "Keane, I ask that you not dance with my sister anymore. She's a young girl who doesn't understand that you're not looking to marry right now."

"Very well, Wade," Keane said genially. "I find your grandmother's companion more intriguing anyway."

Simon gritted his teeth, but managed to smile. Before he could warn the man away from Louisa, Keane said, "But she is quite good at making her true feelings known. Young Wade, did she send you packing, as she did me?"

Confused, Simon wanted to frown at his brother. What was going on?

Instead he listened as Leo said, "I was fetching her for my grandmother, Keane."

"Oh, I understand too well. Have a pleasant evening, gentlemen."

Simon heard the man's laugh fade as he walked away. He turned to his brother. "What was that all about?"

"I saw him alone with Louisa on the terrace," Leo said in a low voice. "He had his hand on her arm, as if he meant to prevent her from leaving."

Fury coursed through Simon, thick and hot.

"Now, Simon, don't look like that."

"Like what?"

"Like you're going to challenge him. Nothing happened."

"Damn those rumors," Simon said. "She's a target for every man who knows."

"She knows now, too. What are we going to do?"

"I'm the one who accidentally told her."

"For God's sake," Leo hissed in a low voice. "No wonder she looked so sad. I thought it was all about Keane. Simon, how are we going to fix this?"

"I'm surprised you care so much," Simon said distractedly.

"I care because she seems important to my family."

"There's nothing we can do to repair a rumor.

She lives an exemplary life—we can only hope that causes her reputation to subside. But as far as Louisa herself . . ." He trailed off, remembering the bleak way she'd spoken to him. He felt ... helpless.

"Where is Louisa?" Georgie sounded rushed, impatient, just as worried as Simon was.

"With the other companions," Leo said. "She's sitting and talking with an elderly lady. She's smiling—that's a relief."

Simon wanted to groan. "Of course she's smiling. She wouldn't take out her sorrow on an innocent woman."

"We should leave," Georgie said. "I've danced as much as I need to."

"With Keane, I hear," Simon said.

"Ugh," was her only response.

Simon shook his head. "But we can't leave, because Grandmama would be suspicious. I don't want her to know anything about this."

"She'll know when Louisa goes back to London," Leo said.

Simon inhaled, telling himself the sudden pain meant nothing. "She said she was leaving?"

"I'm only assuming—"

"She won't leave," Georgie said with confidence. "I told her I need her. And it's the truth."

"I don't understand what your problem is, Georgie," Leo said, exasperated. "You look pretty; men want to dance with you."

"Well I feel stupid!"

At the heat in her voice, Simon raised a hand. "Enough, both of you. Let's get through this evening without arguing. For Grandmama's sake."

"And Louisa's," Georgie whispered.

Chapter 17

The carriage ride home seemed twice as long to Louisa as it had on the way to the ball, when everything had seemed so promising. She'd imagined Georgie as a success at the ball, dancing with eligible men, and comfortable at last with her place in Society. She'd hoped Simon would feel more at ease with his old friends, that they'd treat him normally and prove to him that he had no reason to avoid such events. Before this evening, she'd thought things were getting better—with Georgie, Simon, and herself.

Instead she'd discovered that she'd understood nothing. Her lessons didn't seem to be helping Georgie, though Georgie insisted that wasn't true. It was a good thing Louisa wasn't going to try to make a living at this.

And Simon—he had only come to the ball to protect Georgie from Louisa's influence. It was a noble reason, and perhaps it had finally allowed him to see that he could function in a sighted world.

"Louisa," Lady Wade said, "I did not see you dance."

Louisa gave a start and turned to her employer with a smile. She wondered how much of her expression the swinging lantern revealed. "But I enjoyed myself, my lady. I met some interesting people."

She heard Mr. Wade give a snort as he turned away. Simon continued to focus on her with that otherworldly concentration that she'd once found so flattering, so promising.

Now she only saw it as suspicious.

"Louisa," Georgie said, "I met up with two of my friends tonight, and they'll be visiting me tomorrow afternoon. I wonder if you would be so gracious as to work with all three of us. They're not very good at talking to men either."

Stunned, Louisa could only blink at her. "Georgie, while it is sweet of you to want to help, I'm not sure their parents would appreciate my interference."

"Interference?" Lady Wade said. "I think it's a wonderful idea. You've done a world of good for Georgie, hasn't she, boys?"

"Yes, Grandmama," Mr. Wade answered dutifully, unable to meet Louisa's eyes.

When Simon didn't answer immediately, his grandmother repeated his name.

"Louisa has a great talent for helping people," Simon finally said softly. "It would be a true shame if she didn't understand that."

So now he was trying to lift her spirits, Louisa thought tiredly. Weren't they at Enfield Manor yet?

"Of course I'd like to help your friends, Georgie," Louisa said, mustering a smile.

When they finally arrived, Lady Wade couldn't understand how tired all the young people seemed, when she herself was energized by the evening. Louisa was able to retire, while the grandchildren listened to the evening's gossip.

When Louisa was finally in her room, she felt exhausted and sick at heart. There were no more tears left to cry, and it was time to figure out what to do with her life, now that she knew the truth.

But nothing came to her, even as she lay in bed and stared up at the dark ceiling. An hour later, she heard a tap on the balcony door, but she ignored it. Simon even tried to turn the handle, but she'd locked it against him.

She didn't know what to say, how she would face him again. Or how she could stop this slow slide into falling in love with him.

When Louisa awoke the next morning, she was grimly determined to finish the job she'd been hired to do. Regardless of what was being said about Louisa, Georgie and Lady Wade trusted her to help. And Louisa wanted to do that above all things. It might be her last opportunity, because when Georgie no longer needed her, Louisa would have to return to her sister's home and hope for the best—either spinsterhood or a marriage based on her dowry.

Neither option overjoyed her, but it was all she had. She would make the best of it.

Louisa spent the morning avoiding Simon, then in the afternoon, she was introduced to her new students. The Misses Chester were twin sisters with twin squints. You could only tell them apart because one wore her black hair curly, and the other straight. The first thing Louisa accomplished was getting them to wear their spectacles.

"Ladies," she informed them, "squinting calls attention to your eyes—and not in a pleasant way. With your spectacles I can see how lovely your blue eyes are—and even better, you can see me. Correct?"

They leaned toward each other and giggled.

"Besides that, what do you need help with?" she asked.

"Talking to men," said Miss Chester of the curly hair.

"Georgiana says you are very good at it," said the other Miss Chester. "Although I'm quite jealous because Georgiana has gotten better at it, too."

Louisa glanced at Georgie, who looked surprised, though pleased. It was good for her to know others saw her improvement.

But didn't Georgie understand that Louisa had only *thought* she could talk to men? Maybe Georgie hadn't considered how Louisa was affected by these rumors. Or perhaps to Georgie, the only thing that mattered was how Simon and Louisa fared together.

Louisa set them to practicing their conversation using riding, a topic men found interesting. But during the exercise, Louisa silently questioned everything she'd ever said to a man. Hadn't Simon warned her early on that men didn't always converse straightforwardly? How could she tell that to innocent girls?

She felt so alone, so sad, because everything she'd ever assumed about her life was not as she remembered it. Striding calmly to the windows, she looked out, only to see Mr. Wade guiding his brother through the garden at a pace that Simon must surely be protesting.

Louisa's sadness deepened, and she wondered if this was how Simon had felt when he became blind, like his whole life had changed.

But how could she compare her situation to losing one's sight?

She thought of his inability to roam his own grounds at will. If only there was some way that he could walk outdoors like he did indoors.

She pressed her hand to the glass as she watched him disappear around a turn of the path. She'd only been avoiding him for less than a day, and already she missed him.

An hour later, Louisa suggested to the girls that they walk the grounds, in hopes that they'd run into the Wade brothers for extra practice conversing. Louisa begged off, then went to see if she could be of help to Lady Wade. The woman was sitting in her morning room, writing a letter.

Lady Wade looked up with a smile when Louisa entered. "Well, Louisa, how did your new pupils do?"

"They're lovely girls, Lady Wade. All they need is confidence."

"Just like my Georgie."

Louisa smiled. "Exactly."

"And you, my dear, what do you need?"

Louisa opened her mouth, but for a moment was too shocked to reply. "I need nothing, my lady."

"Well I think we need to find you a husband."

She gave a choked laugh. "I don't think that's part of your duties as my employer."

"Perhaps not, but in the absence of your mother, I could help with that."

"My mother was once very determined to see her daughters married."

"Of course. A mother's worst fear is that her daughter will not have her own home, her own happiness. You need to meet more young men. I should probably host a house party, but for now I think we should host a musicale. Georgie can play, you and Simon can sing, and of course you'll all have to practice together for several hours every day."

Louisa closed her eyes on a sigh. "You must

stop trying to get your grandson and me together, my lady. It will not work. He thinks I'm—" She bit back the words, embarrassed, heartsick, yet already so tired of secrets. She had tried to explain everything to her sisters in a letter this morning, but she couldn't bring herself to do it. It was only fair that this kind lady know the truth.

"He thinks what, my dear?" Lady Wade asked. "I can tell that he appreciates you."

"Not for any good reasons," Louisa said in a low voice. "He thinks I'm ... fast."

Lady Wade straightened with a gasp. "Simon said that to you? Why ever would he—"

"It's not his fault, my lady. Apparently there have been rumors about me for years that I knew nothing about. He's been worried about my effect on Georgie's reputation. That's why he stayed close to us, why he came to the ball. I should go back to London, before Georgie's chances at a good marriage are hurt."

When Lady Wade said nothing, Louisa couldn't bring herself to look at her and see disappointment or condemnation. She wondered how soon she could pack and leave. Her eyes burned with tears she didn't want to shed.

"Simon's first instinct might have been to protect Georgie," Lady Wade said kindly, "but that's not the whole truth."

"My lady—"

"You forget that I know my grandson far better than you do. Your presence has changed him,

Louisa, and you must never doubt that. I will not
hear of you leaving."

"But my lady—"

"I'm too old to care what people think. Upon
meeting you, anyone who believes such outland-
ish rumors is not worth our consideration. You
have earned our loyalty, Louisa, and I will not
abandon you—or allow you to abandon yourself."

Louisa wiped a tear from the corner of her eye
and tried to smile. "You are too good to me," she
said faintly. "But I have to leave sometime."

"Not yet, please. Give it some thought and
promise me that you'll make no decision until
you consult me."

"Of course, my lady."

"Good. Now why don't you read this letter
back to me, because my eyes are quite tired today,
and I've lost my place."

Louisa humored her, even though Lady Wade's
eyesight was sharp, and she saw too much.

The Chester sisters stayed for dinner, and Mr.
Wade charmed them until their faces were red
from laughing and blushing. Louisa watched one
of the sisters glance repeatedly at Simon, who,
though quieter than normal, still participated.
Perhaps this was what Lady Wade meant by Louisa helping Simon. Was she supposed to make
him see that women found him intriguing?

Or had Lady Wade had a third reason for hiring

Louisa from the beginning—for Simon himself?

Now that Lady Wade knew the truth, surely she couldn't believe such a union possible.

Louisa's self-assurance was taking a beating, and she was disgusted with herself. She made an effort to converse normally during dinner. After dinner, feeling wide awake, she browsed the library for a book. She didn't flee when Simon found her and closed the doors behind him, leaving them alone with each other.

He said nothing, just waited. Though she wanted to deny them, her feelings for him overwhelmed her. In just a day she'd missed being with him, missed enjoying his beauty and laughing at his humor. He rarely felt sorry for himself—as she was doing today. She'd missed how he'd made her feel aware of her body, aware of its response to him. Regardless of the motives for his kisses, she'd responded to them like a starving woman.

How was she supposed to forget that? How could she keep reminding herself that those same kisses surely meant nothing to him?

She cleared her throat. "May I help you, Simon?"

"At least you're not 'my lord'-ing me."

He moved smoothly around the furniture and came toward her. She wanted to back away, but held her ground, though her heart pounded with both desire and sadness.

"And you're speaking to me," he continued.

She heard uncertainty in his voice, and her own tension eased.

"You thought I'd ignore you?"

"You did last night," he said.

"I—I needed to be alone, I guess, to think about everything that had happened."

"Did Keane hurt you?"

"It's too late to rescue me, Simon."

He grimaced, and she realized how that sounded.

"Keane said you rescued yourself," Simon said.

"With help from your brother."

"If Keane bothers you again—"

"I've always been bothered by men, Simon," she said, trying for humor but hearing bitterness in her voice. "I thought it was because I was pretty, and because my company was pleasant."

He ran a hand through his hair. "You are, and it is."

"Ah, but there's more. Thank you for making me understand, before something worse happened."

He stepped closer, and she took another step away but found herself in the corner, books pressing into her on two sides.

"I never wanted you to know, Louisa. I may have been trying to protect Georgie, but damn it all, I was protecting you, too. The way your voice sounded when I told you, the hurt—God, maybe it's a good thing I couldn't see what was in your eyes."

She closed them now, feeling the tears escape and slide in silent paths down her cheeks.

"Louisa," he said gruffly, reaching out a hand.

"I'm all right," she whispered, wondering whom she was trying to convince.

She meant to only pat his hand, but when she touched him, he held on, sliding both his hands up her arms to cup her face.

She stiffened, trying to pull away, but when his thumbs brushed her wet cheeks she stopped fighting.

He inhaled and whispered her name again, leaning down to her. "I didn't want you to feel this way. I would take away every bit of your pain if I could."

His thumbs continued to stroke her cheeks, then to her shock, he leaned down and kissed her tears, kissed her eyelids. His gentleness was her undoing. She clutched his arms to keep from falling into him. She had no defense against him, no anger.

When he continued to kiss her face, she tipped her head and their mouths met. He froze for only a moment, as if he hadn't meant to go this far.

But she wanted him to. She wanted his closeness, his comfort, things to use in her battle against the bleak loneliness that might fill the rest of her days. She moved her mouth against his, then suddenly he was kissing her back. Their lips parted and searched, their tongues met and mated with a rising need that made her feel frantic to be closer to him.

She slid her arms around his waist, then let her palms press up against the heat of his back. He felt solid and real and so wonderful. His mouth was an intimacy that still surprised her. This was her third kiss—why did it still feel so glorious?

Perhaps because she knew that there was more, that his hands and mouth could work magic on her skin. She pressed even harder against him, and this time he was the one who broke the kiss. He lifted his head, his breathing still unsteady, his lungs filling to press against the ache in her breasts. She wanted to be touched there, but didn't dare ask such a thing.

"Louisa," he murmured her name, eyes half closed. "I shouldn't have—I never want you to think that I am using you as someone like Keane would."

"I don't." She kissed his chin, tucked her head against his neck and just let herself hold him. "Don't give me explanations or defenses for what we feel. Let me just enjoy it, and not think about tomorrow."

Simon held Louisa close. Though he desired her, though their kiss still wreaked havoc on his control, there was a comfort and a peace in holding her that he never expected.

He couldn't understand why she didn't hate him, but he was grateful at the same time. He should back off, not confuse either one of them with this intimacy, but the feel of her in his arms was more powerful than even passion.

He didn't understand himself and what he was experiencing—he certainly didn't want to look too closely. He saw himself as outside accepted conventions, knew he would never be a husband or father.

But when he held Louisa, he was lying to himself. For these brief moments he could pretend that his eyes were only closed, not blind, pretend that there were possibilities in the world.

But he forced himself to remember his reality—he was a blind man, and he'd allowed Louisa to be hurt. She wanted his comfort, and instead all he could think about was her body, and forgetting himself in the heat and the softness of it.

He lifted his head away from hers. She stirred and moaned and burrowed even closer against him. He drew a deep breath, so easily seduced by the possibilities. But he'd only hurt her worse.

"Louisa." He whispered her name, tried to draw away.

"I don't understand how I feel."

She spoke the words against his throat, and he shuddered.

"But when I'm with you," she continued, "everything else just goes away."

She took his hand and placed it on her breast. He couldn't breathe, couldn't think of anything but the soft mound hidden beneath corset and gown.

He stood on the edge, teetering, imagining taking her when she was so willing.

But they would be using each other to forget—him to forget his disability, his feeling of forever being on the outside, and her to forget her pain and uncertainty and worry.

He moved his hand from her breast, slid it up to cup her face. "Louisa, you would regret this. You would consider yourself as having finally proved all the rumors right. And you would think that I had used you. I don't want to be that memory for you."

He felt her tremble, felt her mouth open as if to deny his words.

Then she sighed. "No, we would be using each other," she whispered. "You are too good to me, Simon."

He forced a chuckle. "I don't feel very good. Go to bed, Louisa."

"Alone."

He closed his eyes and stepped away. "Yes, alone."

When she'd gone, the room felt cold and empty and lonely, and for the first time, he questioned whether that was what he wanted for the rest of his life.

Chapter 18

The next morning, Louisa awoke feeling almost at peace, even ... hopeful. She could not change what people had said about her in the past; she could only live her life proving that she was a good person doing her best. Dreading the future only brought heartache; she would take each day as it came.

And as for Simon's family, she could not leave them, not in hurt and defeat. For now, she would remain and finish what she'd started, helping Georgie, helping Simon.

Simon.

Even thinking his name made her shiver. He could have taken advantage of her weakness last night, but he hadn't. He was such a good man. She could not deny herself the rare pleasure of his company, even if it was only temporary.

But somewhere inside her grew a hope that she dared not contemplate or give a name. A hope that she meant more to him than he realized.

Louisa was helping Lady Wade cut flowers

for the manor early that afternoon when she saw Simon being escorted past her by Manvil. They were headed for the lake, and Simon's daily rowing. He probably knew these paths as well as the layout of the house, but without walls to follow, he could not navigate.

So what could he use that would guide him down a path?

When an idea came to her, she gave a gasp of surprise. Lady Wade, who'd been behind a rhododendron, peered around the foliage and gave Louisa a puzzled look from beneath her bonnet.

"Oh, don't mind me," Louisa said, smiling. "I just had a wonderful idea to aid your grandson. Might I be excused?"

Lady Wade reached for the basket that Louisa was holding. "By all means. It doesn't take two of us to cut flowers. I just didn't want you to be alone today."

Louisa smiled at her. "You are too good to me, Lady Wade."

A stable groom offered Louisa as much rope as she wanted, and she took several stakes as well. Down by the pier, she waved absently in response to Manvil's shouted greeting from the middle of the lake, then used a rock to pound her stake into the soft earth just off the pier. She tied the end of the rope to the stake, then walked back toward the terrace, leaving the rope to trail loosely behind her on the path. She explained her plan to every gardener she passed, so that no one would remove the rope. When she reached the terrace, she tied the end to the balustrade that lined the stairs.

Basking in satisfaction, she looked over her work. It felt good to have done something useful. Now if only Simon would think so, too.

She was waiting at the pier when Manvil and Simon left the boat. While Manvil bent to tie it up, Louisa called, "Lord Wade!"

He turned swiftly around. The sunlight shimmered through his blond hair, and she enjoyed the sight of his deepening dimples when he gave her a slow smile. She was suddenly very warm, and she knew she blushed when Manvil glanced at her.

"I have a surprise for you," Louisa said as Manvil escorted him down the pier and onto level ground.

Manvil gave an innocent smile. "I should be going."

Louisa and Simon spoke at the same time.

"Oh, no, I didn't mean—"

"You can't believe that—"

Manvil rolled his eyes. "I have real work to do, my lord."

Simon shook his head, grinning. "Then go do it. Louisa will see me back to the house."

"But I won't need to," Louisa said, feeling quite proud of herself.

Manvil hesitated.

"You want me to leave with Manvil?" Simon said doubtfully.

She blushed. "No, but I've done something that will help you walk about outside unassisted—well, actually, the end result will help. This is just preliminary."

Though Manvil obviously saw the rope tied to the stake, he said, "I imagine we're going to station all the servants at various points in the garden to call to you, my lord."

Louisa stared in shock at the forward valet.

But Simon only laughed. "Don't keep me in suspense, Louisa."

She took his elbow and guided him to the stake. "Bend down and feel what's at your feet, my lord."

He leaned over, and she couldn't help but watch the way his damp shirt hugged the muscles in his back, the way his trousers outlined—

She looked quickly at Manvil, but thank goodness he was watching his master instead of her.

"I feel a stake and a rope," Simon said. "It is a rather loose rope. Do you mean me to follow it?"

"Yes, for now. The ropes will serve as a guide for the servants to build a railing."

"A railing," he echoed doubtfully.

"A railing could follow a path and lead you to the lake. Another one could lead you to the stables. You wouldn't have to be confined to the house."

Simon looked thoughtful. "You are good to

think of me, Louisa, but surely that would be too much trouble—"

Manvil interrupted. "Trouble to put up some pieces of wood? It's not terribly difficult work. I think it's a brilliant idea, and I'll talk to the head gardener about it."

"I already mentioned it to him," Louisa said. "Once I have your approval, I only have to lay out some paths, and they'll build whatever I want—whatever *you* want, my lord."

Manvil looked between them. "I have some ideas for paths. I'll go consult."

He left them, and Louisa watched Simon. She wasn't sure what he was thinking. Was he upset that she hadn't spoken to him first? She wanted to take his arm, to lean into him, to have him confide in her. Instead, she repeated his name softly.

He glanced her way. "It is an idea with merit, Louisa. I appreciate that you want to help."

"So you will let the staff build this for you?"

He grinned. "I will think about it."

"Then I will have to convince you," she said firmly.

He took a step closer to her. "And how will you do that?"

"I will show you all the places you could go unassisted about this large estate."

"Go with you, you mean?"

His voice had deepened, roughened, and it made her think of intimacies they could share.

"Not with me," she quickly said, trying not to

let him hear how flustered she was. "I'll leave you clues."

"Clues," he repeated dubiously.

She lifted her chin. "Be patient, Simon. You'll see."

An hour later at the archery field, Louisa stood back, watching Georgie take aim with her bow. The sky was overcast, and occasional drops of rain had begun to fall, but Georgie had stubbornly wanted to finish her lesson. She was becoming quite skilled at the sport.

She released the arrow, and it hit the target only inches from the center. "Soon," she mumbled.

"Soon what?" Louisa asked.

Georgie glanced at her, wearing a cool smile. "Soon I'll be able to challenge Leo."

Louisa laughed. "*That's* your goal? Not self-improvement, or the satisfaction of knowing you've succeeded in challenging yourself?"

"Those things are nice, but I really want to defeat Leo."

"I have another way you can show up your brother," Louisa said slyly.

Georgie released another arrow and glanced at her with interest. "How?"

"At the village assembly this weekend. Dancing and socializing are some of Leo's talents. To defeat him at *those* things would really bother him. Now before you say you don't want to attend—"

"I'm attending."

"—I think you should—oh."

Louisa studied Georgie. She didn't seem nervous or uncertain, just determined. A little too grimly determined.

As bigger raindrops began to fall, Georgie gathered together her equipment, and the two women quickly walked back toward the house.

"I've come to the realization," Georgie said, "that if I would have continued avoiding Society functions, I would have ended up as my mother's permanent companion."

"And that's your only motivation?" Louisa asked dubiously.

"No, of course not." Georgie grinned. "But it's important."

"Simon has many homes, any one of which he'd be happy to let you live in."

"Simon doesn't want to be in his own household—that's one reason he's still with Grandmama."

Louisa frowned. "Georgie—"

"No, I can already see I haven't explained properly. The family seat of the viscountcy is in Derbyshire. Even if Simon weren't blind, he would never go there. It's a lonely bachelor household, and he has always liked having people in his life, even if he won't admit it. That's why he's living with Grandmama. I need my own life, my own home. So I'll go to the assembly."

The rain began in earnest, and they ran the

last few yards through the garden and up the terrace stairs. Only when they were safely inside, looking back out the window at the rain, did Louisa glance at her pupil with a new respect.

"I'm proud of you, Georgie," she said softly.

"Don't be." Georgie wasn't smiling. "It's still very hard for me to attend these events. I am more competent now, I know. But I don't feel the same as everyone else."

"You don't know how they feel." Louisa rested her shoulder against the window frame so that she could face her pupil. "At the beginning, it's hard for everyone."

"But I'm no longer at the beginning, am I?" She gave a sad shake of her head and smiled. "I don't feel ... comfortable having men look at me. Oh, I feel prettier now in my new stylish clothes, thanks to you."

"Georgie—"

"Louisa, I know you want to help, but in this I don't think you can. But I'll make it all work, don't worry."

The next morning, Manvil handed Simon a folded piece of paper that had been left under the door.

"I believe it is from Miss Shelby," Manvil said. "She sprayed perfume on it."

"She did not," Simon shot back, but found himself smelling the paper.

When Manvil laughed, he tossed the paper back at him.

"So read it."

Manvil cleared his throat. "'Lord Wade, you'll find your next clue at the left of the terrace balustrade.' Oh, she's made a rhyme."

Simon snorted. "Is that all?"

"That's all."

While Manvil shaved him, Simon tried to rationalize his excitement—who wouldn't want to spend a morning with Louisa Shelby? She was trying to help him, just as she was trying to help Georgie. But for some reason, he wasn't bothered that he was her special project. Anything that kept him alone with her seemed a good thing.

He found the tethered rope she'd indicated in her note and followed it, feeling rather foolish because he had to walk hunched over. Every twenty feet or so he had to bend even farther to follow the taut rope down to another stake in the ground. But as he paid attention to the direction the rope was taking him, he was aware that he knew where he would end up. The stables.

He gripped the railing of the wooden enclosure, listening to the neighing of the horses and the calm voices of the grooms working patiently with them. He had thought he would feel annoyed or frustrated with having to follow a rope, but he felt only a touch of melancholia for how things used to be.

"You made it," Louisa said from above him.

He turned, perplexed, and felt the nudge of a horse's nose against his shoulder. She was riding.

For only a moment he remembered what had happened the last time he'd gone riding. But then he found himself stroking the horse's nose, running his hands down the neck. The next thing he felt was the hem of a petticoat.

"No farther," she said softly. "Call no attention to me—I'm not riding sidesaddle."

"What a daring woman." He thought of where his hands had almost roamed, and he was immediately aroused.

"I have a picnic meal," she said, as if he needed more enticement.

"Shall I walk beside you?"

"I could lead your horse."

He had vowed never to ride again—and she knew that. Yet here she was offering, as if she thought he should try. He imagined what the servants would think watching their master led around like a child. Of course he'd just followed a rope around the garden.

He even considered riding on the same horse with her, but that would set the rumors flying.

Not to mention what just the thought of her between his thighs as they rode was doing to his ability to think.

"This is Ladyflower," Louisa said. "I'm assured that she is the most gentle mare in the stable. Would you like to ride her?"

"All right." He said the words before he could change his mind.

She must have thought the same thing, because she dismounted quickly. "She's all yours."

"I should adjust the stirrups."

She paused. "They're already adjusted for you."

"Ah, I see."

She said nothing.

"All right, I don't *see*," he continued, smiling, "but I understand your prearranged plan."

He found the stirrup and put his foot in, grasped the pommel, and mounted. The horse danced beneath him, and instinctively he calmed the animal. He was breathing too quickly, and he'd lost his sense of direction when Ladyflower had circled.

"Louisa?"

"I'm right here. Would you like me to take her head?"

"No, get a horse. I'll wait."

"I have a horse right here."

He heard the creak of the leather saddle as she mounted. "So prepared," he said dryly.

"I hope you don't mind."

"You seem to be having your way with me," he said.

She made a choked sound.

He couldn't help but smile. "I meant about the railings and riding a horse, but you can interpret my words any way you please."

"You've taught me too well," she said.

Not everything I'd like to teach you, he thought. But he was the one who'd made the decision to take their relationship no farther. As she took his reins, he didn't ask where they were going. He tried to tell himself he was making the right choices, but it was difficult. If he had ridden with her, right now he would be feeling her backside between his thighs. He could have held her waist in his hands, reached around to the front of her and—

She didn't deserve to be the object of his lustful thoughts. There was a truce between them, a friendship that was more than physical. And she'd been so hurt. Now when she worked with Georgie, he heard a hesitation in her voice that had never been there before. He wondered if she'd lost faith in herself and saw helping him as a way to recover it.

He didn't care why she was with him; he would just enjoy it for as long as it lasted. He let himself move with the horse as he inhaled the scents of grass and flowers.

Before long, she said, "We're at our perfect picnic place."

"And where is that?" he asked.

"A hillside overlooking the manor. The green pasture seems to go on forever here."

"I think I know the place."

He dismounted slowly so that he wouldn't misjudge the ground and fall on his face. Although he wanted to help her down, he didn't trust himself to keep his hands from lingering.

She spread a blanket and guided him to it, then served him foods easily eaten by hand—fruit, chicken, and cheese. The lemonade was still cold, and he guzzled it until it ran down his chin. She just laughed and handed him a napkin.

This could not last, he told himself. She would be gone someday, and these would be memories that he cherished. He didn't mind her constant need to help him; he liked being the focus of her energy, of her attention.

Always, there was her scent, teasing his senses. He lay on his side, head propped on his hand, content to be with her, to pretend that his life was as it used to be. The desire for her that was always with him simmered just beneath the surface. He tantalized himself imagining how he would spread her out on the blanket, the ways he would delve beneath her garments.

"Simon?"

He realized that she was calling his name—might even have said it more than once. Rolling onto his back, he flung an arm over his eyes and smiled. "Just wool gathering," he said.

"So will you agree to allow the servants to build railings? Surely you can see how handy they would be."

"They'd be in everyone's way," he said.

Louisa could not decipher Simon's mood, though his words were thoughtful. He seemed lazy and content, now that he'd at least made himself ride again. Did he protest her plan just to argue with her?

"Everyone would get used to them," she said, glad she didn't have to pretend not to watch him. He looked big all stretched out on the blanket. His feet hung off, his elbow bumped a plate of chicken, but he didn't move.

"I'll think about it."

She wanted to groan her frustration. She saw his mouth quirk up in laughter.

"All right, if you won't discuss the railings, let's discuss the village assembly this weekend."

"More people watching us? I vote we don't go."

"I understand that," she said softly, picking at a piece of grass between her fingers. "I don't want to go either."

"You know Keane won't bother you again. I'll make sure no one else does either."

"You can't always be my protector, Simon." She only wished that. "And you can't hide in the manor either."

"So you think insults will work on me?"

"Georgie told me she wants to go. I think she's braver than both of us."

He grunted his answer.

She told him about her conversation with his sister. "But oh, I can't repeat all of it."

He sat up, leaning back on his hands. "Just say it."

"Georgie said that although you may not want your own household, she does."

"I have my own home!" he said crossly.

"I told her that. And her response was that it's a lonely bachelor home and that's why you're living with your grandmother."

He frowned. "So much for shyness, and wanting to help me any way she can."

"I think she *is* trying to help."

"Like you are?"

Louisa looked away, not knowing what answer he wanted to hear.

In a soft voice, he said, "I'm getting used to people helping me, you know that."

"Yes."

"But that doesn't mean it's not difficult."

"I know. You can return the favor and help your grandmother."

He cocked his head. "Why am I suddenly suspicious?"

"She wants you to be happy, to be back in Society where you've always thrived. And she wants me to overcome these rumors."

"You told her about them?" he said in obvious surprise.

"I hadn't planned to, but she is such a dear lady, and she wants to make things better for me, as well as you. So we both need to go."

"And how would this make her happier, since I've already accompanied her this week?"

"Because I think you should dance." She let out her breath.

To her surprise, he didn't answer right away.

"With you?" he finally asked.

She couldn't look at him, had to concentrate on not betraying with her voice how good that sounded to her. "I was thinking with Georgie."

"She steps on my feet."

"You two could practice."

"You and I don't even need to practice."

She closed her eyes, remembering being held in his arms, moving across the ballroom floor. She shivered.

"Unless you believe it will not look good for you to be dancing with your employer's son," he added.

"Or are you worried because of my reputation?" she shot back.

He grinned. "Then we'll dance."

Chapter 19

∽⟳∾

The village assembly was held in the public room above a prosperous tavern, and like any other dance, it was crowded and hot and loud. Louisa watched as Simon and Mr. Wade at first kept their sister with them as they conversed their way from group to group. Now that it was Simon's second public event, more people approached to speak with him. And those tended to be his male friends, whom Georgie was then lucky enough to be introduced to.

When Lady Wade's back was turned, Louisa retreated to the corner with the other companions and chaperones. She felt safe there, until one of the young girls beside her gave a gasp. "Lord Wade and his brother are coming right toward us!"

Another girl said, "Oh, Mr. Wade will dance with you, Emily. One of us will occupy the blind one for you."

Feeling her muscles stiffen with anger, Louisa opened her mouth for a retort, but it was too late.

"Ah, Miss Shelby," Mr. Wade said.

Though he saw her every day, she still felt that he seemed vaguely uneasy around her. Did the rumors about her bother him so much?

She curtsied to them both, and she saw Simon's wide grin.

"And yes," Mr. Wade said with a roll of his eyes, "she curtsied to a blind man."

Several ladies gasped and tittered with laughter, while Louisa simply shook her head.

"Miss Shelby," Simon said, bowing his head, "I believe you owe me this dance."

Shocked silence followed this announcement, but Louisa stepped forward with rising excitement. She hadn't thought he'd actually do it—they hadn't even found time to practice during the week.

"You're welcome to my brother," Mr. Wade said, releasing Simon to Louisa, who took his arm. "I have more than enough partners to choose from right here."

That distracted all the giggling, blushing wallflowers, and Louisa was able to lead Simon away. She was impressed that Mr. Wade could be thoughtful.

"Well, *he* caused quite a stir with the girls who never get to dance," Louisa said.

"And we're not?"

"Shall I lie to you?"

He sighed. "No."

"Now I know how it feels to be watched, and out of curiosity rather than approval."

"We both used to receive a lot of approval," he said softly.

She glanced at him. "And we miss it."

"Sometimes."

"Sometimes," she agreed. "Shall we give them a reason to approve of us again?"

"And it's as easy as a simple dance?" he asked.

He was smiling at her, but she didn't know what he was truly thinking.

"I don't know," she answered. "But it will make me feel better to remember other times. Maybe for you, too."

"My advice is not to live in the past," he said firmly.

"Then let this be about our present."

"And our future?"

When those words left his mouth, there was a sudden tension between them, part pleasure, part desire, and part uncertainty. She wasn't sure what he meant, but when he turned and put his arms around her, every coherent thought fled her mind except one—it was too late; she'd fallen in love with him.

The most handsome, generous man in the room had asked her to waltz, had taken her into his strong arms and was about to sweep her to a reality of only their bodies moving in sync across the floor. Frozen, she stared up in wonder at him, shocked at her emotions, full of awe, but not yet ready to remind herself that he was not in love with her.

"Miss Shelby," Simon whispered, "I believe you have to lead."

She blushed, knowing she'd been standing still, caught up in the way he made her feel.

"And please make sure we don't run a shy couple right off the floor," he added.

"Then I'll steer clear of your brother."

Simon gave a bark of laughter. Heads turned, couples paused, and Louisa used that moment to begin the sweeping circles of the waltz. Simon's smile faded as he concentrated, and she knew he couldn't be very at ease, but his triumph was in the attempt. If only he'd see that.

She used the pressure of her hand in his to turn him, pushed against his shoulder, and once even pulled, but it was Mr. Wade they were avoiding.

"Your brother is deliberately getting in our way," she said with amusement.

"He didn't think I'd dance," Simon said. "Even I can't believe it. But I couldn't stand to have you sitting in a corner, when you deserve to be in the center of the room."

She blushed but couldn't answer—her entire attention needed to be focused on keeping Simon from being humiliated. She was shocked to remember how her partners had easily kept up a conversation while waltzing about a crowded floor. Thank goodness only four other couples were dancing with them. Another twenty or so people were openly gawking.

When the dance finally ended and Simon released her, she sank into another curtsy and he bowed.

When she took his arm again, he leaned down and said, "You're trembling. Is something wrong?"

"Only the stress of leading," she lied. "I am filled with admiration for you men who have to do this all the time."

"And there's nothing else?"

She hesitated. "We are quite on display here. I hope—"

"Just stop right now," he said firmly. "You're going to spout nonsense about me suffering for having to be seen with you. If I ever discover who tarnished your reputation, I'll destroy him with my bare hands."

She warmed with pleasure.

"What about your suffering?" he continued. "I know I stepped on your toes twice. You have to put up with a blind man, for heaven's sake."

"But it was an honor," she said softly.

His smile faded, and she found herself trapped in his awareness of her, enjoying being the center of this man's attention.

"You know," she said breathlessly, "I saw several mamas pointing you out to their daughters." Did that sound as if she was trying to marry him off to someone else, she wondered? Or maybe the more she reminded him that he was an eligible mate, the more he might think of himself that way.

"Don't even bother," he said.

Simon wasn't going to listen to her foolish words about other women or other dances. He was happy where he was. Wondering what Louisa was thinking was a pleasant obsession. She was treating him like a normal man, and it was a rare feeling these days. He had spent the past months telling himself that everyone else had changed, not him, that his life could go on as always.

But finally, here on the dance floor with the only woman he could dance with, he had to admit the truth to himself: he was different, he'd changed, and he didn't know how to go back to the man he was before. If not for the many challenges Louisa had presented him over the past several weeks, he still would have been in his grandmother's home, conducting his business in solitude, telling himself that everything was all right.

So where was he supposed to go from here? Blindness had changed him, but he was beginning to forge a new life. It was yet incomplete, as he lacked any clear understanding of his future. All he knew was that Louisa Shelby was important to him. He found himself torn between protecting her and pursuing her for his own selfish pleasure.

At this moment, he was living his life in the present, and that was all he could offer.

"I see Georgie with Mr. Reyburn," Louisa said.

"You sound hesitant."

"No, it's just that she's seemed ... confused the

last few days, and she hasn't been able to tell me why. I've thought she and Mr. Reyburn had a special relationship, but now I'm not so sure."

Simon found himself turning his head, as if he could gaze about the room looking for his sister. "What do you mean?"

"As she's gained confidence in herself at these events, she's lost confidence when she deals with Mr. Reyburn. Oh dear."

Her voice had grown concerned.

"Louisa," he began in a warning tone.

"I'm sorry. I can see the two of them together against a wall. Wait, someone got in my way." She gave Simon a pull to the side. "Now I can see them better. Oh my, he's lifting her hand. He kissed it!"

"Paul?" Simon said in surprise, then felt a growing worry. "This is a public place, and he's always considered her a little sister."

"Simon, I've tried to tell you that things have changed. Oh dear."

"Now what?" he demanded, exasperated.

"She's run away and left him there alone. She looks distressed, and he looks confused. If only she could tell me what is wrong!"

Simon was the confused one.

After an hour of casual conversation with neighbors, Simon was surprised when Louisa told him that Paul Reyburn was approaching.

"Miss Shelby," Paul said, "would you mind if I speak to Simon for a moment?"

She released her hold, and Simon missed her already.

"Of course, Mr. Reyburn," she said. "All this talking leaves one very thirsty."

Simon put his hand on Paul's shoulder and let himself be led through the crowd.

When Paul finally stopped, Simon said, "So where are we?"

"There isn't anywhere else to go, so I've picked the quietest corner of the assembly room."

Simon raised his voice over the small orchestra. "Quiet?"

"Private anyway."

"Is something wrong, Paul?"

"I'm worried about Georgie."

Simon stiffened. "Don't tell me Keane is here."

"Nothing like that. She's just ... ignoring me."

"Ignoring you? She's always treated you the same as she'd treat any member of the family. But of course, now you've kissed her hand."

"You saw that?"

Simon laughed. "No, but everyone else here did."

"Damn. But that doesn't seem enough reason for her to be angry. Embarrassed, maybe, but she seemed upset with me. Could there be another man whose attentions she wishes to attract?"

"I don't know what to say, Paul. I don't think there's a particular man she's trying to impress. She's not very good at these social things."

"Well, who would be, next to you and Leo?"

Simon appreciated that Paul discounted his blindness, but his ease in Society was long gone.

"So may I visit her tomorrow?" Paul continued.

"Are you asking my permission?" Simon asked slowly.

"I never thought I needed to."

Paul sounded baffled, and Simon felt the same way. What was going on?

"Visit whenever you'd like," Simon said.

The next afternoon, Paul did indeed come to visit, although it was to Simon's study that he came first. The butler announced him and departed, along with the secretary who'd been transcribing a letter. Simon waited with his hands folded in his lap.

When Paul said nothing, Simon finally said, "I thought you were coming to visit Georgie."

"I am. But I thought you should come in with me."

"Don't worry—we won't leave you unchaperoned with her."

Paul made a disgusted sound. "But I always used to be able to talk freely to her. What happened?"

"You kissed her hand."

"But—"

"Louisa and my grandmother are with her. Go pay your respects."

Paul grumbled something as he left the room, and Simon found himself curious enough that he couldn't concentrate. Paul and Georgie? That didn't make sense. She had known him as a friend her whole life. She hadn't even given herself a chance to consider another man.

He walked out into the corridor and only took a few steps when he heard, "Hello, Simon."

Louisa's voice could always make him smile. "Hello. Is Grandmama still with Georgie and Paul?"

"They all went to the library together, and now she's waiting inside while they walk the conservatory."

"Let's you and I look in on the conservatory, too."

"Simon," she said in a warning voice.

"I'm Georgie's brother. I want to know what's going on."

"Would you like people watching you and me?"

"They would get quite an eyeful, would they not?"

She groaned.

"There's a little balcony overlooking the conservatory from the first floor."

"So you want me to narrate everything for you."

"Not everything. I just want to know that she's comfortable."

When they reached the balcony, Simon remained just inside, while Louisa peered over the balustrade. The humid warmth of the indoor garden was more intense here, the scents more potent.

"They're standing still, talking," she whispered. "No, Paul is talking, and Georgie is keeping her head down, listening."

"Georgie always talks to Paul," he whispered back. "Maybe she really is bothered by the hand kissing. Maybe she doesn't think of him like that."

"Simon, you're playing the protective big brother again. I know you always want to rescue her, but you can't this time. Oh dear."

"Louisa—"

"He's leaving and he doesn't look happy. Do you mind if I go to her?"

"Of course not."

When she was gone, Simon made his way back downstairs and to the library. No one spoke to him, so his grandmother must have gone somewhere else. He walked to the conservatory, wanting to help.

He hadn't meant to eavesdrop, but when he reached the door, he heard Georgie speaking in a forlorn voice.

"I shouldn't see him again. He wants more from me, and I'm hopeless."

Simon rubbed his hand down his face in frustration. Louisa had worked tirelessly with Georgie— why was she not more confident?

"Why do you feel this way now?" Louisa asked. "You and Paul always did well together."

"But that was ... before. When I was just a

friend and not a woman. I don't make a good woman."

Simon gritted his teeth together, wanting to help somehow, but he just ... waited.

"Why ever would you say that, Georgie?" Louisa asked with gentleness. "Surely you've seen how successful these last few parties have been. Men have wanted to dance with you, talk with you."

"But shouldn't it be easier? It always is for my brothers, for my mother."

"And you want to be like her?"

"No!" Georgie said vehemently. "I know I can't be a woman like her."

Simon leaned his head back against the wall, full of sorrow.

"Did your mother tell you that?" Louisa continued.

Georgie drew in a breath, and Simon wondered if she were crying.

"Yes, but I didn't think I had listened," Georgie said with a sad laugh. "I thought I didn't care. But now when I stand there between Simon and Leo, I feel like ... nothing."

"You mean 'nothing 'in other people's eyes—or your mother's eyes?"

Georgie remained silent.

"Perhaps your mother didn't know how to show you understanding or compassion as a little girl, so you grew up thinking you had to do whatever you could to please her."

"And I never could," Georgie whispered.

"And you still think you have to please everyone, that it matters how you compare to Simon and Leo. The people who truly love you don't care that you might not be the best at everything you do. So should *you* care so much what acquaintances think?"

There was a long silence before Georgie spoke. "I hadn't thought I cared so much about making a good impression on people."

Simon went back to his study and shut the door behind him. Was that also his legacy from his mother, caring too much about what people thought, how they viewed him? He'd thought he'd retired his need to be "the entertainer." But he'd spent his life trying to amuse his parents, keep everyone happy, and even blind, he'd continued in that pattern. That need to please just didn't go away. Inflicting his blindness on people, making them uneasy, was something he hadn't wanted to do. So he'd retreated, not wanting people—besides family—to see him stumble, to see him eat, to see him dance. Just like Georgie, he'd been pleasing everyone else before himself.

And before Louisa had come, he would have let Georgie continue on in error, trying to please him with her assistance. He'd become like Leo— good at getting people to help him so he never had to ask. He was angry with himself, worried for Georgie—and relieved that he'd discovered the truth, all at the same time.

All because of Louisa.

And when Georgie didn't need her anymore, Louisa would leave.

He tried to imagine his life without her, and it seemed an even darker place. But how could he ask her to stay, to join him in this darkness, when she deserved so much more?

Chapter 20

Over the next several days, Mr. Reyburn called on Georgie regularly, and Louisa was quietly thrilled. After the first awkward day, Georgie seemed to become more confident by the hour. The couple could often be found walking in the garden, or riding through the countryside, an inconspicuous groom trailing behind them. Louisa would have thought Simon would be pleased with this, but he seemed thoughtful around the young couple, and Louisa wondered if he was concealing his disapproval. Why would he disapprove of his own friend calling on his sister?

She couldn't ask him what he thought, because he didn't come to her room at night anymore. And there always seemed to be someone with him during the day. She would have despaired of his interest, if he didn't seem to be so focused on her whenever they were in the same room together. Once or twice Georgie nodded toward Simon while giving Louisa an encouraging look. What did she expect Louisa to do—pay him special attention in an obvious manner? Perhaps that would even drive him away.

But she had to know what he was thinking. For the fourth night in a row, she lay in bed wide awake, frustrated with their relationship, unable to sleep.

If Simon wasn't going to come to her, she would go to him.

After wrapping her dressing gown over her nightdress, she stepped outside onto the dark balcony. Rain was falling in soft waves that soaked into her loose hair. There was no moon tonight, so instead of running she had to follow the building.

But she knew which room was Simon's. She tried the door and found it unlocked. Slipping inside, she put her back to the door and just breathed heavily. It was as dark inside as it was outside and she felt vulnerable, hesitant, even foolish.

"You shouldn't have come."

She gasped, because she hadn't heard him, hadn't sensed him. But he was before her, looming over her. She was aware of him in the darkness as he was of her. The heat of him was a solid wall she wanted to lean into, to surround herself with. Instead she shivered and waited, alone.

"You didn't come to me," she whispered.

"Let us not pretend anymore, Louisa. I can't be alone with you, because I don't want to be a gentleman when I am. I want to touch you."

She felt his fingers in her hair, pushing the damp locks off her shoulder.

"I want to taste you."

In the darkness, she felt a stir of movement a moment before his hair brushed against her face. She tilted her head as he pressed his mouth below her ear, then licked a tantalizing path down her neck. She groaned, reaching for him, but he held her hands away.

"I want you in my bed, Louisa." He spoke the words against the hollow of her throat. "I have no defenses left against you."

She was helpless against the need they both shared. Could he be falling in love with her and not know it? But regardless of her reputation, she was inexperienced in the ways of men. She knew a man did not have to be in love to desire a woman.

But was it worth the risk to discover the truth?

A knock sounded on his door, and he suddenly backed away from her. She held her breath in panic. Much as she wanted to explore Simon's feelings for her, she didn't want him trapped in a marriage he hadn't planned.

"Simon?" It was Mr. Wade. "I just returned from Paul's. Let me in."

She fumbled for the door handle behind her. Simon brushed her aside and opened it for her.

"Don't come back, Louisa," he whispered. "You can do better than me."

By the time she ran down the balcony, she was

soaked to the skin, chilled—and very angry. How dare he think that his blindness should be a reason to deny her feelings for him!

She wasn't going to avoid him; she wasn't going to find someone else. She had met many men, and none had ever made her feel like Simon did. If he wanted her, however briefly, she would take those moments of happiness and make no demands.

It was time she took the risk of loving Simon.

The next day, she kept a close eye on Simon's activities, and when she saw him head down to the lake with Manvil, she followed. She waited until Simon was already seated in the boat before she called the valet's name.

"Yes, Miss Shelby?"

"You're needed up at the house, Manvil," she said. "I can navigate."

"Manvil—" Simon began ominously.

The valet only glanced at his master with a grin on his face. "You heard Miss Shelby, my lord. The housekeeper must need me."

Whistling, he walked away from them. Louisa untied the rope and climbed down into the boat. It rocked beneath her weight, so she settled herself carefully.

"So who needed Manvil more than I did?" Simon asked doubtfully.

"No one. I lied." She kept her voice cheerful. "Go ahead—row."

With the oar, he pushed away from the pier and began to row in slow, even strokes. She settled back to enjoy the view of Simon. She let her feet rest between his spread feet. Though he had to feel the spill of her skirts, he said nothing, his jaw set.

Just let him try to ignore her, try to ignore the awareness they'd both known of since their reacquaintance a month ago. She put up her umbrella and began to hum.

Simon broke first. "I've given the order to have the railings installed. It is a good idea, and I appreciate it."

"You're welcome." She kept her voice soft, intimate.

The boat was veering to the east, where the lake narrowed and curved away toward a copse of trees that hung over the water's edge. Louisa didn't bother to correct his course.

Simon was rowing harder now, faster, as if he was in a race. She wondered with amusement if he was trying to get away from her.

He couldn't make everything go away by ignoring her, and if she had to teach him that, so be it.

"I was thinking about having a dinner party," he said stiffly.

"Lovely." And it was a step forward for him to consider eating among people, but right now, he was just trying to distract them both. She trailed her fingers in the water, then flicked droplets at him.

He blinked when they hit his face. "Very funny."

Laughing, she leaned back on one hand, letting her foot brush against his.

He inhaled, but said nothing. The pace of his rowing said it all.

"What do you think about Paul and Georgie?" he asked.

She sensed his relief at having found a topic.

"I think it could turn out well," she answered, still trailing her foot along his. "If she becomes too busy to assist you in the mornings, you know that I will."

"Be careful, Louisa," he said softly. "I can be selfish. I've been selfish with Georgie."

"It's not selfish if she wants to help you."

He stopped rowing, then reached down and grabbed her wandering foot. She didn't try to pull away.

"Is that what *you* want, Louisa—to help me?"

"If you're asking if I pity you, that is the most ridiculous—"

But he suddenly stiffened and cocked his head. "You never corrected my course once. I always pull to my left."

"I know," she answered, distracted by his hand surrounding her foot. "I've never come to this part of the lake, and the trees are quite beautiful near the bank."

"Trees!" He shouted the word, dropping her foot, and in that moment, the boat hit something submerged in the water.

Surprised, she fell forward and caught herself on his thighs. She looked up into his face.

He pushed her back to her own seat. "Are we taking on water?" he demanded.

She looked behind him and saw that the wood of the floor was cracked and raised up. Water seeped in.

"Yes. Oh, I'm so sorry, Simon."

"It's my fault," he said shortly. "I never told you about the submerged trees in this part of the lake. How far are we from shore?"

"Not far." She blushed. "I was enjoying the view of the trees hanging over the water." And her view of him. She wasn't worried—surely she could swim if she had to.

"Is the hole small enough to cover with your hand?" he asked.

"It's pretty jagged, but I can try."

"Then I'll keep rowing. Do you see anyone?"

From beneath her bonnet brim, she searched for signs of life, but they were totally alone. "There's no one, Simon."

He leaned to the side while she stood up. The boat rocked wildly, and she grabbed his shoulder. Carefully she stepped into the bow to kneel down. Three inches of water already filled the bottom, soaking into her skirts. Using her umbrella, she tried to push the damaged pieces of wood back in place, but they broke off completely, leaving an even larger hole.

"Simon," she began hesitantly.

"My boots are already wet," he said with a sigh. "The water is coming in too fast for me to row to shore."

She told herself the chill of foreboding she felt was silly. "We're not that far. I can swim." Once again she used his shoulder for leverage as she moved past him.

"Your heavy clothes will be a problem, but I'm a good swimmer. I can help."

She bit her lip and looked toward shore. "It really isn't far."

"I'll row as far as I can. It's too bad there isn't a bucket to bail with."

"I'll use my umbrella!"

"You can try. But first, remove as many petticoats as you can."

She stared at him. "What?"

He kept rowing. "I don't know how many you have on under there, but it will be easier to swim without them. And who's going to see you?"

She blushed. "Very funny."

She reached up beneath her skirt and fumbled at her waist with the ties to the first petticoat. Water was up well above her ankles now, and the boat moved slower and slower.

"Hurry, Louisa," Simon said, as sweat poured down his face.

She lifted her bottom and pulled the petticoat down. "You should remove your coat."

"Good idea."

She took off two more petticoats, leaving her

skirt looking strangely deflated. Her wet legs felt almost bare with only her drawers and skirt covering them.

The boat was now at a dead stop, and the water lapped at her seat, soaking her hips.

"Are you ready?" he asked. "You'll have to navigate for the swim as well."

"I'm ready. Let me swim alone first. Maybe I won't hold you back."

He said nothing, although he didn't look convinced.

In silence, they sat still as the water rose higher, faster.

"Let's jump," he said. "I don't want either of us getting caught on something and pulled under with the boat. I'm going in first so that I can help you swim. Then stand on the seat and jump toward me."

Before she could even speak, he'd jumped in and come sputtering to the surface.

"Can you stand?" she asked.

"No. Hurry!"

She gathered her wet skirts in her hands and stepped up onto the seat. The boat still rocked though almost completely submerged. Then she leapt. The shock of cold water was followed almost immediately by Simon's flailing hands. She caught one and let him pull her to the surface, where she gasped. He put an arm around her ribs, and she could feel him kicking his legs to remain above water.

"Are you all right?" he said near her ear.

She spat water. "Fine. We need to swim toward the shore behind you. You go first."

"I'm not leaving you behind me."

"It will be easier for me to guide from behind. Just go!"

When he let her go, she felt a moment's panic at the feeling of the water pulling on her. Next to them, the boat disappeared silently. But she kicked her legs and started to swim. It wasn't long before her legs and arms felt heavy, but she continued to swim alone to conserve Simon's strength in case she needed him at the end.

"Veer to the right!" she called out, then coughed as she swallowed water. She couldn't seem to get enough air.

"Louisa!"

"I'm all right!"

He suddenly cursed.

"What is it?" she demanded.

"I hit my shin on something," he called over his shoulder. "We must be almost there, aren't we?"

As she grew more tired, the shore seemed just as far away, but she couldn't say that. "Almost!"

And then she couldn't talk anymore because it required too much effort. She hadn't realized how much her corset would restrict her breathing. She was beginning to feel light-headed.

"Louisa, I hit bottom!"

Thank God. She saw Simon's head bobbing in the water, saw his hand reach back for her, and with a last flail, she grabbed it. He pulled her against him, and she clung to him, her arms wrapped around his neck, her head pressed to the side of his, her legs bumping into his. She was breathing in gasps.

"You're a strong, stubborn woman, Louisa Shelby," he murmured against her hair.

"Simon, I can't ... get enough air."

His head lifted. "It's that damned corset. Hold on." He took several long strides until his shoulders were out of the water. "Can you stand?"

She nodded, her lungs straining, aching as she held her chin above the water. He spun her around and went to work on the buttons of her dress.

"Damned wet material," he mumbled.

She swayed, heaving, telling herself that panicking only made her breathe quicker. If she just calmed down, she'd be all right.

"I can feel the corset," he said. "The strings are so tight, Louisa. Why does a small woman like you torture herself like this?"

"To fit in ... the dress."

He tugged and tugged, and then she felt his fingers moving up her back, loosening the laces, spreading the garment, and at last she was able to take a deep, satisfying breath. The shoulders of her gown drooped forward, and she held them up.

"Did I hear grateful breathing?" he asked.

She smiled at him over her shoulder. "You did."

"I'll help you walk."

"I don't need—" But she broke off as she stumbled. "Maybe we can help each other."

He laughed. Arm in arm they pushed through the water, stumbling over rocks. In waist-deep water, they both fell over a submerged log and came up sputtering and laughing. When she tried to reach Simon to guide him to the shore again, she tripped over her skirts and sprawled on top of him. He went under beneath her, and as his face broke the water, he coughed. Slapping him on the back only submerged him again. They were crawling and laughing and less than ten yards from shore when suddenly the bed of the lake was gone again, and she went under. Her feet hit the bottom rather quickly and she bounced back to the surface.

Simon caught her and pulled her against him, treading water. "I should have warned you. You mentioned overhanging trees. This was where we used to swim. This hole was formed by uprooted trees long ago. It was deep enough for a boy to dive into and still be near shore."

Louisa couldn't answer. As they bobbed in the water, chest to chest, she was suddenly very aware of the fact that her corset had slid down around her waist. One shoulder was bare but for her chemise strap because the bodice of her gown had fallen forward. But the most startling sensation of all was how few clothes there were separating them, and how pleasant the ache was where her nipples were abraded.

Simon had finally stopped talking. He was breathing quickly, his mouth inches from hers. She stared at his lips, and hers felt parched for the taste of him. The movement of his legs keeping them afloat was distracting somehow, and it dawned on her that it was because there wasn't much left to separate her from him. Their legs entwined with each movement, and when his thigh bumped high between hers, the shock of pleasure made her gasp.

They were breathing harder and harder, the air mingling between them.

"Where's the shore?" he asked with a hoarse voice.

"Behind you." She stared at his mouth, wanting to be kissed.

"Hold on."

He rolled onto his back and she clung to him, riding on his chest as he took several strokes toward shore. They slid beneath the low overhang of willow trees, and the light became muted. Even the air seemed quieter, as if they were cut off from the world. All she could hear was the gentle lap of water, and the frantic sound of her own breathing.

She could tell when Simon could touch ground again. He stood upright, then caught her legs and pulled them up around his waist. She could feel the long, hard ridge of him riding against her in the most intimate way. For but a moment she hung in his arms, her head back, her body pressed hard to his. He buried his face in her neck and with a groan, rubbed against her with a slow roll of his hips that made her shudder with a dark, wicked delight.

There were no words, no hesitation after that. Their open mouths came together as if they couldn't taste enough of each other. She held him with her arms and legs wrapped around him, wishing she never had to let him go. As he kissed her he walked backward, then turned and pushed her up against the uneven slope of loose rock at the water's edge. She was not quite standing, not quite lying back. But he was able to push hard against her, while she enjoyed the wet, warm weight of him as the water lapped beneath her breasts.

With his mouth he worked his way down her neck, sucking and nipping. With his hands he tugged at her bodice, baring her shoulders. When he tried to slide the straps of her chemise down, they popped in his hands, and he was able to pull the wet garment down.

As her breasts were revealed to the light of day, and the air felt cool across them, she knew she should stop this madness—but she couldn't. They were in their own world of water and low-hanging trees, and she wanted him. Even if she couldn't have him for a lifetime, she wanted these precious moments.

With a soft, welcoming moan, she encouraged his exploration. He moved down her body with wet kisses, and she sighed with relief when he licked her nipple with a long, flat stroke. She held his head against her, wrapped her legs even tighter around him as if that would ease the restless ache that wouldn't go away. She couldn't get close enough, didn't have what she needed.

While his mouth was busy worshipping her breasts, beneath the water his hands followed her legs around his waist and then dove beneath her hemline, sliding back up along her inner thighs that were clad only in thin silk drawers. Then he caught her knees and pushed her lower body away from him, holding her legs spread wide, her back riding against the embankment. With nothing to rub against, she felt rising frustration and desire and helplessness. She didn't know what to do.

"Simon—" She broke off when his hand cupped between her legs, long fingers sliding down and back. She whimpered and writhed as he stroked her and found the slit of her drawers to move deeper. When his fingers slid inside her, she arched back, desperate, churning water around her. Still he kept her pinned to the embankment, his mouth at her breasts, his fingers circling and teasing, then sliding upward to make her burn with an even sharper pleasure. Every flick of his fingers against her stoked a painful desire.

"Please, please," she whispered, her mouth against his wet hair.

He let go of her, and she groaned.

"Wait, wait," he said.

She couldn't see what his hands were doing beneath the water, but she wanted them on her. Just as she reached for him, he tried to pull her legs back up around his waist, but her skirt had floated and bunched between them. Swearing, he tossed them up to her waist. At last he slid back against her, his mouth coming up to kiss her, his body pushing between her thighs. And it wasn't his fingers, which were still cupped against her bottom. Their bodies slid together intimately, naturally, bare flesh against bare flesh, and she felt him part her, ease inside her.

Against her mouth, he whispered, "I promise the hurt won't last."

And then he pulled hard on her hips, sheathing himself. The pain was a burn that faded as her need reawakened and surged higher, stronger, taking away her will with its demands. She held him and kissed him, letting him know with touch and taste that she wanted everything he could give her.

And then he began to move inside her, pressing her against the embankment with each deep stroke. The water splashed with their movements. They surged together and came apart as in battle, each desperate for the release only the other could give. He took her nipple into his mouth. Both hands played her body, his fingers sliding between to stroke her just above their joining.

Pleasure exploded within her, shocking her as

it raced outward through her body. He continued to plunge inside her, drawing out the aftershocks until he suddenly groaned and shuddered in her arms. His movements slowed and eased, her legs floated at his waist.

When he lifted his head, she didn't understand all his changing expressions, but regret and shame were mingled. She cupped his face in her hands and held him.

"Don't pull away," she whispered, holding him close for a kiss.

"I have to sometime."

Kissing him, she clutched his hips with her thighs, desperate to remain a part of him. Because she knew once they were separate people, his regrets would begin.

But not hers. She had held him and showed him her love, and if it wasn't enough for him, she would have to accept that. But she would continue to do everything in her power to be the only woman he wanted—that he loved. He *had* to love her—how could she be feeling this way, so tender, so full of wonder, if he didn't love her?

Chapter 21

~~~~~~~~ ∞ ~~~~~~~~

Simon could barely think, barely reason. He was buried in the heat and comfort of Louisa, while all around them peaceful water lapped. It was as if his body had assumed control of his mind and taken the pleasure so long denied. He was embarrassed and worried for her and wondering what she might be thinking.

But she held him so close, her thighs clutching his hips to keep him inside her. Her wet hands on his face were a comfort and forgiveness he didn't deserve. He cupped her cheeks, and swept his thumbs across her lips before he leaned in and kissed her.

"I'm sorry," he whispered.

"I'm not."

Two simple words, so heartfelt, but it was like a knife being plunged deeper.

"Your first time should be special," he continued, "where you could be treated as you deserve."

"I will cherish these moments with you for a

lifetime. Whenever I am beneath willow trees, this is what I will remember."

He felt her back arch, knew she was looking over their heads at their private bower, but in doing so, she brought him deeper inside her. A groan escaped him, and mindlessly, he pulled out, then sheathed himself once again.

And felt her flinch.

"I've hurt you," he said in a low voice.

She chuckled. "Isn't it that way for every woman the first time?"

He pulled out of her and suddenly felt very alone. "We need to get you out of this water. You could take a chill."

"I don't feel very cold."

He sighed. "Me neither."

But he buttoned his trousers and straightened his shirt.

"I'd take off this corset, but then I'd have to carry it," she said ruefully. "Can you help me dress?"

"You're asking the blind man?" he said, attempting to be light and amusing, when all he felt was confused.

He took her arm and helped her climb the steep embankment. They were both shivering now that their intimacy had ended.

"Were you able to pull your corset up?" he asked.

"Yes. My back is to you."

He found her easily enough, and tugged at her laces.

"I'll never get the dress buttoned if you don't pull tighter," she admonished him.

"I don't want to hurt you." There was a wealth of meaning in those words, and she must certainly know it.

"Now, Simon, I've tied myself into this corset my entire adult life. I will be fine."

He pulled tighter, dreading a whimper of pain.

But she laughed. "You should see your expression. Tie me off, Simon, and button the dress. We need to get back, before they think we've drowned." After a few minutes, she continued, "I wish you could tell me how I look—or maybe I should be glad I don't know. My hair is in snarls all the way down my back."

"You almost drowned. I don't think anyone will suspect a thing."

Arm in arm, they began the long walk around the lake. He knew when they left the shelter of the trees because he could feel the warmth of the sun steaming their damp garments.

"I have always loved willow trees," she said as they walked. She tugged him to the side. "No tripping on rocks."

"So you foundered our boat so you could be near willow trees?"

She laughed. "Maybe that was it. When I was growing up, we had a special place in our garden, way at the back, a pond surrounded by walls and shrubs and overhung with willow trees. My sisters and I used to hide there and tell secrets and plan our futures."

He wondered if she regretted the lost innocence of her girlhood. Discovering her reputation had taken some of it away, and he'd just taken the rest. But all he said was, "I can't imagine you'd want to tell them why you'll now associate willow trees with me."

"You never know. We share everything."

"Ah, then it will be my turn to have a reputation."

They spent an hour talking about nothing and everything, and to Simon it passed far too quickly.

"Oh, look, I think I see Georgie!" Louisa said. "Wave!"

He lifted his arm once, and then left the waving to her. It was as if she was leaving him, being pulled back into the world away from the intimacy they'd shared. And the selfish bastard that he was, he wanted to keep her all to himself.

And that would only hurt her worse. He couldn't let her fall in love with him. It wouldn't be fair.

Maybe she felt sorry for him; maybe she thought she was helping him. He felt like the world's biggest fool.

He heard Georgie's cry. "You two look terrible! I thought you went boating!"

"We ended up swimming," Louisa said. "I was not a very good navigator."

"The boat sank?" Paul Reyburn said.

Simon felt startled and guilty, knowing that someone beside his naïve sister was seeing their disheveled condition. What did he and Louisa truly look like? And could Paul tell what had transpired?

"I didn't know what could possibly have happened to you when I saw a petticoat floating in the water," Georgie said, "and no sign of the boat!"

Oh, God, this was worse than he had feared. He steeled himself to appear sincere, but Louisa beat him to an explanation.

"It was Simon's idea," she said.

He could have groaned. He was glad he couldn't see Paul's face.

"He was worried I would drown if I tried to swim in so many layers of clothing. So I had to remove my petticoats. And he was right. I felt so heavy when I was trying to swim. If we hadn't been near shore . . ." She trailed off.

Still holding her arm, he could feel her shudder.

"How frightening!" Georgie said. "You both need to get into the house at once. If you take ill, Grandmama will be beside herself!"

Louisa spent the day coddled and fussed over by Lady Wade and Georgie, and she was grateful for the distraction from her tumultuous thoughts. After her hot bath, they made her stay wrapped in blankets all day. They sent a tray up for dinner, insisting that the dining room was full of unhealthy drafts.

She never saw Simon, but he was much in her thoughts. She did not regret their lovemaking, although momentarily she worried that he only felt he could be intimate with her because her reputation was already stained.

But no, he was not that kind of man. She knew he felt guilty over what they'd done. Somehow she would have to make him see that the blame for their indiscretion must be shared.

Sleep came too easily to her that night. The swim and what happened afterward must have exhausted her more than she'd realized, because she never blew out the candle, never even awoke when Simon came into her room. She only knew he was there when she half opened her eyes and saw him sitting in a chair beside her bed, his head resting in his hands, his blond hair shining in the candlelight.

For one moment, she let herself believe he had changed his mind, that he loved her and wanted to marry her.

He lifted his head. "I can tell by your breathing that you've awakened."

"Very clever of you," she whispered.

"I didn't mean to come here."

She said nothing, but her hopes faded away.

He sighed. "I can't sleep for thinking about how poorly I introduced you to lovemaking. Have you forgiven me?"

She drew in a breath, shocked by how quickly her skin flushed with heat at just the memory of what they'd done together. "If that was poor, then no wonder people can't help themselves from seeking out pleasure." She reached out to touch his arm. "As I told you earlier, there's nothing to forgive."

He put his hand on hers, caressing gently, almost absently. She stared at him in sorrow. He was going to leave things as they were. There would be no proposals of love, no talk of weddings. She only had this last night with him, this last chance to be happy in his arms.

And she was going to take it.

She sat up in bed and pushed the blankets down. After unbuttoning her nightdress, she pulled it over her head and tossed it at Simon. It hit his face and slid down his arms. He reared back, and in his expression she saw understanding—and passion.

How could he feel this way for her and not love her? Was she fooling herself to think this would show him?

"Louisa."

He said her name in that low, throaty way that made her insides turn to mush.

"That was my nightdress," she said.

"I could tell. It was warm and smells like your skin."

She sighed, letting rising pleasure wipe away any sad thoughts. "I'm sitting naked in the middle of this big bed."

He didn't move, only closed his eyes.

"And now I'm lying back and stretching my arms wide."

He groaned. "What else?" he whispered.

"I'm unbraiding my hair and spreading it across my pillow."

"Does it look like a fiery sunset?"

She blushed. "Yes."

"Do the curls curve around your breasts?"

So he wanted even more detail. She warmed to the task. "Yes. And they tickle."

"So your nipples are hard."

She covered her face with her hands. Talking about such intimacy was more difficult than she'd imagined. "Yes," she whispered.

"Touch them."

She gasped, but she was caught in the spell of his intensity, the way he was leaning forward in his chair, so close to the bed.

She cupped her own breasts, but it was not the same as his hands on her, his desperation to have her. She needed him to touch her.

"I'm parting my thighs."

With a growl, he rose to his feet, hovering over the bed.

"I need to see you," she whispered, then realized how that might sound to a blind man. "Oh, Simon, I shouldn't have said—"

He pulled his shirt over his head. "I take no offense, believe me. I'm flattered."

His chest took her very breath away. It was

wide, and scattered with blond hair, and sculpted with muscle from his rowing. They'd shared the most basic intimacy between a man and woman, yet she hadn't even seem him nude.

"Now your trousers," she said, and her voice was almost a squeak.

He grinned. He unbuttoned and dropped them to the floor. His drawers poked toward her in a very obvious way. "Don't tell me you want me to leave these on."

She licked her lips. "Remove them."

He bent over as he slid them down, and she was disappointed that she didn't see the rest of him yet. She knew he was shedding his shoes and socks. When he stood up, she sucked in her breath. His penis hung large and full and it was a shock to think it had fit inside her.

And then he walked away, down to the end of the bed. She came up on her elbows to appreciate the movement of his buttocks. He ran his fingers along the bed, then rounded the post to the end. He put both hands on the bed, leaning toward her.

Her breath faded away in excitement.

"Are your legs still spread?" he asked.

She nodded, then cleared her throat. "Yes."

"Spread them wider."

Not for the first time, she wished he could see her. But there were other things he could do, and he began them in a slow climb onto the bed. On hands and knees he crawled toward her, looking so big and male. He trailed one hand out to the side until he found her foot. Then he bent and placed a kiss there.

She moaned his name, never imagining that such a simple thing could feel so wonderful.

He continued to crawl, kissing his way up the inside of her leg. Her tension mounted as she realized his aim. She could barely lie still when he tasted her inner thigh. His head accidentally brushed her cleft, and she gave a startled jump.

He chuckled and retreated, beginning again with her other foot. She was trembling by the time he reached her hip. For just a moment, he paused above her, as if giving her time to consider—or imagine. With his hands he gripped her thighs, his thumbs dangerously close to the moist depths of her.

Then he bent his head and placed a gentle kiss on the curls guarding her entrance. She bit her lip to keep from crying out. Though she shook under him, he didn't stop, kissing deeper and deeper. Pleasure swirled and rose higher, faster, clutching at her chest, restraining her breathing.

Then he licked her. His hot tongue circled and explored until he sucked the tip of her into his mouth.

She came apart then, convulsing and rocking, but still he didn't stop, only moved lower until he tasted the inside of her. He spread her thighs, tilted her hips higher, taking everything she had.

When she lay gasping and sated, he crawled

farther up her body, until his hands rested on either side of her shoulders. His erect penis hung suspended above her hips, and before she could think about being shy, she reached out and took him in her hand.

He arched his head back and shuddered.

"That feels good?" she whispered.

"You have no idea."

"Well after your demonstration, I think I do."

She played with him, stroking him, learning the softness and the strength of his very male body. His arms gradually bent at the elbows, as if he could no longer hold himself up.

"Enough," he said harshly.

She pulled back, uncertain, but all he did was lower his hips to hers and thrust deep inside. It didn't hurt this time, but she felt stretched and filled, as if she were meant to accept only him.

He held himself still and leaned down to take her mouth in a deep kiss. "If you had continued to touch me, I never would have made it inside you."

She smiled and settled back into the pillows, feeling wickedly satisfied. When he started to move, he reawakened her own passion. She gave herself the freedom to touch him, to stroke his face, to memorize the muscles of his chest and arms. When she plucked at his nipples, he trembled and stroked harder, faster.

He found his release before she had a chance to catch up to him, but she didn't care. She held him as his shudders subsided. He was big and heavy, and she had never imagined so enjoying the weight of him.

But finally he rolled off her and settled back amid her pillows. When he pulled her against his side, she sank happily into the crook of his arm, her head resting against his chest as she looked up at him.

His expression was pensive, even sad, though he stroked her hair gently. The spell of their love-making faded, and the sorrow returned.

"Louisa, I need you to understand that this hasn't changed things for me. I don't mean to marry."

It was no surprise, although her heart broke all over again. She put her finger to his lips. "Shh. I know. I don't expect it of you. And I would never want to force you into marriage. I told you how much I cherished our time together, and it's true."

But oh God, she felt the tears rise unbidden into her eyes. As they started to spill down her cheeks, she pulled away from him, patting his chest so he wouldn't think her too abrupt.

Simon stilled as Louisa left the bed. He heard the sound of water pouring into a washbasin. He told himself she had entered into this affair with a clear understanding of his intentions.

But as she'd left him, he'd felt a tear splash to his chest.

Did she think she was in love with him?

Didn't she understand that he would always think of it as pity? If ever he gave in and married her, someday she would regret it. The novelty would wear off, and their marriage would die.

And then he would be the only one in love.

Though he might be breaking her heart right now, she would be the better for it in the end.

Chapter 22

❦

The next afternoon, Louisa sat alone on the terrace, looking out over the garden to the lake beyond. She could just see the curve of the far shore, and the beginning of the copse of willow trees. She knew she had to learn to forget what had happened there.

Sipping her tea, she contemplated her future, proud of the logical way she was dealing with her life. After Simon had dressed last night, his sad regrets did not change anything. He'd left her to sleep alone, and she'd lain awake long into the night.

Her love was hopeless; she understood that now. She'd helped him grow and change and accept that his blindness didn't mean an end to his old way of life. She had to give herself some small congratulations on that.

But he could not "see" himself as a married man. Intimacy with her had not changed that.

It was time to return to London, to try to find her own life, because it wasn't going to include

Simon. She could not quite give up hope that her dream to help girls prepare for their first Season wasn't dead. The women she daily encountered here knew nothing of her reputation; why would the newly rich industrialists have heard? Or at least their wives, the ones who mattered as far as hiring Louisa. If the men in the families knew otherwise, she would deal with it as it happened. She was no longer an innocent, and she could take care of herself.

She even had an alternate plan; she could always live with her sister Victoria in London. Louisa had a dowry at her disposal, and there would be men who wanted to marry her. She would have to accept one of them eventually, but she was confident she could choose a decent man who would accept her good intentions for the marriage, though she did not come to him a virgin. She would never love him, of course, but she had the memories of Simon to sustain her.

Her grief welled up again, surprising her. She had already decided to turn him away the next time he came to her. She had taken the risk of loving him, and had failed. Giving herself over to the pleasure of him could only lead to their being caught in a compromising position, or worse, leaving her with child. In her early plans, she hadn't considered the innocent life of a baby. She'd been swept up in her excitement, in her need for Simon. Might she even be pregnant now? She would not allow herself to panic un-

til she had to. But she could not be so careless
again.

So she would leave, and soon. She was surprised how sad she found the thought of leaving
this wonderful family. Lady Wade treated her
as a granddaughter, and Georgie shared confi-
dences as a dear friend ... or a sister. Even Mr.
Wade—Leo—had brightened her days. She had
long since put aside the immature ways he had
once pursued her.

As if she had conjured him, Leo came out of the
manor and stood beside her, arms folded over his
chest. He glanced down at her with amusement,
then out across the grounds.

"Well, is the view as lovely as your preoccupation with it suggests?" he asked playfully.

She smiled up at him, patted the chair beside
her, and hoped he could amuse her. She had to lift
her spirits, or be reduced to crying.

"Well, that's interesting," Georgie said.

Simon was sitting at his desk, but he knew his
sister stood at the window. "What's interesting?"

"I can see Leo and Louisa laughing together on
the terrace."

A knot congealed in Simon's stomach, and he
told himself to ignore it. After all, Louisa could
have any friends she wanted. And by insisting
that they would never marry, he'd freed her to
pursue a life without him.

But with Leo?

Simon knew he was overreacting. She had always been a woman at ease with men. That would do her in good stead finding a husband.

But the pain in his heart burned steadily, and learning to ignore it might take a lifetime.

There was always Georgie to worry about.

"Paul has been visiting quite a lot lately," he said.

"Yes."

She was doing a good job of sounding perfectly normal.

"And it seems like more than a friendship might be developing between you."

"We'll see."

"Do you think that's a good idea?"

He heard her flounce into the chair beside him. "I can't believe you're saying this to me in that dubious-sounding voice. You've wanted me to go out in Society, to find my own life. A man starts calling on me—a good friend of yours!—and now you have reservations?"

He sighed. "I'm worried that you're settling for him because he's an old friend, and therefore less intimidating than a stranger. You've barely had a chance to meet men."

It was her turn to sigh. "Simon, you've wanted me to grow up and live my own life. Well I am. As long as I choose a man acceptable to you, you need to allow me to make my own decisions. I don't need rescuing anymore. Unlike Louisa."

He was startled and uncomfortable at the sudden change in topic. "Louisa? This isn't about her. She's strong and independent, and doesn't need rescuing, especially by me."

In a disdainful voice, she said, "You must be blind."

He opened his mouth, but couldn't think of a retort. What did Georgie see about Louisa that he didn't? Did Georgie actually think he should ... pursue Louisa?

She left him sitting there alone.

Louisa spent the afternoon as she'd begun her stay at Enfield—doing embroidery with Lady Wade and Georgie. It was a comfortable, peaceful, sad feeling, and Louisa didn't converse much as she tried to find the best way to tell the two women that she was leaving.

The butler interrupted before she spoke, and intoned, "Ellen, Viscountess Wade."

Louisa saw Georgie and her grandmother exchange shocked glances, but both swept to their feet and Louisa followed. Georgie's mother strode into the room, full of purpose and command, and came to a halt, wearing an intimidating frown. Her blond hair, lightened with white strands, was swept up elegantly. She had a handsome face in a remote, cold way that might have been truly beautiful with a more pleasant expression.

She opened her mouth to speak, and then she saw Louisa. Her eyes widened, then narrowed, and Louisa felt the first whispers of unease. Ellen, the younger Lady Wade, did not look exactly friendly.

The dowager viscountess smiled at her daughter by marriage. "Ellen, you've come so quickly from Scotland. I would have thought my invitation had only just arrived."

Georgie stared at her grandmother in shock. "Mother, I didn't think you needed an invitation to visit Grandmama and us."

Lady Wade—Ellen—looked at her mother-in-law. "The invitation to the house party only just reached me, but I had already packed to come ... visit."

She glanced at Louisa, who felt that cool regard like an icicle dagger.

Georgie turned back to her grandmother. "House party?"

Lady Wade smiled. "Ellen, first allow me to introduce my companion, Miss Louisa Shelby. Miss Shelby, my daughter-in-law, Ellen, Lady Wade."

Louisa curtsied silently, submitting to Ellen's deliberate perusal. Ellen nodded and turned away.

Well, Louisa thought, as they all sat down, Simon's mother would be thrilled that Louisa wasn't permanently joining her family.

"House party?" Georgie prompted again.

"This weekend," Lady Wade informed them. "I took the liberty of inviting several couples—and many eligible young men."

Georgie groaned. "Grandmama—"

"I decided this before your recent preference for Mr. Reyburn, Georgie my child. Do not be angry with me. And if you do not wish to enjoy the attentions of bachelors, Louisa certainly can."

Louisa felt her face redden as they all turned to stare at her. "Lady Wade," she began.

Ellen interrupted. "So you are matchmaking for the servants now, Mother Wade?"

"Louisa is my companion," Lady Wade said coolly, "not a servant. She is a gentlewoman."

Ellen's glance in Louisa's direction clearly showed that she was doubtful.

And then Louisa understood—Ellen must know about Louisa's reputation. And she was obviously not happy that Louisa was in such close proximity to her children.

Louisa would have gladly packed and left before the house party, but she knew that Lady Wade would be hurt. And the older woman had been so kind to Louisa. No, Louisa would have to endure the house party—and leave immediately afterward.

"What is this about Mr. Reyburn?" Ellen said to her daughter.

"He frequently visits because he lives nearby," Georgie said firmly. "You know how close he is to Simon and Leo."

"And now to you?" Ellen said with obvious doubt in her voice.

Louisa stiffened at the insult, even though

she already knew how poorly Ellen had treated Georgie.

"We are friends," Georgie said simply, hands folded in her lap.

Louisa was proud of the calm way Georgie was responding to her mother.

Lady Wade leaned toward Georgie and patted her hand. "Your mother would want to know that you might be more than friends, my child."

Georgie smiled at Ellen. "If we are, I promise I'll let you know, Mother."

"But you should take advantage of meeting eligible men this weekend," Ellen said. "Probably nothing will come of it, but you never know."

Louisa bit her lip to keep from defending Georgie, and then was thrilled when her student spoke up for herself.

"I'm finally learning to enjoy Society, Mother. We've been attending many parties. I'm dancing, conversing, and in general proving that I've grown up. I hope you will accept that."

Ellen looked surprised, but before she could speak, Lady Wade said, "Georgie has been enjoying the companionship and assistance of Louisa. They've worked well together, and I think the combination has been a success. We've even gone to London to have a whole new wardrobe made for Georgie."

But Ellen didn't look at her daughter, or admire the lovely gown she was wearing. Once again,

Louisa was the focus of Ellen's icy green gaze. Louisa only continued to smile pleasantly.

Footsteps echoed on the marble floor outside the drawing room, and Simon entered, his cane held before him. Louisa knew she should look away, because she was certain she was blushing. He was clothed elegantly in dark green, but when she looked at him, she remembered him naked in her bed.

"I hear we have company," he said.

Ellen rose to her feet and hurried to him. "It is your mother, dear boy."

He leaned down for her kiss as if it were natural between them. Ellen had not kissed Georgie.

"Has your servant left you utterly alone?" Ellen asked, aghast. "Let me take your arm, Simon."

"Good day, Mother," Simon said. "Please, such attention is no longer necessary. Are you here for a visit?"

"Here for a house party, Simon," Georgie told him. "This weekend at our own Enfield Manor."

His eyebrows rose. "So Grandmama, you decided to surprise us?"

"Your sister and Louisa need to meet young men," Lady Wade said.

Louisa stilled at the mention of her name. What did Simon think of her meeting other men? Did he even care?

But this time Ellen ignored the mention of Louisa's name linked with her daughter's. She had Simon's arm, and was trying to lead him, but if he hadn't had the cane, Ellen would have run him right into a low table.

Simon cocked his head. "Matchmaking, Grandmama?"

"Bringing together old friends," Lady Wade said, her grin saying otherwise. "There will be eligible young ladies for you and Leo. And I invited your good friend Lord Thurlow."

Louisa couldn't withhold a thrilled gasp. "My sister is coming?"

"She accepted. As did your other sister, Mrs. O'Neill."

Louisa could barely keep from clapping her hands together with glee, or enveloping the dear old lady in a hug. Instead she said, "Lady Wade, you are too generous. Thank you so much."

"Your sister married an Irishman," Ellen said.

Ellen looked at Simon as if this was only further proof, but of course he could only hear her.

"His brother was the duke of Thanet," Simon said. "And now he is guardian for his nephew—the duke."

"I see," his mother said softly. "And will the duke be attending?"

"He's only seven, Lady Wade," Louisa said.

"But he's coming," the elder Lady Wade said.

If Louisa was smart, she would have all her belongings packed so she could leave with Victoria.

She looked at Simon. She had to be smart. She had to leave him. Her heart was already broken;

the longer she stayed, the harder it would be to mend.

"We have so much to do," Georgie said with a groan.

Lady Wade smiled. "Perhaps you and your mother could take care of the menus. Louisa, if you would make certain that the staff has already prepared all the guest rooms."

"That is my place, Mother Wade," Ellen insisted.

Lady Wade's smile faded. "As you wish, Ellen. I'm sure I'll find plenty of things I'll need help with."

"Grandmama," Georgie said, "show me what entertainment you've planned."

"I have a list in the morning room. You'll be thrilled."

As they both rose, Ellen said, "Miss Shelby, please see that my room is prepared. I usually use the green suite."

"Right next to yours, Louisa," Lady Wade said helpfully. "But I'm sure the housekeeper has already—"

"No, that's all right," Louisa interrupted. "I would be pleased to make sure everything is ready for Lady Wade." She curtsied to them all and began to walk across the room.

Simon realized that he must have missed quite an exchange, because Louisa sounded glad to escape. As she moved by him, the air swirled with the current of her scent, roses in summertime.

He inhaled and said softly, "I'm certain you curtsied when I entered."

"Always, my lord," she answered back.

And then she was gone, and the room seemed colder. For her sake, he was glad her sisters would be coming.

"She is a polite girl," his mother said, as if that was all that could be said about Louisa. "Simon, I would like to speak to you in private."

Damn. He'd really been hoping that his mother had left with the others. "Has everyone gone?"

"Yes," she said.

"So we're alone. I'm glad you were able to attend the house party."

"So many people had already left Scotland for the London Season. But I was coming here even before I received your grandmother's invitation."

"You missed me?" he said lightly.

"I heard that your grandmother hired that Shelby woman." Her voice was full of outrage.

Simon's smile faded, and he clenched his jaw. "She has been of great help to Grandmama."

"And to your sister, I hear."

"Yes, she has. How can you have any complaints, when Georgie finally seems to be blossoming?"

His mother was very good at ignoring what she wanted to. "Has that Shelby woman tried to be alone with you?"

He frowned. "Excuse me?"

"You may not be aware, Simon, but that woman has a *reputation*."

"What kind of reputation?" Simon asked. He felt a little ill, knowing that he himself had once had the same reservations.

"She is known to be of ... easy virtue," she said primly.

"Once you know her, you will see that the rumors are just that—rumors."

"Surely Leo told you—"

"Hell, he told *you*!"

"Simon, your language!"

"He was drunk when he proved himself less than a gentleman by repeating such gossip to me. What excuse did he have for telling you?"

"I admit that he did not realize I was close enough to overhear his conversation with you."

"That's because he was drunk," Simon said with disgust. "I wonder why I didn't see you. Were you hiding?"

"Simon!"

"Regardless, please treat Miss Shelby with the respect she deserves."

She sighed dramatically. "I fear I am already too late."

"Too late to treat her well?"

"Too late to keep her from ... attaching herself to you."

Simon sat back, surprised and disturbed. What did his mother know—or guess? "So what happened between you ladies before I arrived?"

"Nothing, but I am very good at guessing people's motivations."

Or ascribing nasty motivations to something clearly innocent, but he knew better than to say that aloud.

And what he had shared with Louisa was hardly innocent, but that was his fault.

"And what would Miss Shelby's motivations be beyond the obvious?" Simon asked. "Grandmama employed her, then asked her to help ease Georgie's shyness."

"That woman's father was a mere banker!" she said, as if the career were no better than that of a chimney sweep. "And he lost everything!"

"And Louisa had to look for work in order to survive."

"You call her by her Christian name?" his mother said, aghast.

Ignoring that, he continued, "So you're judging her for faults not her own?" ·

"It is certainly her own fault if she came here specifically for your money and family connections."

Simon had once wondered the same thing. Was he really so much like his mother?

At least he learned from his mistakes. Louisa only had the best, most generous intentions in everything she did. But he could hardly say that to his mother. "Louisa is not—"

"She knows you can't do any better," his mother interrupted. "How cruel of her to take advantage of you like this. I just refuse to let it happen."

If Simon could stare in shock, he would be doing it. His mother didn't think a woman could want him as he was. At least Simon himself only thought he'd be a burden to a wife.

He shouldn't be surprised—his mother's behavior toward him had vastly changed after his accident, as if she didn't know how to treat him anymore. He was no longer her socially successful son.

She'd obviously decided on a course of action. She'd protect him from unscrupulous women—as if he couldn't protect himself.

And she wanted to protect him from Louisa. It was almost laughable. Who was going to protect Louisa from him?

He was the one who'd hurt her.

He was the one who was in love, and didn't want to take the chance that she might love him in return.

He was worried about accepting pity—God, was he really so much like his mother?

That eased his anger somewhat. "Promise me that you will not bother Louisa. She is a good woman with only the best of motives. She doesn't deserve your censure."

She remained silent.

"Mother."

"Oh very well, Simon, I will say nothing to her. But if she betrays herself—"

"I will handle it."

"But Simon, the house will be full of people! I know how difficult that will be for you. You need me."

Maybe she was trying to make amends in her own misguided way. He sighed. "Mother, you'll be pleasantly surprised at how well I'm getting used to people again. At the last ball, I even danced a waltz."

"You *danced*?" she said, not sounding happy about it.

That revelation might have been a mistake.

Suspiciously, she said, "I didn't think Georgie capable of such confidence."

He just smiled. But his mother was clever.

"Your grandmother doesn't waltz anymore. It had to be—oh Simon," she said with heavy disappointment. "It is a good thing I'm here."

Chapter 23

That night, Louisa was glad to finally retreat to her room. During a tense dinner, Ellen had stared daggers at her. Leo had obviously found the whole thing amusing, and paid more attention to Louisa than normal. Their mother almost had apoplexy, so red in the face had she become. Simon had seemed quieter than normal—except whenever his mother overstepped her bounds.

Louisa had wanted to sink under the table at being the object of so much attention. Yet the sweet way Simon continued to distract his mother in protection of Louisa almost brought tears to her eyes.

She would definitely be going home after the weekend, for her fragile heart couldn't bear anymore.

But her room contained no solace, for it was full of memories of Simon: the night he'd lost his way and she'd brought him inside to comfort him; the nights they'd sat and talked in the dark; and the tender way he'd worshipped her body with his lovemaking.

And then she heard a tap on the balcony door. Before she could run to lock it against him, he was inside. He said nothing as she stared at him, feeling the swell of desire and the sweet ache of love that suffused her. But she couldn't give in to these feelings; the consequences could be worse.

"Simon—"

"I know you didn't want me to come."

She folded her arms over her chest. "Then why are you here?"

"I came to apologize for my mother's behavior. Her treatment of you was appalling."

"I expected nothing else from her."

He lowered his head. "I think she's trying to make amends by protecting me."

Louisa sighed. "Well, she won't need to worry for long. I'm going to return to London with my sister after the weekend."

His head came up and then he went still. "I—does my grandmother know?"

"I told her I'd be leaving eventually."

When he said nothing, she lost the fragile control of her emotions. "Simon, what did you think I'd do? Stay here and fall into bed with you every night? Risk the possibility of a child?"

He frowned.

Her voice lowered, grew husky. "Or did you think we'd be able to resist each other, as if our intimacy had never happened?"

He took a step toward her, reaching for her with that uncanny accuracy he had.

She ducked away from his hand. "There's nothing you can say or do to make this situation any better. You have to leave right now, and I have to leave on Monday."

"Louisa." He whispered her name.

"Just go, Simon," she said tiredly.

And after he'd gone, she cried.

As the guests began to arrive on Friday afternoon, Louisa made herself scarce by conferring with the housekeeper for Lady Wade. But when one of the downstairs maids came to tell her that her family had arrived, she practically ran through the house.

In the entrance hall, she slowed to a stop, taking in the wonderful sight. Meriel and her husband, Richard, were talking to their little nephew, Stephen. Victoria and David were walking toward Simon.

"Well look at you!" David said to Simon. "The last time I saw you, you were holed up in a dark room."

"It's still dark, but I'm used to it," Simon said.

To Louisa's surprise, David hugged Simon, then stepped back, clearing his throat in obvious embarrassment. "So, you're going to visit London again?"

"I just might," Simon said with a grin. "Would your wife still want to see me?"

Victoria Thurlow, Louisa's sister, gave a laugh. "Always, Lord Wade."

"You could call me Simon after all this time."

"I'll try."

Simon in London—visiting the house Louisa might be staying at? He'd chased her away from Enfield Manor; now would he chase her from her own sister's home?

And when had she become such a coward?

"Victoria!" Louisa cried out. "Meriel!"

The three sisters came together in a laughing hug.

"How was your honeymoon?" Louisa asked Victoria. "I thought you would still be gone."

Victoria blushed. "We cut short our trip."

Louisa glanced at Meriel, who only grinned and shrugged.

"Not because of this house party," Simon said in disbelief. "I would have thought Rome had more appeal than Enfield."

"No, a much more personal reason than that," David said cryptically.

Louisa stared at Victoria, and for the first time noticed the dark smudges beneath her sister's eyes. "Are you ill?" she asked, feeling a rising panic.

Meriel laughed. "You are so blind, Lou." She winced and glanced at Simon. "She's with child. And I'm terribly jealous."

Louisa gasped and hugged Victoria, rocking her back and forth. When she released her, Victoria looked even paler than before and put a hand to her stomach.

"I cannot believe how even the simplest thing affects me," Victoria said ruefully.

David put his arm around her. "She's been dreadfully ill with it."

"I'm afraid I quite put a damper on our romantic escape," Victoria said, blushing as she leaned into her husband.

Louisa took one of Victoria's arms, and after shouldering David aside, Meriel took the other. "We'll need to pamper you," Louisa said.

"Aunt Louisa!" Little Stephen rushed up to tug on her skirts.

Louisa was touched that he would use such an endearment when they'd only met at his uncle's wedding. She put a hand on his unruly hair. "Yes, Stephen?"

"We rode on two trains, Aunt Louisa!"

"You are so lucky!"

His uncle, Richard, said, "And maybe that wasn't such a good idea. I never saw a woman need her privacy as much as Victoria did on the brief train ride from London."

Victoria shuddered.

Meriel grinned. "Makes one almost want to avoid a similar fate. And there's only one way . . ."

Richard gave a snort.

Louisa blushed, hoping her sisters thought her reaction due to ignorance.

Leo, Georgie, and Paul Reyburn came to see what the commotion was all about.

After the introductions were made, Leo eyed

Richard O'Neill. "It is uncanny how much you look like your brother. My condolences on his passing."

"Thank you," Richard said.

"He always enjoyed a good game of billiards," Leo continued. "Can I interest you gentlemen?"

Simon laughed. "Leo, I'm certain Lord Thurlow would be uninterested. After all, I could still defeat him even blinded."

"I think that's a challenge," David said.

The three sisters glanced at each other, shaking their heads.

"I could guide your hand, Simon," Leo said. "For a cut of the winnings."

"Definitely a challenge," Richard said. "Do you ladies mind?"

"By all means," Meriel said. "You men go find something to do. Stephen, you too! We ladies have lives to catch up on. Louisa, surely you have somewhere private we can talk, like our Willow Pond."

Louisa could not help but blush at the thought of willow trees and water. Simon was surely close enough to have heard, but he said nothing, only led the men away.

Leo's voice trailed down the corridor. "I'm the one who taught Simon to walk by himself."

As the laughter faded away, Georgie shook her head and said to Louisa, "I need to get back to Mother and Grandmama. I think there will be open war over the plans for dinner seating. It's so nice to meet you both," she said to Victoria and Meriel.

Victoria watched Georgie walk away. "She seems very nice. I can see why you enjoyed working with her."

Louisa slid her arm through her sisters'. "It's been fun and fulfilling."

Meriel frowned. "But . . ."

Louisa shook her head. "Let's go outside. It's a beautiful afternoon."

Though several houseguests strolled through the garden, the sisters had the terrace to themselves. Louisa sent for refreshments, then sat on a bench between her sisters and took turns grinning at them.

"What?" Meriel said.

"I'm just so happy to see you both. And Victoria, your news is such a blessing."

Victoria put a hand to her small stomach. "It is. Mama is thrilled. Lady Wade invited her to come this weekend, but she had already made plans to travel to Scotland with a friend."

"She might have passed Simon's mother on the way," Louisa said. "Wait until you meet her."

Victoria frowned. "You don't sound enthused."

"She's not enthused about me. I'm quite positive she thinks I'm here to take advantage of her poor blind son and force him into an unwanted marriage."

Meriel gasped. "Our reduced circumstances of last year made her think so poorly of you?"

Louisa bit her lip. She did not want to worry them by explaining the revelation of her reputation as a fast young lady.

"Papa's death changed so many things," Victoria said. "But we have survived and come through it for the better."

"But it took me a long time to forgive him," Meriel said quietly.

Louisa took a breath. "And it took me a long time to forgive myself."

On each side of her, her sisters took her hands.

"What are you talking about?" Victoria asked in disbelief. "You have nothing to forgive yourself for."

"I know. But ... Papa used to talk to me, and after he was gone, I thought perhaps I should have seen his despair and done something to help."

"We've all thought that, Louisa," Meriel said patiently.

"But Simon made me see ..." Louisa trailed off as her sisters leaned forward to give each other a knowing glance. "What?"

"What about Simon?" Victoria asked with obvious hope in her eyes.

Louisa ignored it. "When I first arrived, I thought he was in despair too, but he wasn't. He made me realize that until someone asks for help, it's hard to know just what they're thinking. In the end, I don't think any of us could have helped Papa."

"And you had an actual discussion about such a personal topic with Lord Wade—or Simon, as you call him?" Meriel asked.

She was saved from having to answer by the appearance of little Stephen, running from the house toward the garden. Meriel came to her feet, but Georgie was right behind him.

"We're going down to the lake to watch the race," Georgie said. "Do you ladies want to come?"

"Race?" Louisa said.

"Leo bet Simon he could beat him in a rowing race," Georgie said, laughing. "I told Leo he was too scrawny, and a bet was born. I think the gentlemen are already down at the lake."

"If you don't mind," Meriel said, taking hold of Louisa's arm, "we'll watch from here."

"I can't see anything from here, Aunt Meriel," Stephen said. "Can I go to the lake?"

"I'll be with him," Georgie added.

Meriel waved them off.

"You don't want to watch the race?" Victoria asked. "It's so wonderful to see Simon back to himself again."

"There are two very handsome, eligible brothers down at that lake," Meriel said, turning to look at Louisa.

Louisa sighed, feeling the tightness creep back into her chest.

It was Victoria's turn to give Louisa a stare of understanding. "But *Simon* is the one who seems to be doing so much better. I wonder if our dear sister had an effect on him?"

Louisa planned to distract them by saying how hard Simon had worked to improve himself. But then she started to cry.

"Oh dear," Victoria said, taking a handkerchief from within her sleeve and handing it over. "Louisa, I didn't mean—"

"No, no," Louisa said, waving her hands. "I told myself I wouldn't cry, wouldn't … Victoria, I'd like to return to London with you."

Victoria and Meriel simply stared at her.

Louisa only wiped her eyes, fearing words would give everything away.

"You are welcome in our home any time you want," Victoria said softly. "You know that."

Louisa sniffed and nodded.

"Mine, too," Meriel added. "But you have to tell us *something*. Your letters have been all about Georgie and her progress."

"But always you mentioned Simon," Victoria added. "I thought . . ."

"That I was foolish enough to fall in love with him?" Louisa whispered.

Meriel shook her head. "Love is not foolish."

"It is when it's not returned."

"How could he not love *you*?" Victoria asked. "I always thought you two were so very alike."

"So you've said. But while Simon has finally come to realize he can have a normal life, he doesn't believe he could ever have a normal marriage."

"I imagine a proud man like him would now think himself a burden to a wife," Meriel said shrewdly.

Louisa shrugged. "I've even been too afraid to tell him what I think. And I don't want him to feel guilty, so I've just … let him go."

"Then he's not worth having," Meriel said bluntly.

But that only made the tears start again.

Victoria gave Meriel a cross look. "That is not helpful. Louisa dear, perhaps when you return to London, he'll miss you so dreadfully that he'll change his mind."

"No, I think he'll settle back into what's easiest for him," Louisa said bitterly. "He was doing that with the rest of his life before I challenged him. Last night I even told him I was leaving. He had the chance to ask me to stay. He didn't."

Meriel narrowed her eyes as she stared down at the lake. In the distance, they could see two boats racing each other across the water. "Perhaps I could—"

"No." Louisa dried her eyes and told herself she was done crying. "I won't let him be forced. Forget I mentioned this. I want one last good weekend here, without thinking about regrets."

When Meriel would have spoken, Victoria reached across and touched her arm.

"We're here for you, Louisa," Victoria said simply.

And Louisa was grateful. She stared down at the lake, where she could see Simon's boat far in the lead, heading away from her. She would get through these last days. The rest of her life was a blank canvas that she would someday fill, but not now, not when her heart was in pieces.

Chapter 24

Twenty people gathered for dinner that evening. Louisa was grateful for the noise and the distraction. She kept her mind off Simon by ignoring him, studying all the other guests. She was angry with herself for worrying her sisters, who kept watching her with too much revealing sympathy. She saw David frown at Simon for no reason, and wondered about what Victoria might have told him. Simon's mother watched her as if Louisa might attempt to compromise Simon in front of everyone, just to have her for himself.

What a hollow victory that would be.

And then there was Leo. He was normally such a carefree, lazy, amusing man. But he was wearing a rather nervous expression. He kept looking at his mother, then at Simon, then at Louisa, then looking away. He tapped his fingers, sipped his wine, but then his gaze would wander to the same three people again. What had Simon told him?

After an evening of conversation—thank God no one suggested any singing!—guests began to retire to their rooms one by one. Soon all that was left were family—Louisa's and Simon's. Even Paul Reyburn had stared at them all in bemusement and retired to bed.

An uneasy silence descended on the group, as if there was something hidden that no one wanted to mention. As usual, Louisa was watching Simon, knowing every moment was precious. He seemed distracted, too.

Leo rose to his feet and began to pace, drawing all eyes. He ran a hand through his hair, looked at them all, opened his mouth, then fell to pacing some more.

"Leo, you're wearing out my carpet," Lady Wade said gently. "Do tell us what's bothering you."

He put his hands on his hips, then looked directly at Louisa. "Ever since my mother arrived, Louisa, she's made it a point to remind us what a bad opinion she has of you."

There were gasps from several of the women. Louisa blanched, hating the way every gaze in the room settled on her. Why would Leo speak so forthrightly?

"Leo!" his mother cried, aghast. "I never—"

"Be quiet, Mother," he said tightly.

From his chair, Simon spoke in a low voice. "I don't know what you think your purpose is, Leo, but I suggest—"

"Just listen," Leo said harshly. "God, this isn't easy."

Louisa stared between an angry Simon and an overwhelmed Leo. Meriel and Victoria wore wide-eyed, confused stares. Of course they didn't know anything about the rumors, so Louisa offered them a hesitant shrug.

Only Lady Wade gave Leo an encouraging smile. "Go on, dear."

"So I've been thinking that Louisa is stuck with this terrible reputation she didn't deserve."

"Reputation?" Meriel demanded.

But Louisa could only stare at Leo. "What are you saying?"

"I didn't think there was anything I could do to make it better, so I've waited. But that didn't work either."

"Leo, it's not your place—" Simon began.

"Just be quiet!" Leo's hair now stood on end from his nervous fingers. "There's one thing I can offer, and that's the truth."

The murmurs died away, leaving an expectant silence. Louisa stared hard at Leo. "Go ahead," she said, feeling strangely calm.

"It's my fault, all of it." Leo sprawled into a chair, staring at the floor. "I was a drunken fool—you know that better than anyone, Louisa."

She couldn't miss the way Simon stiffened. Quickly, she said, "Leo, that was several years ago. All you did was try to persuade me to dance. And you were a little forward about it."

"I even chased you down a hall," he said glumly. "My friends knew we'd disappeared together."

A chill slithered down her back. "We weren't together," she said slowly.

"They thought we were. They thought—" Leo grimaced and swallowed, then finally met her eyes. "They thought you had let me kiss you. And when they congratulated me, I let them think it."

Her jaw dropped.

"I was a coward, and I enjoyed being the center of attention. It's my fault that some men believe you fast; it's my fault that my mother has a poor opinion of you; it's my fault that Simon—"

"Shut up, Leo," Simon said, coming to his feet. He had his cane held low before him, and he took only two steps before it caught on the table between him and his brother.

Ellen sniffed. "He was young. He didn't mean—"

"Mother!" Leo said, also standing. "I did a reprehensible thing. To my shame, there's nothing I can do except apologize." He looked at Louisa sincerely. "And I deeply apologize, Louisa. I did not see how my actions would someday affect you. Can you forgive me?"

Louisa stood, embarrassed that her reputation was out in the open before her family. But everyone—except Ellen, who sulked—regarded her with compassion and understanding.

And it was enough. She looked at Leo, who still watched her with anguish. "I forgive you, Leo. We've all been young and foolish before."

"Foolish?" Simon said, still focusing his anger at his brother. "He cost you so much."

Leo looked away.

"But I know the truth now," Louisa said, "and I will be the better for it. Some things hurt worse than others. I will go on."

Simon took a deep breath, and she regretted her words immediately. She hadn't meant to hurt him—or maybe she had. "I'm sorry," she whispered.

"You have nothing to apologize for, my dear." Lady Wade still reclined across her chaise lounge, looking unperturbed. "I am disappointed in Leo, it is true. But he was incorrect when he said that he could only apologize. In fact, he can make everything right again. Leo can marry you, Louisa, and restore your reputation."

As gasps echoed around them, Louisa and Leo stared at each other in shock. Her thoughts were awhirl as, for just a moment, she actually considered it. But how could she possibly remain close to Simon, loving him as she did, and not have him? She didn't love Leo. She'd be imposing a chasm between the brothers that might never be crossed.

Simon seemed frozen in the center of the drawing room. She couldn't read his expression, but he didn't protest. Did he think she would actually marry his brother? Why wasn't he saying anything?

But Leo's shoulders were back, his head lifted,

and he was beginning to look resolute. As if he were considering the crazy idea.

Ellen recognized his expression and raised both hands in panic. "Leo, you didn't tell anyone that you kissed her. You never lied; you don't have to do this."

Leo rolled his eyes. "Be quiet, Mother."

In his own dark world, Simon could feel people all around him, but in many ways, he was alone. The thought of Louisa marrying someone else—marrying Leo—seemed incomprehensible. Simon was in love with her.

But didn't she deserve happiness? Wouldn't she be better off with a normal marriage to a sighted man?

Someone gently squeezed his arm, and for a moment, he didn't know who it was. Then he remembered Georgie, who'd been sitting beside him. Was she trying to give him strength to accept what he couldn't change?

Or strength to take his life back? How could Louisa be happier with Leo than with him?

"Louisa, you can't be considering this," he said suddenly, forcefully. "You are not marrying anyone but me."

He heard whispers and murmurs and gasps, and his mother trying to speak, but being hushed.

What was Louisa's reaction? God, if only he could see her. Did she think he was proposing out of collective family guilt?

"Louisa, come here," he said.

He smelled the sultry scent of her a moment before her skirts swished against his legs. He let his cane drop, oriented himself by running his hands up her trembling arms, then cupping her face.

He felt her tears, wet against his fingers, and a great relief went through him. "I love you, Louisa. I've never met anyone with your compassion and your gift for helping people. I'd still be in my own private hell of a cave but for you. I'm done living my life by what other people think. My love isn't about gratitude. It's very selfish and demanding and will only be appeased if you never leave my side again."

Her cheeks lifted in a smile and she put her hands on his waist. "I love you, Simon, and I would be proud to be your wife. You see inside me where others only see what they want to see. You make me feel so precious and loved."

"Not damn near enough, and that will end right now." He drew her into his arms and kissed her. She responded with the unabashed passion he so loved about her.

A man cleared his throat. "This is a lovely display," Leo said dryly, "but you're making a mockery of my grief, Simon."

Louisa laughed against Simon's lips and broke the kiss, though he wouldn't let her leave his embrace.

"Leo," she said, "I can see very well how relieved you are."

Suddenly they were surrounded by people

wishing them well, by laughter and pats on the back and kisses from Louisa's happy sisters. Georgie hugged him about the neck so hard he had to pry her away to breathe. His grandmother, sounding like she might be crying, announced that the house party had turned into an engagement celebration.

Through it all, Simon held on to Louisa, and knew that for the rest of his life, they had each other to light the darkness.

Epilogue

Derbyshire
1846

Louisa came into their bedroom and saw Simon in his usual chair by the window, holding their infant son. As always, the love on his face brought tears of joy to her eyes. She had never imagined she could be so happy, so fulfilled, so in love.

Simon lifted his head. "Louisa?"

"Yes?"

"Is your newest young student settled in?"

"Yes, but I'm afraid she's feeling rather shy."

"Then don't start your lessons by telling her about the conversations of rakes."

She smiled. "I won't. I've learned my own lesson. I left the girl with Georgie to cheer her up."

"A fate worse than death—nothing but talk of wedding plans twenty-four hours a day."

"Georgie can restrain herself," Louisa insisted, though inwardly she doubted it.

He shook his head. "Come here."

She went and sat on the arm of the chair, leaning against her husband's shoulder, looking at the precious innocence of their sleeping baby.

"I still can't believe how lucky I've been," Simon said softly.

The baby arched lazily, and opened his mouth in a tiny yawn. As usual, Louisa couldn't resist stroking the soft skin of his little hand.

"How lucky we've been," she corrected him.

"I already know you're lucky," he said, grinning. "How could you not be?"

"Simon!"

His laughter faded into the sweet smile she'd come to adore. "But I'm lucky. All those months ago when I went blind, I thought my life as I knew it was over. Although I was right, who would have guessed that my new life would be more rewarding than anything that came before it? You did that for me."

Louisa smiled through her tears. She swept the blond curls off Simon's forehead, then cupped his cheek, adoring the rough feel of his skin.

"The love I feel for you and this baby—" After his voice grew hoarse, he broke off and swallowed. "Tell me again."

"Again, my love?"

"Again. Describe everything about him, and don't leave anything out."

"You already know he's perfect, just by being our child."

"Well of course," Simon said, smiling up at her. "But I love seeing him through your eyes."

She leaned down and kissed them both.

Avon Romantic Treasures

Unforgettable, enthralling love stories, sparkling with passion and adventure from Romance's bestselling authors

DISCOVER
ROMANCE *at its*

SIZZLING HOT BEST FROM AVON BOOKS

Return of the Highlander   by Sara Mackenzie
0-06-079540-9/$5.99 US/$7.99 Can

Hysterical Blondness   by Suzanne Macpherson
0-06-077500-9/$5.99 US/$7.99 Can

Secrets of the Highwayman   by Sara Mackenzie
0-06-079552-2/$5.99 US/$7.99 Can

Finding Your Mojo   by Stephanie Bond
978-0-06-082107-4/$5.99 US/$7.99 Can

Passions of the Ghost   by Sara Mackenzie
978-0-06-079582-5/$5.99 US/$7.99 Can

Love in the Fast Lane   by Jenna McKnight
978-06-084347-2/$5.99 US/$7.99 Can

Beware of Doug   by Elaine Fox
978-0-06-117568-8/$5.99 US/$7.99 Can

Arousing Suspicions   by Marianne Stillings
978-0-06-085009-8/$5.99 US/$7.99 Can

Be Still My Vampire Heart   by Kerrelyn Sparks
978-0-06-111844-9/$5.99 US/$7.99 Can

One Night With a Goddess   by Judi McCoy
978-0-06-077460-8/$5.99 US/$7.99 Can